MONARCHS

Table of Contents

PROLOGUE

An excerpt from the historical chronicler, Ra's Al-Awati's, 'A Story through Time.'

'' Historians have recorded with great fascination the emergence of the African Union (AU) and its dominance over world politics since. The staging point for the emergence of this super state came during failed European conquest of the Western part of the continent. Powerful leaders arose to combat the harmful territorial practices of these invaders from the North.

The development of powerful biological weapons made from strains of the malaria pathogen are credited for the successful campaign against the Europeans who had developed powerful conventional arsenal of their own. Rival empires in the African peninsula rallied together in a defensive contract to form the prosperous AU superstate as we know it. Its creation was unprecedented in history up until this point.

A chronological timeline of historical facts through time from the 13th century to the present is as follows:

1235 AD: The Mali Empire was founded by Sundiata. It formed the largest and richest empire in all of West Africa.

1312-1337 AD: Mansa Musa seizes power, doubling the size and strength of the empire. His general, Saran Mundian, leading an armored calvary of 100,000 strong calvary troops seizes land from its neighbors. The price of the Gold Dinar in Cairo plummets by 20% as King Musa made his way on pilgrimage to Mecca.

1471-1483: Portuguese sailors first make contact with the Akan people. A trading partnership consisting mainly of gold is established.

1624: The Monarch Queen Nzinga of Andongo takes the throne. Her reign sees the defeat of Portuguese invaders at Ngoleme in 1644. The first instance of targeted biological agents to destroy the invading armies are recorded in this battle. Historians and personal accounts from both sides describe the battlefield as follows:

'In the middle of the battle, Queen Nzinga ordered her troops back from the front lines. The fighting had been going on for hours, staining the lush green vegetation a satin reddish hue. The Portuguese forces marched forward, seemingly assured of victory; their red pikes emblazoned with flags adorned with the lion coat of arms which could be seen in their numbers from atop the battlefield.

Safe within the intricate web of mud trenches located under the battlefield, Queen Nzinga lay ready as the last of her troops rushed into the hidden caves and sealed the metal doors behind them shut. Troops within the caves hurriedly handed the last of the retreating troops specially crafted masks made from charcoal and tree resin as a precaution for when the toxin was released. Queen Nzinga knew its deleterious effects would not harm her troops but she would not take the risk regardless. With a strong nod of her head, the order was given.

Entwined vines hanging from the top of the mud caves were pulled down, triggering a release of gaseous poison from airtight fish skins on the battlefield. A greenish mist surrounds the bewildered Portuguese troops, stopping them in their tracks. The effects were instantaneous. Several infantry collapse on the battlefield and shake violently as blood profusely runs down their noses and eyes. Screams from Portuguese troops sear through the air as a full retreat is ordered. Queen Nzinga grins in content as she hears the Portuguese orders being given. She knows it is already too late. The heat from the tunnels and the mask covering her face causes drops of sweat to form on her forehead. She closes her eyes, heaves a deep sigh and imagines the carnage occurring on the surface.

She has seen the effects of the toxin firsthand. They made sure to amply test it on captured European soldiers before deploying it on the battlefield. First, blood begins to issue from every opening of the hosts' body. Then the toxin induces seizures which paralyze the victim instantaneously. The process proceeds for another few seconds where the victim convulses on the ground experiencing pain equivalent to several bones breaking but is unable to scream; only to lay on the ground with eyes wide open as his life slips away.

Queen Nzinga waits several minutes for the gas compound to dissipate then orders her troops out of the trenches. The carnage on the field is evident from the hundreds of Portuguese troops who lay dead on the grassy floor; their faces contorted in horror even in death. The battle has been won. The Queen would retain her kingdom.'

1648: The last of the European invaders are driven back at Al Hociema. A collective war treaty is struck between Queen Nzinga of Andongo, the Ooni of Ife of the Yoruba Kingdom and Emperor Susenyos II of Ethiopia. Queen Nzinga's biological arsenal proves instrumental in the warfront against the Europeans.

1738: Shaka Ngaba takes the throne. A period of expansion known as 'Mfakane' sees the expansion of the Zulu empire and cuts across much of Southern Africa.

1742: Queen Nzinga III marries King Ishaka of Mali, forming the amalgamated Republic of Luanda. The Yoruba Kingdom is given independent autonomy in the newly formed ''Super- State.''

1884: The Mbanza peace accord is signed between the five powerful kingdoms in Africa. Delegates from the Zulu Empire in the South, the Luandan Empire of the West, the Aksum Empire of the East, the Mazighen Empire to the North and the Central Kongolese Empire descend on the city. The African Union (AU) is formed. A 10-year rotational rulership is established.

1912-1925: Land rights disputes in the Chinese, Slovia, and Austria-Hungarian colonies of North America cause a 13-year long conflict on the continent. The fallout leads to the precipitation of war on the Eurasian continent as home states seek to capitalize on the chaos by annexing more territory in the region.

1965: The Treaty of Vienna is signed between the major world powers prohibiting the use of biological weapons in large scale conflict. The fledging English-French alliance are not signatories to the agreement

1989: Renewed tensions on the Eurasian continent sends waves of migrants from ethnic minority groups to the AU. Among the majority of these are Jewish settlers.

2009: A temporary seize fire is agreed upon by colonies in both Slovian and Chinese colonies. ‘’

THE TIES THAT BIND US

'An exert from an article in The Observatory, dated February 10th, 2015,'

- ''Luandans are not known for their modesty. Their intricately patterned, flamboyant outfits are laced with gold embroidery which are woven into various designs on the fabric. Like regal crowns, the women tie scarfs on their heads forming various impressive shapes to complement their outfits. Uniquely shaped diamond necklaces which sparkle brightly under the tropical sun are a common sight amongst these women. Their entire wardrobe seeks to match the affluence of the region rich in gold and precious metals. Comparisons are quickly drawn to their Arabian counterparts who dress with similar expensive fashion sense…'' –

Tife Berkowitz was known by her father's friends as a precocious and gifted child. At the tender age of four, she had already become fluent in several languages including her mother's tongue of

Afrikansi and her father's Hebrew tongue. Her mother would listen on with deep interest as Tife would recite the Shacarit prayers during the Synagogue's morning service. Although Kifunji did not share in the religious practices of her husband, she quietly indulged her daughter's interest in the Jewish practices and customs.

At home however, Kifunji would have her way as she adorned the walls of her house with religious symbols unique to the Christian faith. One of such decorations which caused numerous clashes between her parents was the image of Jesus Christ which hung on the wall overlooking the dining room table. The picture depicted Jesus with his right arm raised in a dignified pose. His two fingers were outstretched as an angelic halo formed around his head.
Eli was furious over the addition of the picture to the dining room wall but tolerated it for respect of his wife. He did however ask Abigail, their live-in nanny, to take it down each time his friends came over for a traditional Jewish meal.

Eli was what his peers described as a 'modern Jewish man.' He did not wear the traditional shtreimel fur hat which adorned many men's head in his area and reserved the tallit, his long-fringed shawl, for use at morning prayers in the Synagogue. He did however insist on wearing a Kippah wherever he went. Kifunji would chide him daily that it was merely an attempt to hide the growing bald spot on the top of his head, but Eli insisted it was solely for religious purposes.

Over the weekends, Eli would have Tife read bits of the Torah out loud in the living room as her parents watched on from the couch with delight. One night for her was particularly memorable as her father asked her to put down the Torah after reading a length of scripture from Deuteronomy.

''Tell me Tife, why did God prevent Moses from entering the land of Canaan as he had originally intended?'' Eli asked.

''Because he had disobeyed God at Kadesh,'' she replied, remembering the verse in Numbers she had read many weeks ago, ''God instructed him to speak to the rock to bring forth water. Instead, he used his staff to do it.''

But Eli probed further, ''But what difference did it make if he used his staff rather than his words? Was the result not the same?''

Tife paused for a long time, mulling the question over in her head. Her mother watched on, beaming with pride at the wisdom her six-year-old daughter already displayed. Finally, Tife spoke up again.

''By striking the rock with his staff, he demonstrated his unwillingness to believe God's word. He showed a lack of trust in God who had shown him no reason to doubt his Word.''

''Yes, and on another note Tife, you must understand that the ends do not justify the means,'' Eli added. '' If I steal money and give it to the poor, does that make me a good or a bad man? The poor may benefit from my generosity but that does not excuse the crime I committed. Do you understand, Tife?'' She nodded in agreement, her frizzy hair bouncing in unison.

''Very good, my flower,'' Kifunji said with a smile. ''Why don't we call it a night, darling?'' Eli rose from the couch, planting a kiss on his wife's lips before kissing Tife on the forehead. A hoarse, wet cough echoed throughout the living room. Eli turned to see his wife coughing loudly into a white handkerchief. The center of the handkerchief was stained red with droplets of blood. Tife looked worryingly at her mother as Eli steadied her up and took her upstairs to her room.

Over the next couple of months, Tife would watch as her mother's health deteriorated over time. Her doctor recommended a battery of antibiotic medication to keep the raging infection at bay. When that proved abortive, chemotherapy was advised to help with her ailing condition.

Kifunji grew paler and weaker with each round of treatment she received. Her symptoms became increasingly worse as the cancer raged through her body. A walk to the bathroom would leave her gasping for air. Abigail was increasingly on hand to assist Kifunji with tasks around the house. Finally, it became clear she needed greater attention for her deteriorating health and was admitted on bed rest in Queen Nzinga's National Hospital, the premier hospital in the capital for various diseases.

Tife would stop by the hospital after school and remain by her mother's bedside as she slept. She regularly read poems she had written in school as her mother laid in bed and would paste them on the walls of her hospital room.

Kifunji had now grown frail, with the last bits of grey hair falling off her head. The hum and buzz of the machines filled the blinding white hospital room. Several tubes ran from her mother's arm to machines which clicked on rhythmically. Some of the tubes had colored fluids which ran intravenously into her mother's body.

On a certain day, Tife had raced back from school to be by her mother's side as she always did. Eli was sitting in an armchair at the corner of the room with one arm propped against his face to keep it upright as he had now fallen fast asleep. He had relinquished the role as chairman of his company to his vice so that he could remain by his wife's side in the hospital.

Tife inspected her mother's face as if meeting a stranger for the first time. Red, splotchy raised marks of varying sizes dotted her once smooth face in several places. She had also become ghostly pale and breathed shallowly as she lay in her hospital bed. Tife began reading a poem titled 'Love Lost' that she had written in school when her mother's eyes flickered open. Kifunji beamed weakly at Tife from her hospital bed and moved her hand slowly to touch her daughter's arm.

''My flower,'' she said softly, ''I thought you would be in school today.''

''I finished early today, Mama. Look, I wrote this poem for you.''

Kifunji smiled broadly, ''that's lovely, my flower. I want you to read it all for me.''

Tife cleared her throat and began reading the two-page poem for her mother again. She listened on intently until her eyelids fell heavy and she slipped back into a deep sleep. Tife finished the poem and looked up to see her mother fast asleep again. She kissed her mother on the forehead and fixed her sheets till they rose to her chin. She remained there gazing at her mother's serene face in the yellow glowing haze of the hospital lights.

Kifunji passed away a few days later. The doctors said the disease had progressed too far and had damaged key organs in her system. Over the next couple of days, Tife remained in her room donning a simple black Aso'ebi with a matching scarf which was tied into a bow on her head. Abigail remained inside with her as relatives poured into the house to offer their condolences.

The entire mood was somber and grim with the muffled cries of mourners piercing the air. Eli wore a simple black suit and stood at the front door to greet members of the family who had come to mourn with them. Kifunji's parents had just arrived at the house. Her mother, Uvewa was well into her years. Her face was framed by her wrinkly, leathery skin and her hair was white as snow.

In tow was Mefele, her husband of fifty-three years. His lean frame was barely visible in the flowing black kaftan which ran down to his legs. He steadied himself with a brown walking stick which had a lion's face carved at its top. Uvewa wrapped her thin arms around Eli as she walked through the door.

''I'm sorry I couldn't save her, Mama Uvewa,'' Eli said through gritted teeth as tears flowed down his cheeks. ''We did everything we could to help her...'' but Uvewa interjected, clasping his cheeks with her bony fingers and wiping the tears from his eyes.

''My daughter is not suffering anymore, Eli. She is in a better place now,'' she said with a weak smile on her face. ''You are a good and kind man. I am glad my daughter built a life with you.''

The mourners gathered at the cemetery to lay the body to rest. Kifunji was placed in a simple wooden casket with an engraved tombstone which read, 'Kifunji Berkowitz, a loving wife and mother. September 1969- November 2010.'

The air was humid and wet with heavy, dark clouds forming overhead. Family members gradually gathered around the gravesite waiting for the service to begin. As were Kifunji's wish's, a priest was present to officiate the ceremony alongside a Rabbi.

The Rabbi was a rather large, pudgy man who donned on a kippa which barely covered his head. Draped over his shoulders was a cream-colored tallit that ran down to his waist. The priest on the other hand wore a black, floor- length cassock with an embroidered cincture of the same color around his waist. Abigail held Tife in her arms as the service wore on. Her father stood beside her clutching a folded piece of paper in his right arm as he wiped away tears with his left.

''And now, I would like to call on Mr. Berkowitz to share a few words about his wife on her passing,'' the priest announced. Eli stepped forward to the pulpit which stood at the forefront of the mourning crowd. He unfolded the white paper he had in his arm and spread it out on the pulpit. Breathing in heavily and choking back tears, he began reading it.

''I was married to Kifunji for seventeen beautiful years. She was a fierce woman who always saw the brighter side of life…''Eli paused as he began to well up in tears again. He put aside the piece of paper he had laid on the pulpit and faced the crowd with tears streaming down his face.

''She was my life and my soul, and she gave us a beautiful daughter. She was kind and gentle and I still can't believe she's gone…'' The priest moved forward to gently pat Eli on the back as he began sobbing loudly. Uvewa stepped forward and helped Eli from the pulpit as he could no longer finish his eulogy.

The Rabbi continued the ceremony, allowing for members of the family to a lay a bit of dirt over the casket which had been lowered into the grave. Family members stepped up one by one to take a fistful of dirt which lay in a mound beside the grave and sprinkled it over the coffin as it lay in state. Abigail helped Tife walk over to her mother's grave. Both took fistfuls of dirt and showered it over the coffin. Tife watched as the balls of dirt bounced off the brown casket and rested on either side of the six-foot deep grave. The rest of the red earth was filled in with shovels as family members dispersed the grave site.

The days and weeks following Kifunji's death passed slowly. The loss weighed especially heavy on Eli who spent many hours in the dining room, sitting across from the picture of Jesus hanging on the wall. Abigail walked in on him one day as he reclined in the chair. Eli held a glass of bourbon in his hand and took sips periodically from it. His eyes were bloodshot and red as tears still trickled down his cheeks.

''Are you alright, sir?'' Abigail inquired as she entered the room. Eli breathed in heavily, taking a long sip from his glass again.

''I gave her so much grief over that picture, Abigail. Over a damn picture!'' he spoke through gritted teeth. ''If I could do it all again, I would tell her how much I loved her instead of arguing over a stupid painting.'' Abigail stepped up till she was standing opposite Eli across the huge oak table. She had her hands clasped behind her back and had a kitchen apron tied across her waist.

''I have been with you for over twelve years now, sir. I can say with the utmost certainty that Kifunji loved you deeply. I also know she would want you to be strong in this time for Tife's sake.'' Eli looked up at her with reflective eyes. His eyes had become a renewed red tint, reflecting in it the golden shade of the bourbon.

Their heads turned as a creak from the front door echoed through the house. Tife stepped into the dining room to see her father sitting deeply in his wooden back chair. The sharp smell of alcohol which Tife had grown accustomed to over the years filled the room. Eli quickly put his drink aside and stood up to embrace her. His breath reeked of the bourbon and his face was red with grief.

''How was school, angel?'' Eli asked with a weak smile, brushing

her curly, dark hair and pushing her hair behind her ears. Tife paused before moving in to kiss Eli on both cheeks before embracing him tightly in her small arms.
''I miss her too, daddy,'' she said comfortingly, tightening her grip over Eli's shoulders.

Streams of tears ran down both of their cheeks as they stood in silence in the dining room.

Tife returned to school to rejoin her classmates who expressed their condolences at the loss of her mother. Eli slowly began to reassert his leadership over his trading firm. His company was a leading exporter of refined fuels to the largely Chinese and Slovian colonies across the Atlantic. They had also formed partnerships with fuel exporters in the South American colonies, several of which belonging to the Middle East kingdoms in the Qur'anic Alliance.

Eli routinely hosted business partners in his house many of whom visited him regularly. Tife returned one day from school to see his father in intense conversation with an older gentleman in the living room. They both stopped talking and turned to the door once they heard it open. Tife shuffled into the room and Eli quickly rose from his chair to plant a kiss on her forehead. Holding her lovingly by his side, he introduced her to the man seated on the couch.

''Tife, I would like you to meet Mr. Zhang Wei Chan. He is the new distribution manager in-charge of retail distribution in the Chinese provinces of North America,'' Eli explained. The man quickly rose up and gave a curt bow before out-stretching his arm for a handshake. He was a short, pale man who had several blisters and callouses across his palms. He attempted a smile which revealed yellowing teeth in his mouth. His cheeks were sunken and deep which grew even more pronounced the longer he smiled. He sported a fading black suit which was nearly two times his size and which hid his small frame.

''Nǐ hǎo,'' Tife said. Mr. Zhang's smile was replaced with an amused grin. ''Nǐ hǎo ma?'' he replied ebulliently. He shook Tife's hand with greater fervor.

''Wǒ hěn hǎo, xiè xiè nǐ,'' Tife said in response. The man let out a raucous laugh of amusement which rang throughout the house. Eli hugged Tife tightly in deep admiration.

''Your daughter can speak Mandarin, Eli?'' Mr. Zhang asked, his eyes widening in curiosity.

''She's learning it as part of her school's curriculum,'' Eli explained.

''I'm going to be a diplomat one day!'' Tife declared in a loud voice. Mr. Zhang smiled broadly and bent down on one knee to face Tife.

''Would you like to visit my country one day, Tife? I think you would like it there.''

''Maybe when things quiet down there, Wei,'' Eli replied. Mr. Zhang nodded affirmatively before taking his seat once more. Eli of course was referring to increasing tensions in the Chinese colonies which made business especially difficult. The landmass was largely claimed by Slovian and Chinese interests and fortified by an increasing military presence which separated the borders of the two nations.

Claiming a large section of the Western coast of North America were Slovian colonies which grew over the years into successful and booming cities. Hugging the Eastern coast was a patchwork of Chinese interests with several bases in key islands scattered in the Caribbean. Austria-Hungarian interests on the other hand spread to the South-Eastern region flanking the Atlantic Ocean.

The significant control of oil deposits in the North American region held by the Austria-Hungarian empire had caused deep tension with Chinese agencies seeking access to those oil fields. Of equal interest to the competing colonies were the significant mineral deposits in the Rocky Mountain region; a key geographical feature dividing the separate colonies from each other. Military patrols in that region had become increasingly violent, with regular bombing raids carried out on military installations. The Chinese Emperor famously touted the strength of his military in his annual speech to his constituents.

''We only use a fraction of our military might in our pursuit to defend our interests and our people. Foreign governments will do well to deter their military forces from showing further aggression in the region. We will protect our people at all costs and use the full weight of our military might if necessary,'' he declared. Repeat broadcasts of the speech were played across Luanda as it was of interest to several businessmen in the region including Tife's father. Eli struggled to hear the translated speech through the crackle and buzz of the radio receiver during the evening news bulletin.

News of military action in the North-Atlantic colonies was not the only topic of concern for residents in Luanda. Closer to home was the upcoming change of leadership expected to happen in January when Queen Yaa-Yaa of Luanda would pass on leadership to King Dinga of the Zulu kingdom. Dinga was set to take over as the Sovereign Leader of the African Union (AU).

The ceremony was set to hold in Teke, the state capital of Luanda. A large festival was to be held with residents from every region in the African Union (AU) expected to attend. Many local businesses in Teke sought to capitalize on the large inflow of tourists by raising prices on everything from rent to farm produce. Adverts for short term rent were on full display on many buildings in the capital. On a walk to the local produce market with Abigail, Tife saw large, wooden banners boasting of the best deals for short-term room and board options.

A parade leading to the Queen's residence was planned during the ceremony. The 'Irin Ajo Oba' or 'Royal March' was a ceremonial event which had the two monarchs, the current Sovereign Leader and their successor, march together in the streets as a symbolic sign of unity. Merchants hurried about purchasing many lucrative spaces designated for the parade march. Items for purchase were set to be displayed along these routes and businessmen and women seeking to make large profits were keen to have monopoly over these spaces.

The week leading to the big event saw tourists swarm the capital of Teke. Tife's school was closed for the week to mark the royal occasion. Chaperoned by Abigail, Tife had the chance to roam the capital and see the event take shape herself. Many sightseers filled the streets looking to catch a glimpse of the preparations. People from all over the AU and the world had come to witness the ceremony. Some wore traditional garbs which announced their countries of origin.

Tife immediately recognised the traditional attire worn by people of the Zulu empire. It was worn by a large group of men wearing polka dot leopard prints passing by on the street. They each donned knee-length, white-hide material made from sheep skin which they tied around their waist. Each held a shield made from dried raw cow hides. They stopped in the city square to perform lively action scenes depicting famous battles from centuries passed.

With loud grunts and thrusts, the men attacked and jabbed the air with their pointed sabers whilst throwing themselves in the air in complicated, acrobatic movements. This delighted many sight seers who swarmed in large crowds to watch the performance unfold. Many avid sightseers were also fascinated by the unique sculptures that adorned many street corners along the capital. Most were depictions of various warrior kings and queens from times past.

A popular attraction was of course the many statues of Queen Nzinga which dominated the artistry in the capital. Prominently featured at the foot of the stairs leading into the palace was a large, gleaming gold statue of Queen Nzinga seated on her throne. The statue showed an ornate, beaded crown adorning the top of her head. She also had similar beads tied around her wrists and ankles.

Two lions with their mouths open in fierce growls were carved on either side of her throne. Carved beside her in bronze were warriors in full military attire. The ends of the spears which they held tightly in their grasp were raised proudly into the air. A dozen warrior men carved opposite each other were set up in this way leading to her throne. The impressive carving shone brilliantly in the tropical sun and was a prime attraction for tourists visiting the capital.

The palace itself was a beauty to behold. Situated at the top of the highest elevation of the city, it was visible from several directions no matter how far away you were from the city's center. The beautiful combination of polished stone facades and mud masonry gave the palace an imposing presence for many to enjoy.

The Queen's residence was by far the largest building in the walled compound. It was primarily made from polished stonework with intricate straw roofing affixed atop wooden supports. Three separate large buildings of various sizes but connected to each other made up the expansive estate.

The first was the large antechamber where the Queen had events for royal guests and a larger courtyard outside for proclamations to her people. The building to the right of this one was the Queen's quarters where she would have one of her seven male concubines spend the night with her. The smaller building to the left of the courtyard was reserved for these concubines who had adequate living arrangements within the palace.

The big day arrived with much fanfare in the capital. Tife's school was closed to mark the holiday and allow for the children to be present for the ceremony. She awoke to the noise of drums and music being played outside her window. A merry group of musicians with various instruments danced joyously down the cobblestone road. Abigail helped Tife to get ready for the parade.

''Rose bud, are you ready?'' Eli called out from downstairs, ''the car is waiting downstairs.''

Tife's head popped out from the top of the stars. ''I'm almost ready, Papa,'' she replied gleefully. She was dressed in a bright, white flowing kaftan with intricate gold embroidery patterns across its side. Abigail rushed out and ushered her back into her room.

''I'm not done with your hair yet, Precious. Don't you want it beautiful for the parade?'' Abigail asked as she braided portions of Tife's hair to run down her back.

''Papa is waiting for us outside, Abi. We need to go with him now. I don't want to miss the Queen!'' Tife moaned while fidgeting uncomfortably.

''Your father can wait, darling. The parade happens all day. Besides, you'll be in the motorcade behind the Queen. You will not miss her,'' she assured Tife. Abigail brushed her shoulders one last time and with a large smile, beamed brightly at Tife.

''Look how beautiful you are now, darling. You'll be the pride of the parade.'' Abigail motioned Tife to the floor length mirror to get a better look of herself. Tife smiled brightly at her reflection in the mirror. Abigail's expression suddenly changed to one more pensive and reflective.

''Your mother would be so proud to see you now, rose bud,'' she said finally. Wiping a tear from her eye, she ushered Tife out of the room and into the waiting car downstairs.

The streets were jampacked with parade goers dressed in colorful outfits and instruments of various kinds. Tife looked out the window as a troop of men dressed in flowing kaftans and armed with talking drums passed their car. Their upbeat tunes were complemented by the high- pitched ululation of the women who accompanied them. They too were dressed in large kaftans and gele's of matching color. Tife took her seat in the back of the car with Abigail. Her father sat up front in the passenger seat and quietly gazed out the window.

''Papa, why do we get to ride in the motorcade with the Queen?'' Tife asked inquisitively.

Eli turned back to face his daughter with a wide smile.

''Because I'm a prominent member of the Jewish community, rose bud,'' he explained. ''Only a privilege few get to take direct part in the ceremony.''

''Your father made a special request to have us all join in the parade with him, darling,'' Abigail continued. ''He knew you would be especially happy and wanted you with him.'' Tife beamed brightly with all her pearly white teeth showing. Eli stretched into the back of the car and planted a large kiss on her forehead.

They arrived at a large square located in the heart of the city. Hundreds of people dressed in magnificent traditional attires surrounded the square as they waited for the festivities to begin. A group of horses with their handlers stood to the side eating hay and whisking flies from their bodies with their tails.

No sooner than a couple minutes passed when two men blowing ivory horns appeared in the crowd. They were accompanied by six dancing masquerades who moved in circles around the square. Each wore a unique attire and performed a mixture of acrobatic and aerial dance moves to the delight of the crowd.

Tife was mesmerized by what appeared to be a headless masquerade who approached where she stood. He had loose strips of vines attached to every part of its body and moved with unearthly dexterity. He also did several backflips in the air before throwing its body in several aerial arches. The other masquerades with face masks circled around this masquerade and performed several menacing gestures at him. In time, they circled him and placed him in a wooden box in the center of the square. Tife watched on with delight and apprehension.

''Do you know what they are doing, Tife?'' Abigail asked. Tife shrugged her shoulders. ''This is a traditional dance performed at every Irin Ajo Oba. The masquerade with green vines attached to his body is the embodiment of evil and bad tidings which the new monarch would have faced during his tenure. This ritual serves to drive the evil away and into that box. The new Sovereign leader will be free of these evils and will have a trouble-free reign.''

''Does the ritual really work?'' Tife probed innocently.

''Some say it does. Others are not so believing. Nonetheless it is tradition and must be performed at each ceremony.''
The men with ivory horns blasted their instruments in the air again, this time with even greater fervor. It was immediately clear why they this was happening. The crowd had parted on the far-left side to reveal Queen Yaa-Yaa and her successor, King Dinga march through the crowd. They were accompanied by a large troop of men and women dressed in traditional warrior clothing and who held an assortment of weapons. They were ushered unto the stage which was erected on the same side of the square. Queen Yaa-Yaa rose to the podium while King Dinga took his seat beside her. Silence fell in the crowd as the Queen delivered her speech.

''Welcome to all our guests from far and wide who have come to our glorious kingdom to witness this monumental event. Today, I will be transferring all my authority to the new Sovereign leader of the AU, King Dinga of the Zulu Kingdom.'' The crowd erupted in a thunderous rush of claps and screams. King Dinga rose from his chair, waving his gold-studded walking cane in the process before returning to his seat. The Queen continued.

''It is my hope that his reign will usher in even greater peace and prosperity for the people of the AU. Our role as leaders in an ever changing and violent world cannot be overstated. We must remain steadfast and strong so that we may continue to fulfill our responsibility as a bastion of hope for all the world to see.'' She turned to King Dinga in his seat behind her.

''May you live long and prosper. May your reign be good and just. May we continue to have peace in our lands as you take up the mantle of leadership this day.'' King Dinga smiled and bowed courteously in reply as the crowd erupted in another raucous bout of applause. Several ladies dressed in colorful beads walked unto the stage carrying various items on velvet pillows. They formed a straight line behind Queen Yaa-Yaa who remained at the podium. She motioned to King Dinga who rose from his chair and knelt down facing her on stage.

The first girl brought forward an ornate shoulder piece made entirely of gold. It gleamed and sparkled brightly in the tropical sun. The Queen took it and rested it across Dinga's shoulder.

''This shoulder piece represents the weight of responsibility you will carry on your shoulders from this day forward,'' She bellowed. ''May you carry it with the same strength as the monarchs of old.''
Another girl stepped forward with several gold bangles atop her pillow. The Queen took it and attached it to the King's outstretched arms.

''These bangles represent your link to the people. You will remain bound to dispensing their will until the end of your reign as Sovereign. You will be just and fair and will always do what is in the best interest of the people.''

The next girl came up with a golden sceptre resting on the top of her pillow. The Queen took it and handed it to King Dinga who took it in his outstretched hand.

''This staff symbolizes the power of this great title you will bear from this day. You will command the great resources available to the AU and will wield it absolutely from this day until the end of your reign.''

Last to approach the podium was a girl with a beautiful gold crown balanced atop her pillow. It was a stunning piece of headwear with seven rubies affixed around its center. Queen Yaa-Yaa took it and placed it on the King's head.

''This crown has been passed down from generations of monarchs before you. It is the quintessential representation of unity and strength that this position offers. With this, you are now the new Sovereign of the African Union. May your reign be long and prosperous.'' The crowd of people gathered echoed the same words in solemn harmony. Queen Yaa-Yaa took a step back as King Dinga rose from his kneel. She in turn fell to her knees and bowed in deference to the new leader. The crowd erupted in a joyous frenzy of screams and applause. The new Sovereign had now emerged.

After their speech, the parade began in earnest. The sweltering tropical heat would not dampen the joy of the crowds gathered for the ceremony. King Dinga and Queen Yaa-Yaa took their positions at the head of the parade alongside troops of performers and bands with various instruments.

Conveying them slowly through the streets were the horses which were equally dressed in festive attire. They were quickly followed by members and leaders of various communities alike invited for the parade. The monarchs themselves were pulled along the parade route by twelve horses atop a raised platform. Tife marveled at the crowds of people lining the streets, hoping to catch a glimpse of the new Sovereign of the African Union.

The air was buzzing with excitement and screams of delight from the crowd. The people lining the parade route threw flowers at the feet of the Sovereign. In return, he waved his scepter to the crowd. They progressed slowly through the streets until the golden statue of Queen Nzinga peaked from the top of the hill.

The imposing castle filled the view ahead as the parade goers proceeded to the gates of the Queen's residence. The bright sun overhead was slowly replaced with storm clouds which gathered in thick plumes in the sky. Tife watched the sky with unease as thunder began to rip through the cumulonimbus clouds one after the other. Eli noticed the nervousness of his daughter and stroked her hair gently. The parade was nearing the Queen's residence as the first drops of rain began to shower from above.

Suddenly, an explosion ripped through the crowd sending several people flying through the air. Screams of panic and terror quickly followed. The bodies of parade goers on either side made frantic attempts to escape the ensuing chaos of the raging crowd.

The second explosion quickly followed. This time, it emanated from underneath the caravan carrying the King and Queen. The horses carrying Tife's float bucked and neighed in anxious reply. The entire train of the parade stopped now with several of the horses rushing dangerously into the barricades which lined the parade route. Several of the people on the parade floats jumped off in an attempt to flee the violence. Eli rushed to grab Tife who had frozen up in fear; her eyes wide open and fixated in complete shock. Abigail jumped down from the float and waited on Eli to pass Tife down to her.

''It's going to be ok, rose bud,'' Eli muttered under his breath as he helped to hoist her down from the raised platform.

The third explosion upturned the float, sending a shockwave of dirt, shrapnel, and concrete flying through the air. The force from the blast threw Tife several feet into the parade barricade, knocking her unconscious. The obliterated remains of the parade float drifted into the air before landing several feet in the direction of the fleeing crowd.

Tife was awoken by the continuous deluge of rain which swept down from above. Her black hair was matted and stuck like glue to the sides of her face. She opened her eyes slowly to see the ground awash with blood and dirt. The horse which had been conveying them in the float had been split open and lay on its side. Its blood tainted the rushing water a reddish tint. Tife turned her head to the side to see Abigail crumpled to one side on the ground. A large gash ran down from her forehead to her right cheek. It was hard for Tife to determine if she was still alive or not from where she lay.

The parade route was deserted in either direction she looked. Only lifeless and unmoving bodies lay strewn across the ground in contorted positions. Some of the injuries sustained on the bodies looked worse than others giving hope that some of those people may yet still be alive. Tife looked down to her own body to give it a closer inspection. Only then did she notice the metal piece which had lodged itself deep inside her upper right thigh. She was still in shock and hadn't even felt the pain from the shrapnel. Blood flowed continuously from the spot which was promptly washed away by the rain.

Tife now had time to notice the screaming coming from just ahead of her. Queen Yaa-Yaa was kneeling in the rain with her gown fully drenched in blood. Laying lifeless on the ground was King Dinga still adorned with the gold jewelry which he had worn at his coronation. He lay sideways on the ground; his eyes glazed over and fixated on one spot in the distance. His crown had been knocked off his head and lay several feet away from him.

From the corner of her eye, Tife noticed a familiar silhouette behind a large section of the destroyed float which made her heart sink in anguish. Ignoring the overwhelming pain of the shrapnel in her leg, she slowly dragged herself across the rain-washed pavement to the body which lay behind the remains of the wooden float.

''Papa?'' she called out through tears as she winced at the rising pain which began to spread throughout her body. Eli's body was pinned under a section of the wooden float which had fallen on top of him. Tife attempted to push it off him but found it to be far too heavy. She dragged herself one last time and set herself in front of Eli's unmoving body, her face just inches away from his. Half of his face was submerged under the raging torrents of rainfall and his eyes were closed shut. Occasional lightning strikes lit up the overcast sky and thunder echoed in the distance.

''Papa...papa please don't leave me, you're all I have left,'' Tife muttered as she stroked his cheek. The grief mixed with the pain from the metal in her leg overwhelmed her and she slipped back out of consciousness...

Tife awoke to hear the pulsating sound of the ambulance siren. She lay in a bed with medical personnel surrounding her. The continuous downpour of the rain still could be heard across the surface of the ambulance vehicle. A nurse in scrubs stroked her hair as her eyes flickered open.

''Hello, my name is Asha. I am one of the first responders to the incident at the coronation today. I want to assure you that you are going to be okay,'' she said assuredly. ''Can you tell me your name, please?'' Tife hesitated, her eyes darting nervously around the bus.

''It's okay darling. We only want to help,'' the nurse continued. ''Can you tell me who you came with to the parade today?'' she pressed. Tife's mind immediately flooded with images of her father's lifeless body and her eyes instantly streamed with tears.

''Papa, Papa!?'' she screamed and thrashed around violently in the bed. The nurse gently held her down while another nurse manipulated the IV drip connected to her arm. Tife quickly nodded off once more, falling fast asleep to the rhythmic beat of the rainfall on the bus…

News of the tragedy began to circulate, with radio transmissions carrying nothing but exclusive updates as details began to trickle in. A group of old men drinking at a local beer parlor gathered around a radio as it crackled to life with the latest news bulletin. The news caster's voice came on and boomed over the radio speakers.

''Nations around the world continue to react to the devastating tragedy which occurred in Teke, the capital of Luanda. It has been reported that several bombs were detonated at the coronation ceremony of the new Sovereign of the African Union, King Dinga of the Zulu Kingdom who is believed to be the target of this attack. He was sadly killed in the attack on that day. So far, no group has come forward to claim responsibility, but many suspect the Slovian hate group to be the instigator of this attack…''

An entire month of mourning following the attack was dedicated to mourn the late King and the two hundred and thirty-three other victims of the attack. Residents in Luanda were instructed to wear black to honor the victims who had passed away. The atmosphere was somber and grim as business activities slowly picked up days following the tragedy. People spoke in hushed tones of nothing but the bombing as military troops poured into the capital. Men dressed in full military fatigue went from house to house asking residents for details on the incident. A considerably large military contingent patrolled the gates of the Queen's residence surrounding the once welcoming quarters of the matriarch.

Tife's grandmother, Mama Uvewa, shuffled across the marble floor as a knock came through the door. Three men in green-colored military uniform stood at the doorway, their guns fully visible on the holster of their belt.
''Can I help you, officer?'' Mama Uvewa asked politely through the doorway.

''Can we come in, Madame?'' one officer asked curtly. Reluctantly, she opened the door and allowed the three men into the parlor. She asked them if they wanted a cup of tea to which they immediately declined.
''To what do I owe this visit, officer? Mama Uvewa probed. She sat opposite one of the military men who reclined deeply in his seat. The other two paced uneasily around the room, occasionally looking out through the window. The officer sat up from his chair, looking deeply into her eyes.

''I am Captain Benga. I lead the investigation into the bombing that occurred at the Irin Ajo Oba that claimed over two hundred lives, including King Dinga's. We have questions for Ms. Berkowitz. We believe she can aid us in our investigation into the bombing which occurred that day,'' he explained.

''Tife is still resting and cannot see anyone at the moment,'' Mama Uvewa replied firmly. The officer furrowed his eyes and gazed at her with consternation. Heaving a deep sigh, he took off his green beret and placed it on the table.
''Madam, this is in the interest of national security. The perpetrators of this attack are still at large. If Ms. Berkowitz saw something at the event, we need to be made aware of that information and act on it swiftly.'' Mama Uvewa stared deeply into the Captain Benga's eyes before getting up from the chair and shuffling across the room to a photo on a makeshift altar with candles. Taking the picture down carefully with both hands, she returned with it to the couch and raised it to the eye level of the captain.

''Do you know who this man is, Captain?'' she asked. Captain Benga sat up from his chair and gazed deeply into the large portrait.

''That is Mr. Berkowitz if I am not mistaken. He was a prominent member in the Jewish community.''

''Tife had to witness her father's death right in front of her eyes. In so many months, she has had to watch my daughter slowly succumb to cancer. My granddaughter has had to bear the loss of both of her parents....'' she laid the picture down as tears began to well up in her eyes. The officers stared back at her with cold indifference.

''Tife is in no condition to answer any of your questions,'' she said finally. Captain Benga signaled to one of the officers standing close to the window. They quickly discussed something under their breath before returning their attention to Mama Uvewa.

''We do not want to exacerbate the condition of the patient until she is well enough to answer our questions. We will return in the coming days. Hopefully that will give her enough time to recover.'' The captain rose up from his seat and motioned to the officers standing in the room. He turned to Mama Uvewa as he reached the door.

''Thank you, Madame for your time today. Please expect another visit from us soon. And if you learn any information from Tife during that time, please do not hesitate to reach out to us. Officers are stationed on every street corner in the interest of public safety. Approach any one of them if you have any information of relevance to the investigation.'' He gave a curt nod and departed the house with the two officers following close behind.

Mama Uvewa slowly made her way upstairs to the bedroom where Tife slept. She found her sitting motionless on the chair nearest to the window, staring out in blank silence. Tife made no notice as Mama Uvewa took a seat beside her. The clouds outside were grey and overcast. The air was humid adding a layer of warmth wrapped in dampness to the room. The spinning ceiling fan overhead did little to quell the rising heat in the room.

''What are you staring at outside, rose bud?'' Mama Uvewa inquired. Tife continued to stare blankly out the window as the rain clouds grew overhead.

‘’My mother and your great-grandmother once told me that rain clouds were a way the gods spoke to their creations. She said the gods sent the rain as a reminder that even when hard times brew and stir in the foreground, a time will come when the light will shine forth from the clouds, signifying an end to the hard times and an opportunity for blessings to flow forth. ‘’

She outstretched her arms to clasp her hands around Tife’s. The scabbing along her arm and leg where shrapnel had punctured her skin was still clearly visible. The doctors had recommended a host of antibacterial drugs to be administered intravenously to prevent diseases like Tetanus from setting in.

There were also fears that the shrapnel contained in the bombs were coated with biological agents to slowly poison their victims if they were not immediately killed in the blast. These fears were bolstered by reports of several patients dying from their non-fatal injuries in the hospital. Mama Uvewa requested her granddaughter be allowed to return home so that she may rest there. The doctors obliged her request with the instruction that Tife remain on her drug regimen until instructed otherwise by the visiting nurse.

She raised one had to touch Tife’s cheek. Only then did Tife turn to look at her. Mama Uvewa looked on with deep concern as Tife’s cold gaze fell on her. Her eyes were distant and glazed over. Her expression was lifeless and empty. She leaned forward to kiss Tife’s forehead and returned her gaze with a weary smile.

They sat in silence for several minutes listening to the rhythmic hum of the ceiling fan. Mama Uvewa cradled Tife's head in her lap and stroked her curly hair.

‘’I miss them both so much, Mama,’’ Tife said finally through tears. "I lost both of them, Mama. It’s not fair…it’s not fair…’’ Tife repeated as Mama Uvewa stroked her hair comfortingly.

‘’I will always be here for you, rose bud. You will never have to be alone. I can assure you of that.’’ The heavy smell of fresh rain slowly dissipated as the thick rain clouds separated, allowing yellow rays of sunlight to beam through and illuminate the sky.

WAR GAMES

General Sumaina was a man driven by his singular love for his country. From an early age, the military appealed to him greater than any other profession. As the only child of a soldier as well, he chose to carry on the legacy his father had inadvertently bequeathed to him.

He would spend much of his adolescent years in the junior cadet ranks of the military where young people were groomed for the harsh life that the army was known for. He quickly rose in the ranks and drew notice from several of the commanding officers in charge of the program. At sixteen years old, he had the rare privilege of leading a squad for a tour of duty in the disputed territories boarding Zaragoza in Western Europe. Queen Salma of the Mazighen Empire had called for reinforcements as they sought to repel attacks on their strategic outposts.

In February of 1965, their platoon was ambushed by a company of allied British and French forces during a routine sweep of the surrounding countryside. The allied troops had seized the opportunity to launch several rocket-propelled missiles filled with a noxious red substance at their company. This was followed by swarms of attacking enemy troops wearing gas masks and firing bullets at their convoy. Sumaina's team had been at the forefront of the company's procession and was gravely affected by the attack, many of whom inhaled the harmful gases.

The next couple of days saw mounting casualties from the effects of the biological substance they were exposed to. Sumaina was forced to slowly watch members of his own squadron succumb to its deleterious effects as he himself writhed in pain from his hospital bed. He learned much later that the severity of the attack had prompted an agreement to be made prohibiting the use of biological substances on the battlefield.

Sumaina had gotten his first taste of war. Despite the personal cost he had incurred, his love for his country never waned and as such, he continued to dedicate his life to the service of his Queen. Over the next several decades, he rose the ranks to become a General of the Luandan armed forces controlling troop movements in installations scattered across the globe.

His fellow Generals would come to know him as a man of very few words who preferred action over lengthy speeches. It was no surprise that he was summoned in times when important military decisions were to be made. His advice became the foundation for many military successes across the many conflicts they had become embroiled in.

The emergency war council meeting was set to begin shortly. General Sumaina stepped down from the car with several of his entourage in tow. He had been duly briefed by the Queen who was still on bed rest only hours prior to the important gathering. Only senior representatives within the Queen's circle would be allowed to the meeting so Sumaina made sure to gather as many high-ranking commanders within the military to accompany him.

They duly presented themselves at the entrance of the non-descript gate at the far edge of town. Security men in full military fatigue welcomed them with a firm salute. They proceeded to give them a full body search, patting down the length of their trousers and checking each of their pockets. The search concluded with each of them surrendering their weapons to the military men at the door. General Sumaina took out both of his pistols and handed it to the waiting soldier. They stored them away in locked black boxes before allowing them into the building.

''Your guest awaits you inside, General,'' said one soldier to General Sumaina. He gave a hard salute which the General returned with one of his own.

The harsh yellow lights in the corridors lit up the stained walls of its interior. The corridors were entirely made from reinforced concrete with the ceiling forming the shape of a semicircular dome. Various pipes and wires ran along the length of these corridors meandering across different paths in the huge underground complex. The entire building itself was housed within a mountain stronghold in the Northern most part of the city.

Located within a deep sea of vegetation spanning several kilometers, the facility was heavily isolated, far away from the prying eyes of the public. The drive to the complex was littered with several military checkpoints. With great displeasure, General Sumaina's convey was made to stop at each of them to verify his credentials. The Queen Regent had handed him a signed document sealed with her stationary mark. He brought it out each time the security guards stepped forward to address his convoy.

They arrived at a room located in one of the many winding corridors in the complex. Inside was a modestly furnished space with couches lined on the edges of the walls, a wooden bookcase housing several pieces of literature and a large lamp holder with a burning yellow light hanging from above.

The four ceiling fans placed in the four strategic corners of the room spun vigorously to drive out the tropical heat. A small man with large glasses and a receding hairline sat in one of the chairs in the room. He had his head hung down with several pieces of paper piled on the seat beside him. General Sumaina cleared his throat loudly which startled the sleeping man from his reverie.

''Ge-General, it is a pleasure to meet you,'' stuttered the man. The General returned his handshake with a limp one of his own. ''I thought I would be accompanying the Queen to the War Council.''

''She is still indisposed after the attack at the coronation ceremony, Emissary Adoke. I will be her proxy in all decisions made during the meeting.'' The Emissary looked stunned but quickly regained his composure.

''She made no mention of this to me during by de-briefing with her,'' he replied. ''I would expect for some written conf---'' The General made a motion with his hand prompting one of the soldiers to unfurl the Queen's signed letter which he handed over to Emissary Adoke. He read through it quickly through his glasses and handed it back to the soldier. He looked warily at the General and the troop of soldiers around him. Although weapons were not allowed at the gathering their presence remained intimidating and unsettling.

The General was a fierce looking man with a trim beard and menacing scowl plastered on his face. A black scar ran down from his right temple down to the corner of his mouth. He towered over Adoke who was a small man to begin with. The rest of the soldiers stood in close formation behind him, completing the terrifying aura he presented.

''We—well I have several medical reports on the status of the patients afflicted by the attack as well as communication sent from my counterparts in the North American territories,'' said Emissary Adoke finally, turning to the crop of papers on the couch. '' I was hoping to share some of the information I learned from them before the meeting began.''

''The War Council is set to begin in a few minutes, Emissary. Whatever you must share, I suggest you do so during our walk to the venue,'' the General replied tersely.

''Yes...yes of course,'' replied Emissary Adoke as he gathered the papers and hurried out the door with the General and his entourage. They marched at a quick pace down several more corridors, all the while Emissary Adoke shared from intelligence reports he had nested in his hands. He pulled out one and handed it to the General as they reached another security checkpoint leading to a large elevator shaft.

''My contacts in the Chinese consulate have informed me of their attempts to get in touch with diplomatic leaders in the Slovian colonies. They are seeking to broker a truce now that tensions have escalated in the region.'' General Sumaina grunted in reply as he handed back the paper to him.

''Diplomacy can only take you so far, Emissary,'' the General said in reply as they reached the elevator platform. Metal grates surrounding the elevator opened to allow them to step forward. The platform was large enough to accommodate them all at once. The General's entourage piled into the elevator first followed by the General and finally, Emissary Adoke. Once in, the metal grates closed behind them and several mechanical gears creaked into motion as the platform began to descend into the underground shaft below.

They arrived at a large, underground chamber deep below the mountain complex. The elevator dropped them down at the far edge of the space with the grates remaining closed behind them. Emissary Adoke looked out over the edge as yellow lights flickered on revealing the true extent of the underground hollow.

The entire chamber was lined with concrete with walls that extended far into the distance. The elevator platform was attached to the far wall overlooking the shadowy chasm below. Emissary Adoke's heart fell at the sight of the darkness which swirled beyond the elevator's edge.

Another set of mechanical noises echoed across the chamber as a singular platform extended from across the chasm to the elevator platform. Once docked, the elevator doors opened leading to a narrow walkway and set of doors at the far end. The group led by the General disembarked and walked across the dark abyss.

The doors opened up into a beautifully furnished hallway with red carpeting lining the floors and paintings of past Sovereigns in chronological order adorning the walls of the space. The end of hallway opened to a large, circular conference room with several people seated inside, many of whom were engaged in heated discussion. Some turned to the door as the General walked through with Emissary Adoke and the other soldiers in tow.

The room was sub-divided into five sections. Filling those seats were delegates from the five confederacies of the African Union. People dressed in military uniforms filled the seats in the front of each section. Behind them were individuals dressed in traditional outfits unique to their region of origin.

Each section was labelled for easy identification of the delegates. On the far right was the Zulu delegation. The delegates filling the seats were stone-faced and largely quiet in the noisy room. Directly opposite them were seats reserved for the Luandan delegation of which the General headed. Several of the seats were already filled with district chief heads who had arrived earlier, ably represented the constituencies in which they led.

Separated by a vacant aisle on the same side were the Aksum contingent who were talking fervently amongst each other. They were known for their oratory prowess and went on long tirades whenever they were called to speak, much to the chagrin of all those seated as it extended meeting times.

Directly opposite them were the people from the Mazighen empire. General Sumaina held deep respect for their people as their military prowess closely rivaled that from the Luandan Kingdom. Easily persuaded to wage war, the General found kindred spirits with them at these types of engagements. The Kongolese delegation were arranged in the gallery facing the podium at the far end. Many had ventured out to engage in conversation with their counterparts in the other seating sections.

The General ushered his entourage into the seats in front before heading up to the raised platform at the front of the room. He stood before the pulpit and waited for the murmurs in the room to quiet down before beginning his speech.

''On behalf of her Excellency, Queen Yaa-Yaa, acting Sovereign of the African Union, I would like to welcome you to this emergency gathering of the War Council. You are all aware of the unprecedented terrorist attack which sadly claimed the lives of two hundred and thirty-three civilians of our great federation. Even more disturbing was the loss of King Dinga of the Zulu empire who was poised to become our next Sovereign. We have gathered this meeting to discuss our response to this cowardly attack. Queen Yaa-Yaa is still on bed rest and therefore is unavoidably absent but she has communicated her wishes to me. I will represent her and the people of Luanda at this meeting. I would like to begin-''

''- I demand the full attention of the War Council,'' interjected a strong voice from the Zulu section of the room. A man stood up and walked to the front pews of the meeting hall commanding the attention of all those gathered.

General Thabiso Masondo was a man well into his years. Several liver spots flecked his wrinkly skin and the hair under his military style hat was ghostly white. Despite his age, his voice remained firm and boomed across the concentric room as he addressed the crowd.

''Our kingdom is the most aggrieved party in this gathering as we have lost our beloved leader, King Dinga, who was set to assume the Sovereign title of our great united territories. It is only right that we begin this meeting by righting this injustice.'' The room erupted in a wave of voices competing to be heard. General Sumaina glared at General Thabiso from the podium with a dour expression etched across his face.

''What do you suggest, General?'' yelled Emissary Asmaa over the sea of voices. She represented the Mazighen delegation at the meeting.

''I demand that council recognize King Dinga's son, Prince Lethabo be crowned the Sovereign of the African Union. Let us honor the succession of the title to our great federation as enshrined in our collective accord.'' Several voices exploded across the large hall at this proclamation. The entire hall descended in a cascade of dissenting voices.

''Silence!'' boomed General Sumaina's voice from the podium. The gaggle of voices slowly died down and calm filled the hall once more. He heaved in a deep sigh before continuing.

''General Thabiso is fully aware that unilateral declarations of that manner are not permitted at these gatherings. The council will decide collectively on such matters at this forum. You may have your seat again, General.'' With a deep sneer on his face, General Thabiso returned to his seat with the Zulu delegation. General Sumaina motioned to the person who had his hand raised in the Aksum delegation. A tall, dark man with a lanky frame rose from his seat and addressed the council.

''I am Emissary Bruk, representing his Excellency, King Berhanu of the Aksum Dynasty. He sends his condolences to all of those affected by the tragedy which struck our great federation. We also lost many of our citizens to the attack that day and share in your grief. In this time of deep sadness, I would like us to reflect on what makes our union strong and resilient. We should focus on our similarities rather than our differences and stand together in one strong voice against violence-''

''-Please make your point known, Emissary,'' General Sumaina interjected.

Emissary Bruk looked taken aback but continued nonetheless, ''I believe we should vote on General Thabiso's proposal. The War Council has extraordinary powers fitted into its mandate to confer this position.'' The room filled with murmurs of approval as Emissary Bruk returned to his seat. General Sumaina gripped his podium tightly; his anger welling up inside. He had lost control of the proceedings of this meeting. He knew General Thabiso had only made his comment to force a vote through in the council. He had no option but to push through with the action.

''The council members will be allowed to confer amongst themselves before a vote is taken,'' General Sumaina said finally. He motioned to Emissary Adoke who joined him on stage.

''I have no instructions from Queen Yaa-Yaa on such a vote,'' Emissary Adoke whispered, ''I think it best for us to discuss these developments with her before we agree upon a vote.''

''Queen Yaa-Yaa has made her intentions very clear with me during our meeting together. We will vote no on this proposition and have an alternative offered,'' explained General Sumaina, who proceeded to inform Adoke of the Queen's wishes on the subject.

Many minutes passed before General Sumaina called to order the gathering, ''I believe it is time to call on the vote. Each Kingdom's Emissary will address the council. The vote began with the representative of the Mazighen Kingdom, Emissary Asmaa addressing the crowd.

''The Mazighen people understand the need for strength and unity in times of deep crisis. However, we cannot entrust leadership to a young prince who is inexperienced in conflict. As such, we vote no on this proposition.'' A similar sentiment was echoed by Emissary

Bruk of the Aksum delegation and Emissary Idrissa representing the Kongolese delegation. Emissary Adoke also declared the Luandan position thereby defeating General Thabiso's proposition. General Sumaina looked on with satisfaction at General Thabiso who was now engaged in deep conversation with soldiers in his aisle.

The air was filled with voices as Emissary Adoke stood up once more. The room quieted down as he began to speak.

''Given the regrettable circumstances that our union finds itself in, we must project strength in these times. That is why I am proposing to extend the term length of our acting Sovereign, Queen Yaa-Yaa. It would send a clear signal to the perpetrators of this heinous attack that we stand united in the face of terrorism and will not be intimidated by violence.'' Murmurs filtered through the crowd as Adoke returned to his seat.

''We shall put this proposition to a vote. Confer with your representatives once more,'' instructed General Sumaina. The vote quickly held, with the Zulu and Aksum representatives voting down the proposition. This was followed by quick votes of approval by the Luandan and Mazighen delegation. The Kongolese Emissary stood up as the council waited on their vote.

''The Kongolese people recognize the power of succession as laid down by our forefathers of old. It was within our borders that the peace accord was signed and sealed between our individual kingdoms,'' he paused to let the full effect of his words sink in to the waiting ears of the council members.

He continued, ''however given the unique times our union finds itself in, we find it wise to have Queen Yaa-Yaa continue in her role as Sovereign.'' His comments were immediately met with dissent in the room with many Zulu chieftains shouting in protest to the vote.

''The motion is carried. Queen Yaa-Yaa will retain her position as Sovereign of the AU for the foreseeable future,'' declared General

Sumaina over the deafening voices.

Over the next few hours, General Sumaina would make a case to strike and establish a greater foothold in the North American territories. He would show them projector slides of troop movements in the area, greater mobilization of resources to specific sites on the continent and pictures of biological weapon systems which their spies had claimed were in development.

''Our intelligence has picked up reports of a new weapon in development, one capable of dispersing harmful toxins over a wide area of land. The result of such an attack would result in the death of millions over a short period of time.'' He had arrived at a graphic slide showing a man covered in boils and pustules over his entire body. Council members gasped at the images displayed over the projector.

General Sumaina knew that fear was a great motivator. Even the most difficult of members in the council would vote to prevent such a weapon from being used in combat. And in light of recent events, they would have no choice but to follow through with his proposal.

The vote was unanimous and swift. Each member in turn declared their intent to strike against biological targets mainly located in Slovian bases scattered across the North American continent and mainland Europe. It would mean a massive consolidation of troops from the individual sovereign kingdoms in the AU. Cooperation and support would be vital to mount an effective offensive against those sites.

The meeting was shortly adjourned. General Thabiso approached General Sumaina as he addressed some of the delegates who had waited behind.

''A word in private, General,'' General Thabiso whispered. General Sumaina excused himself and both found a solitary corner in the room.

''You must be very pleased with yourself, Sumaina. You've gotten everything you wanted. Your distaste for biological weapons is well known amongst the military. You finally have your excuse to wage your holy war against it,'' said General Thabiso.

''You would have us do nothing, Thabiso in the face of this aggression from the West?'' retorted General Sumaina.

''What I would not have are decisions made based on individual sentiments. I would be better suited to lead the war effort.''

''If you are suggesting our Sovereign is incapable of leading our forces in this fight, then I recommend you take your reservations directly to her.'' Thabiso straightened up and took a step back, not saying a word in reply.

''If you'll excuse me, General, ''General Sumaina said finally before leaving the venue with his waiting entourage of soldiers.

The mobilization of troops quickly followed the decision to wage war across the Atlantic. The AU had largely chosen to remain a neutral party in the conflict, never siding with any faction. The direct attack on its monarchs would change that calculus.

The weeks dragged on and General Sumaina would be called alongside other senior members of the combined armed forces to the palace. He noticed a worrying trend in the proceedings which occurred regularly: the number of military generals attending the meetings continued to diminish with each passing day. Whispers amongst senior generals pointed to the Queen's increasing paranoia for the reduction of senior personnel allowed within her inner circle.

General Sumaina arrived at the palace for his weekly scheduled meeting. He was welcomed by guards at the entrance who directed him inside the imposing building. As a man who spent most of his life in the military, Sumaina had lived an austere life, one devoid of many comforts. The splendor of the Queen's palace had therefore amazed him every time he visited.

Lush, evergreen trees were planted along each of the stonework pathways leading into the castle breaking the sun's harsh glare. Manicured shrub-lined statues were strategically placed around the grounds.

One statue of interest to Sumaina was one of a woman carved several meters high. Sumaina understood the statue to be a nude rendition glorifying the female form. The smooth contours of the woman's breasts were the most prominent feature on the statue. It curved generously and proudly, standing firm, and ending in carefully carved nipples. The silky bow of her back arched forward as she held up what seemed to be a light cloth draped across her sensuously shaped buttocks. An assortment of beads was carved and draped over her supple neck meeting the shape of her body as it ran down her chest and stomach. A singular bead string was carved across her hips outlining its buxom features.

The artist had clearly studied female anatomy with boundless delight as great detail was placed in forming the woman's vagina. Like an inverted mountain peak, the carving ended with a singular line parting the woman's lips in two. The woman also wore long braids which were carved to run down the length of her back.

The entire castle itself was made of a polished white stone which gleamed with fierce brilliance. Each stone was intricately laid atop the other to reveal an ornate repeating pattern of stonework. The palace was reverently called, ''Didan Ina'' or ''Shining Light'' in recognition of its luminous intensity in the tropical sun. Historical records claim that each stone was hand-carved and transported from the Zulu kingdom in the southern portion of Africa to construct the palace.

The interior of the palace revealed the ever-greater affluence characteristic of the royal family. Shiny marble flooring covered the entire area of the large castle. Expensive red curtains with golden embroidery hung across all the windows in the expansive space. The staircase balustrade leading to the upper floors were also made from refined gold. The cloisters leading away from the atrium had large courtyards on either side. A select few people would routinely gather to hear the Queen's address from atop the highest level in the castle.

Sumaina never cared for the excesses of riches and seeing it more up-close did nothing to change his indifference for them. He honestly saw no need for them. Why employ the services of an expensive car when a moderately priced one would do, he wondered? The large palace had several rooms filled into each corner. How many beds could one sleep in during the night?

He followed the winding staircase upstairs till he reached the fourth floor of the palace. The advisory chamber was located on the far left of the staircase landing. Large, wooden doors led into the entrance of the room. Inside was a beautifully decorated space with exquisite paintings hanging on either side from the walls and red carpeting laid across the floor. A three-layered crystal chandelier hung in the center of the rectangular room. In front of the room atop a raised platform was a magnificent gold throne for the Queen. It was from here that she would address her advisors who would be seated on the chairs arranged on either side of the room.

General Sumaina was surprised to find the room vacant. At this time, the room would have been filled with generals and military service men and women ready to brief the Queen on the war effort. Troop mobilisation had already begun and the monarch was expected to be informed on daily activities happening on the battlefield.

Although the military took decisions independently, the Queen retained the power to make final decisions boarding on large-scale military engagements. Sumaina found a seat at the far corner of the room as he waited for other service people to arrive. The Queen herself would usually arrive after they had seated themselves.

A dozen men armed with assault rifles filed into the room and arranged themselves behind the Queen's throne. Following them from behind was the Queen herself. Draped around her body was a flowing white cape pinned to her left shoulder by a floral ruby broach. Adorning her neck was a simple cowry laced necklace complemented by pearl earrings. Atop her head was her gold crown, the symbol of her power passed on through her lineage.

Only the women in her family had the right to claim the throne in her family tree. It was claimed that from the time of the great Queens, only women had been borne from the wombs of her lineage. Nothing could be further from the truth. To ensure women retained power in their family, the male heirs were unceremoniously killed at birth, a tradition which was still practiced. A privileged few like himself was made aware to this horrendous custom while the public was fed the story of only women births.

He doubted anything would come of it if the public were in fact made aware of the practice. The Queenship was a revered position, ensuring unity amongst the tribal chieftains scattered across the region. Coupled with the unholy union with the military, the people could not hope to front an insurrection or mount a successful protest. A necessary evil was established through the years to maintain peace and unity or so Sumaina was made to believe.

The Queen seated herself atop the throne as the soldiers moved behind her. Their guns were clearly visible, hanging from straps across their chests.

''General Sumaina, please give me an update to our progress on the battlefield,'' she asked in a pleasant tone. General Sumaina looked at the door, waiting for another service man to enter the room.

''Is something wrong, General?'' the Queen queried, maintaining her friendly demeanor.

''Forgive me, my Queen, I expected more of my colleagues to be present at this briefing.''

''I have decided that you alone shall provide me with military briefings from now on, General. As Sovereign, I have the authority to make you the Commander of our allied troops in the war effort. Information on military progress will be filtered through you and in turn, you will pass it on to me. Are these terms acceptable to you?''

General Sumaina stiffened up in surprise. He had not expected a promotion of this kind. ''Of course, my Queen,'' he answered finally. He stood up and bowed deferentially towards her, ''It would be my honor to serve you in this capacity.''

''Splendid! Now, shall we carry on with the briefing?'' asked the Queen, motioning him to sit down again.

Sumaina had worked with several regents during his time in the military and one quality was common amongst them all: mistrust. The power which they had accumulated over the years was supposed to make them feel more secure. It always ended up doing the exact opposite, placing them in the line of fire of lesser men and women seeking to enjoy the power with which they coveted. This made them feel ever more apprehensive for their safety, putting less and less trust in the people around them. Many became locked in this vicious cycle of fear until they became trapped in their own minds.

Fears for the Queen's continual safety was not the only lingering concern in the air. Her very power of succession was being threatened by her inability to bare a female heir. To that effect, the Queen had become more avaricious in her desire for male concubines. Servants within her palace whispered the rumors of her sexual exploits over the past few weeks. It was said that more and more men were seen leaving her bed chambers at night, a pattern that became more noticeable as the days went by.

The echoes of love making filled the halls at night much to the unease of her night retainers. The batch of male concubines living in the palace were replaced on a weekly basis requiring a constant search for new, virile men in the area.

Sumaina could only come to one conclusion for this new development; the Queen was barren. For a lineage which relied entirely on the fertility of its female regents, an infertile Queen would spell disaster for the monarchy. The Queen's handlers and doctors had attempted to dispel the rumors, stating that the Queen was in perfect health and was very fertile. The problem, they said, lay with the male suitors who she slept with. Fathering a child worthy of being the next Queen would require virile seed from only the healthiest men in the kingdom.

Sumaina knew that even the best spin-doctors at the disposal of the Queen would not allay those fears for much longer. The rumors were spreading through the kingdom already. The instability which would arise from the situation would spell disaster for everyone in the region.

The next logical step would be for the military to seize power by force, an action many Generals already whispered amongst themselves in small gatherings. However, with the Queen enjoying the privilege of the Sovereign position, such action would only result in mutual chaos for all parties concerned.

The Queen's recent actions suggested she would fight till her last breath if an attempt to wrest power from her was made. Spillover from the conflict in the Northern territories and across the Atlantic had the potential of putting the AU at greater risk of invasion from other nations. The calculus therefore favoured the monarch remaining on the throne, at least for now.

After hearing Sumaina discuss the progress of several ongoing military engagements, the Queen interjected, ''- Commander, how soon can we move on the biological weapons installations you spoke about in the Slovian North American colonies?''

''Our forces are coordinating with our Chinese counterparts to launch a concerted attack on each of the identified bases. We risk alerting the Slovian forces of our plans if we strike prematurely, '' he replied. '' In response to our actions, we are also receiving intelligence of Slovian reinforcements arriving from mainland Europe to bolster their forces in the colonies.''

''And how long would it take for us to send additional troops to aid in the war effort?'' the Queen inquired?

''Many weeks depending on the number of troops you are considering, my Queen.''

''Have twenty thousand more troops sent to the frontlines immediately. Expedite their deployment if you must. I want to end this war as soon as possible so that I may focus on more pressing concerns,'' the Queen said with a hint of finality to her voice. ''An attack on the monarchy must be dealt with swiftly and definitively don't you agree, Commander?''

''Of course, my Queen. I will have the plans drawn up immediately.'' The meeting ended with the Queen leaving the hall with her escort of soldiers flanking her on either side. Sumaina would decode the Queen's directive as an escalation of war, a vision he had shared with her but would not propose directly. A swift end to the battle would see the loss of life kept to a minimum and a reduction to any collateral damage on the battlefield.

His persistent grouse with the Slovians were not against its people but lay with its leadership seeking ever more aggressive means of expand its territorial influence across the world. The treaty prohibiting the use of biological weapons had not been signed off by its government and was still in active use in many battlefields across the world. An attempt to increase their stockpile was strongly opposed by world powers across the globe however no territory sought direct conflict with Slovia. Diplomacy was constantly pursued to forestall direct confrontation, but these always proved abortive.

They were all cowards, Sumaina thought, relying on ineffective methods that only delayed the inevitable. Direct confrontation had always been the long-lasting solution to this problem, a thought shared by some of his colleagues in the military. Only after the terrorist attack on the Queen had any concerted effort been made to root out the problem. The final battle to end the proliferation of biological weapons would be fought in the North American territories. War, it was said, is the continuation of diplomacy by other means after all.

Sumaina left the palace and returned to his residence in the military barracks. On the way back, he glanced out the car window to see soldiers armed with rifles patrolling several major street corners in the capital.

Unseen to the public were plain-clothes officers sitting in bars and at roadside cafes spread throughout the city. They would do what the armed soldiers could not achieve: listen in on conversations and gather intel from the public. The crowning ceremony at the Irin Ajo Oba was seen as the perfect staging point for an attack by the Slovian terrorists as many foreign visitors were already expected at the event.

The Red Dawn terrorist group's brazen mandate sought the abolition of the monarchy and an end to hierarchical rule as practiced in the AU and elsewhere. Its leaders worked in secret to spread its message for a more inclusive government, co-opting several high placed members in the society and government to their cause.

It was therefore not be far-fetched that their members had infiltrated the festivities during the Royal March, Sumaina thought. He made it a priority to find any information which would lead to the discovery of its members thought to be hiding somewhere within the city. It would certainly please the Queen to find individuals who she could make public examples of.

Sumaina was awoken by several loud raps to his doorframe. It was 3 am in the morning, a full thirty minutes before he usually woke up for the day. He rushed to the door to meet the face of a wide-eyed soldier dressed in full uniform. He gave Sumaina a hard salute before returning one of his own.

''What is this about, soldier?'' Sumaina asked rigidly.

''Commander, our sources have gathered important intel which you asked to be made aware of immediately,'' he said hastily in reply.

''Have a car ready for me outside. We leave to the site immediately, '' the General replied.

Sumaina draped on his uniform and headed quickly out the door. The driver immediately sped off as he took his seat in the leather-back vehicle. It would seem providence had shone on him today. If the soldier was right, the information he had to share would greatly please the Queen once she was made aware of it.

The drive took them to a heavily guarded prison located on the outskirts of the city. The perimeter was protected by high walls topped with barb-wire fencing. Several soldiers perched atop platforms patrolled the ground for any unusual activity. The entire structure was made of solid concrete giving it the look and feel of a fortified castle.

Inside were several prison cells filled with sleeping men and women. Some stirred awake as the General passed by their cells, menacing through the bars and reaching out to grab the general. Some were more docile and stared disconsolately as he walked by. Many were here for crimes boarding on criminal activity and were awaiting trial.

Others were suspected terrorist members who had been detained and remanded in prison for several years. They were deemed too dangerous for release and would spend the rest of their lives in prison. A judge would not even be appointed to hear their case.

He was headed for the eastern wing of the complex which was dedicated for deep interrogation. Even at this hour, soldiers could be heard hard at work extracting information from their charges. The blood-curling screams from the interrogation rooms became more pronounced as he neared their quarters. The prison ward had greeted him at the entrance and accompanied him down to a room in one of the interrogation cells.

''One of our agents followed this man to a secret bunker thought to be a hideout for the Red Dawn terrorist cell,'' the warden explained, opening a metal door into an interrogation room. '' We sent out an extraction team to the location and were met with gunfire from members of his gang. He was injured in the operation but managed to survive. We brought him here and have been questioning him since.''

The viewing room had one entire wall covered in glass. Outside the glass window was a metal chamber with its flooring several meters lower than that of the viewing room's. General Sumaina looked out the window to see a man strapped to a chair in the center of the circular enclosing. The clothes he was wearing were torn in several places exposing scars and bruises across his body. Streaks of blood tainted the ground around where he sat.

''Has he disclosed anything of value yet,'' General Sumaina asked.

''Negative sir. He claims he was not privy to the planning of the Royal March bombing; that he only delivers supplies to the sect, '' the warden replied, '' We are still attempting to extract any intelligence from him.'' The man tied to the chair looked up to the viewing glass high above him. He had stirred awake at the sound of the door opening in the viewing room. Several black images stared through the glass into his chamber.

''Please, release me,'' he screamed from his chair. The bounds on his feet and legs dug deep into his skin. ''I told you everything I know already! You want me to confess to the bombing? I planted the bombs. I killed all those people. Now please, take me to prison. Stop torturing me!'' The armed soldier stationed beside him struck the back of his head with his rifle. The man's cries continued to escape his lips through whimpers of pain.

General Sumaina looked out the glass window with a general lack of concern etched across his face. This man was reaping the consequences of his actions, he thought. Terrorists like himself did not deserve sympathy or mercy of any kind. Sumaina had made it his life-long mission to rout out these extremists wherever they hid. Only then could the people enjoy the peace and stability afforded to them by the monarchy. He turned to leave the room leaving the warden inside.

''I want you to extract as much information as you can from the prisoner. I need any names and locations he can provide us. The Queen will reward you generously if you are successful in this, warden.'' The warden replied with a wide grin, exposing his yellowing teeth in the process. He pressed his feet together and puffed out his chest in a deferential pose.

''I will not fail my Queen, '' the warden replied swiftly.

General Sumaina left the prison feeling greatly accomplished. In a few short weeks, he had established solid leads linking the Red Dawn to the Royal March bombing. She would seek to make an example of the captured members during one of her public addresses. He made a mental note to update her on his findings the next time he was called in for a meeting.

Sumaina's love for his country was unwavering and he would continue to do everything in his power to safeguard its interests. He was taught from a very young age that one must love his kingdom above oneself. Only then could the empire truly continue to prosper. Personal sacrifice was a direct consequence of this statement.

For this very reason, Sumaina remained a single man understanding that having a family would interfere with his ability to dispense his duties to the kingdom. This coupled with his ascetic lifestyle afforded him with what many men in a similar position did not have: complete and utter focus towards meeting his objectives. He remained determined not to fail his Queen.

JOURNEY TO THE AMERICAS

From the front page of the Royal Inquirer, dated October 12th, 2021'

- ''It was called, 'The War to End all Wars.' The battle raging in the North American colonies has engulfed the entire planet and has caused smaller skirmishes to break out in several regions. What started as a battle between African Union troops and the Slovian army now involves military formations from every major foreign nation on Earth.

The AU formally declared war on Slovia on the 4th of November 2016 and were quickly joined by both the Chinese empire and Qur'anic Alliance to form the 'Allied troops'. Slovia responded by gathering support from Austria- Hungaria and the combined British and French empires to form the 'Axis' troops.

A recent armistice between the major sides has seen a secession of war for the meantime. Plans for a meeting of world powers in the demilitarised zone between the various North-American colonies have renewed hopes for a treaty signage allowing for some semblance of peace to return to a broken world.

Major leaders from all the nations involved in the war effort are set to be in attendance for the historic peace summit. Each of them have been assured of their safety during the event however given the tenuous nature of the armistice, many have opted for a private security detail to accompany them to the summit. Many commentators...'' –

Tife immersed herself in her studies while studying for a degree in International Relations. She devoted a considerable amount of her time to other pursuits alongside her degree including working to feed the less privileged in homeless shelters. The Luandan monarchy made it a priority to feed all its citizens regardless of their socio-economic status and Tife felt humbled to be a part of those aiding its people in their time of need. She had formed a unique affinity with disabled people as well and worked to care for them by offering home grocery deliveries.

One of the people she visited regularly was in fact Abigail who had lost both of her legs to the tragedy at the Royal March. Every week, Tife would bring a basket of fresh produce and grains to her private residence in the city. Abigail would always greet her with a warm smile plastered across her face.

''You come here too often, Tife. You must focus on your studies,'' she had once said on a particular visit. ''I can get to the store well enough in my wheelchair.

''It's really no trouble, Abi. I enjoy seeing you every week,'' Tife had told her. After losing both of her parents, Abigail was truly the only family she had left. Tife made sure her needs were fully met and catered for them personally whenever she could.

Despite her many extra-curricular activities she maintained a stellar academic record, achieving a Summa Cum Laude award for her academic performance. This did not go unnoticed by the monarchy and she was soon called to be the Emissary for the Kingdom, a high honor for a person of her status. She had made history by becoming the youngest person to serve that post to the envy of many of her colleagues.

Her position had put her in close contact with Queen Yaa-Yaa on many occasions, much to her delight. The regal authority exercised by the Queen had always fascinated Tife. That one woman could wield so much power with poise and grace had always inspired her. When summoned to the palace for royal assignments, she would remember the times she played dress up with her father, donning on a paper crown and a white cape while her father acted as one of her royal servants.

Tife remained grateful to the Queen for the leadership and strength she displayed in these times of war. Even as many regions across the African Union were suffering food shortages, the Queen ensured a constant supply of nutrition to her citizens. She made it a constant priority to ensure her subjects like Abigail would always have food on their plates.

Her duties as Emissary for the crown brought its own retinue of daily tasks, one of which was daily communication with local chieftains in the realm. The Queen encouraged constant feedback from these leaders on the needs of the people to which they governed. It was her goal to ensure the concerns of each and every one of her subjects were met. It was for these many reasons that the people loved their Queen and remained devoted to her. She offered peace and security in times of great crisis and this time was no exception.

The turbulent crisis across the Atlantic had ensured her days were awash with news and communiques from her counterparts across the globe. Reports on the number of casualties and battle outcomes piled on her table as each day went by. She had been working with several of her colleagues to broker a peace treaty between the warring sides. It had therefore come as no surprise to her when a formal armistice had been reached between the various parties. The war had claimed too many lives and had resulted in extreme collateral damage to every kingdom involved. A secession of war would be welcomed by all parties involved.

The summit was scheduled to hold in the next few days and preparations were underway to make the trip to the venue. The demilitarized zone separating the North American colonies was chosen as a neutral location to gather the world leaders. Formal assurances for the safety of the monarchs attending the summit were signed by all concerned parties.

Senior military generals had proceeded to try to dissuade the Queen from attending the meeting as her safety could not be guaranteed. She swiftly disregarded their concerns and proceeded with the planned trip. They responded by urging the Queen to double her security personnel for the journey to the peace summit, a request she reluctantly acceded to.

Tife had been invited to attend the meeting as well and was giddy with excitement as it would be the first time she had ever travelled to the North American territories. Even more exciting still was that she would be travelling as part of the Queen's entourage and would experience her royal protocol first-hand. She began planning for the trip well in advance, meeting with Abigail a few days prior with a large batch of fresh vegetables, meat, and other goods she had purchased from the market.

''I'll only be gone for a few weeks Abi,'' she had informed her on her visit. ''I'll have Mama Uvewa come visit you while I'm gone. She can get you anything you need.'' Abigail wheeled herself into the living room as Tife took her seat beside her.

''I am still very worried about you my dear. I follow the news coming from those colonies. It's not safe to travel there with all the fighting going on,'' said Mama Uvewa pointing to the radio on top of her shelf. Tife took her hands and squeezed them comfortingly.

''I will be fine, Abi. I have been assured that every safety precaution available will be taken. We will also be travelling with our own security detail for the summit.'' Tife however did not reveal her inner fears of travelling to the North American colonies. As emissary, she had been privy to reports of fierce skirmishes happening daily on the continent. Despite a secession of violence, the region remained a powder keg set to explode with the slightest provocation. She could only hope for everything to go as planned.

The big day arrived with Tife being escorted to a nearby boat wharf located on the west side of the capital. Extra precautions were on full display as a convoy of soldiers in gun-trucks followed closely behind her for their protection.

Tife had met an interesting woman riding in the same convoy as herself. She was a dark-skinned woman with sharp, alluring eyes and a clean- shaven head. She wore large hoop earrings and a bright leopard print aso-ebi dress which ran down past her knees. She smiled brightly as Tife entered the car with her and promptly introducing herself as Zala.

''You must be the new Emissary for the crown,'' she said brightly. ''I must say you are a massive improvement over her last.''

''Will you be accompanying us to the summit as well?'' Tife asked.

Zala nodded in reply, ''I am a journalist for the Royal Inquirer. I will be covering the entire summit. I have to say, not many journalists get to be a part of history. I feel very honored,'' she said breathlessly. She leaned in towards Tife, bringing her voice down to a whisper.

''Can you give me any insider information on the status of the war? Why is the kingdom so eager to sign a peace treaty now?''

''I am not allowed to divulge classified information with the media at this time,'' Tife replied with a smile. Zala nodded again as if agreeing with her.

They arrived minutes later at the boat wharf. Tife spotted the large shipping vessel as the car approached the waterfront. Measuring several feet across and powered by coal fired systems, the Queen's royal vessel was a marvel to behold. Three large smokestacks protruded from the center of the massive ship. Several decks made up the imposing ship with the highest level reserved for the Queen and her entourage.

Several military personnel littered the boat terminal talking in small circles as they awaited the Queen's arrival. Tife spotted General Sumaina engaged in deep conversation alongside several of his colleagues at the loading bay. As commander of the armed forces in the war effort, his authority was only second to the Queen's. His presence in the delegation only bolstered the significance of this peace summit.

A loud horn in the distance announced the arrival of the Queen's convoy. Several troops dismounted from gun trucks and arranged themselves in tight formations around the pier. General Sumaina marched towards the lead car to welcome the Queen as she dismounted. Her gold crown was elegantly balanced atop her head as she walked towards the waiting ship. Zala rushed over with pen and paper in hand accosting the Queen with questions on the summit. Tife watched from afar, enamored at the poise and elegance displayed by Queen Yaa-Yaa.

The Queen locked eyes with Tife as she stood near the entrance of the ship with the rest of the soldiers. She beckoned her across as the news reporter continued to assail her with questions. General Sumaina still flanked her, his face frozen in a stern expression.

''Tife, are you ready for an experience of a lifetime?'' she asked with a bright smile.

''Yes, my Queen,'' Tife responded quickly, '' I've never travelled so far before.'' They walked across the pier to the loading platform leading into the boat. Each side of it was flanked with soldiers making hard salutes as they walked past. The Queen lowered her voice to a whisper so that only Tife could hear her.

''You see these men, Tife? They believe they are in control of this world. They could not be further from the truth. Only in a woman's body can life flourish. Without women, none of these men would see the light of day. They owe their existence to us. Remember that in your dealings with them,'' she advised.

''Yes, my Queen,'' Tife responded timidly, looking at either side to the row of grim-faced soldiers. They boarded the boat accompanied with several soldiers following closely behind. The captain and ship's crew welcomed them as they came aboard and proceeded to escort them to their separate cabins across the large ocean vessel. Several seagulls squawked overhead, flying in tight circles around the boat.

The ship's horn blared loudly a few minutes later signaling the start of the trip. The boat pulled away from the wharf and glided swiftly over the ocean water. Tife stayed on the ships deck to watch the massive vessel leave the harbor. It gathered speed quickly, escaping the coastline until it became a blurry sight in the distance.

The journey would take approximately ten days to complete. This would give Tife plenty of time to prepare for the summit as they sailed across the ocean. Meeting with several high-powered delegations had always been a dream of hers. The guest list included every major leader in the world including the current King of the Austria-Hungarian dynasty, a delegation from the Middle Eastern Qur'anic Alliance and representatives from the recently amalgamated British and French monarchies.

The Slovian Czar, Nicholas Romanov VI was also said to be

attending the meeting. He was known to be a severe man, commanding a domineering presence amongst his world counterparts many of whom despised him. His aggressive stance in Europe and in the North American territories coupled with his expansionist agenda were drivers of the conflicts raging across the world.

The journey across the Atlantic Ocean offered many interesting sights to the people aboard the ship. Their boat path was set to take them across the Atlantic to the Eastern coast of North America where they would rendezvous with their Chinese allies. As they sailed through the waters, the captain invited Tife to the boat cockpit where she could enjoy a panoramic view of the ocean.

They came across several beautiful islands filled with green vegetation as the boat skipped across the clear blue waters. The Queen would occasionally leave her cabin to join the rest of the crew on the ship. Her demeanor of regal elegance was momentarily replaced with a friendly air that Tife had never witnessed before.

On many occasions Tife had seen General Sumaina and the Queen engaged in lighthearted discussion in a private section of the boat deck flanked by several armed soldiers. Her gleeful laugh would echo across the ship's halls for all on board to hear.

On the last leg of the journey to the summit venue, Zala had joined Tife on one of the ship's deck. Violent wind gusts coupled with occasional precipitation swept across the ship's surface. Like Tife, Zala wore several layers of protective clothing topped off with numerous scarfs wrapped around her neck.

''You shouldn't be outside here Tife, '' she said as she took a place beside her, ''the captain warns the temperatures will drop even further as we make landfall.'' She brought out a cigarette and lit it with a portable lighter. Taking in a huge breath, she proceeded to breathe out thick plumes of smoke from her nose. She promptly offered a cigarette to Tife which she declined.

''Do you think this summit has any chance of stopping the war from raging on?'' Zala inquired. Tife turned to her with an incredulous expression etched across her face.

''Are you asking that as a reporter or as a concerned citizen of Luanda?''

''From both angles, really. I believe the public deserves to know what decisions their leaders make on their behalf.'' She brought out another cigarette and cupped her hands to protect the wind from blowing out the lighter's flame.

''I was part of the team who negotiated the early terms of the agreement. I feel very strongly about the peace treaty.'' This prompted a hearty laugh from Zala coming out in billows of hot smoke.

''Every diplomat I have interviewed feels the same way. They feel that pretty words and promises can solve all of life's problems. That the pen is in fact mightier than a sword. The truth is that this world is run by people who only believe in the power of violence as a permanent solution. They may openly subscribe to dialogue and negotiation but always end up resorting to using bombs and armies to resolve conflicts.''

''Then why do you report these stories if you do not believe in them?'' Zala stamped out her last cigarette and reached into her pocket for another one.

''The people must be given the reassurance that their leaders have at least attempted to make peace. It is armed with this false hope that they may continue with their days.'' She smiled heartily at Tife before strutting back to her cabin leaving Tife alone in the biting cold of the harsh ocean winds.

The boat made landfall the very next day to the delight of Tife and the other passengers. Light powdery snow fell in thick bundles and layered the ground in a fine, white coating. Tife had never experienced snow before and was amused by the sight of frozen water falling from the sky.

Tropical weather with its heat and humidity was all she had known her entire life making her unprepared for the chilling and bitter colds in North America. She had worn several layers of clothing in addition to a thick jacket. Despite being draped in warm clothing, she shuddered violently as a light wind swept across the snow-covered dock.

The Queen disembarked first followed closely behind by General Sumaina. She wore a thick, white cashmere fur coat and substituted her crown for a floral head tie wrapped into an elegant pattern on her head. Outside, she was greeted by a twin delegation from senior members of the Romanov family and the Chinese emissary to the African Union.

Prince Mikhail Romanov accosted the Queen first as she stepped down from the ship. Accompanying him was his wife wearing a thick brown fur hat and a matching coat. He outstretched his hand to welcome the Queen. He addressed her in the regional Afrikaans tongue.

''On behalf of the Romanov family, we welcome you to the North American colonies. I hope your trip here was smooth and without trouble. This is my wife, Olga. She does not speak your tongue fluently so cannot communicate with you directly.'' He proceeded to whisper a few words in her ear making her face brighten up instantly. She proceeded to reach out her hand to shake the Queen as well. The Chinese envoy quickly followed suit offering a generous bow to the Queen before outstretching his hand as well. He began by introducing himself.

''Your presence is very welcome as always here in our borders, your Majesty. My name is Jinhai Wen. The Emperor sends his regards.

He offers his sincere apologies for not being present to welcome you personally. He has urgent matters of state to attend to. He has assured me that he will be present for the summit holding in a few hours,'' he explained.

He beckoned several women who stood waiting in the distance. Each sported a silky, floral pattern dress which enshrouded their entire body. Their hair was tied into a bundle and decorated with elegant hair pins. The blood-red tint of their lips contrasted heavily with the pale white complexion of their skin. In their outstretched hands was a see-through glass box with a stunning painting of the Queen inside.

''On behalf of the Emperor, we would like to offer this gift to you as a token of our deep admiration for your steady rule in these difficult times. We welcome your support in the war effort against our adversaries.'' This comment prompted a deep sneer from Prince Mikhail who stood to the side.

''We have wonderful entertainment planned for your Excellency later tonight. May we escort you to the royal quarters we have prepared in your honor?'' The Chinese Emissary guided them to several cars parked alongside the ship's harbor. Prince Mikhail took his leave alongside his wife citing pressing concerns requiring his attention. He explained he would be leaving immediately for the Slovian colonies in preparation for the summit proceedings.

Tife's father had always mused on about some of the rich cultural sights he had witnessed during his business trips to the Chinese colonies. Tife became quickly enthralled by the distinctive architecture their cities boasted ranging from their unique multi-story timber-work roofs to their large earthen work temples which featured prominently in the distance.

As they made their way into the central parts of the city, they caught a group of children playing in the snow. The children were unkept and barefoot, wearing tattered clothes which hung loosely from their bodies. As the car made their way past, they abandoned their games to chase alongside the vehicle.

Tife's gaze caught one of them; a boy no older than six years old. He had striking blue eyes and a bowl haircut. Dirt and snow clung loosely to his body and his face was ghostly white. His smile revealed several teeth missing in his mouth. The children proceeded to pelt the car with snowballs which prompted angry shouts from the soldiers leading the convoy. Tife watched as the children slowly disappeared into the white blanket of snow fall.

The car took them to a sprawling walled estate in the heart of the city. Inside was a massive ornamental structure with two similarly designed buildings on either of its side. The large campus was replete with snow covered lawns, two reflective pools now frozen over and staff members in gray overalls attending to the property.

''Your highness will be staying here for the night before your flight departs to the summit venue,'' Emissary Wen explained. ''Your entourage will also be welcome to the guest houses adjacent to the guest palace.'' They all quickly settled in for the night and prepared to attend the banquet prepared for them in the amphitheater.

The entertainment proved to be a delightful experience beginning with a traditional fan dance performed by a women's dance troupe. Each wore matching rose colored outfits and wielded intricately designed fans which they waved as they glided across the stage. Tife was joined on her table by Zala who now sported a sheer flowing orange dress with blue polka dots.

''I have always enjoyed Chinese culture, you know. I find their art and history to be fascinating, '' Zala mused. ''Some say in a few years their population will exceed twenty-five percent of the world's total. I guess we should all begin to learn mandarin then.'' She let out a curt laugh before taking in a long sip of gin from her glass.

The entire amphitheater was empty save for a few seats occupied by soldiers in the front. Zala drew Tife's attention to the gallery where the Queen and General Sumaina sat watching the show.

''Those two will be spoken about for years to come in our history books,'' Zala continued swishing her glass of gin around, letting the bronze liquid just wash to the tip of the glass, ''and depending on the outcome of the summit, they will be remembered as heroes or villains.''

''The Queen may have her flaws, but she has done everything to ensure the success of the summit. She is in the best position to broker a truce between the Slovians, '' 'Tife replied assuredly. Zala breathed in a deep sigh before resting her glass back on the table.

''Negotiation between two autocracies have never stood the test of time. They have always used false treaties of peace to buy time in search of greater leverage against their opponents. I see no reason why this treaty will not turn out the same way,'' said Zala wryly. The ongoing performance on stage became even more animated now as the dancing women were replaced with men wielding swords and other dangerous weapons. They performed several acrobatic moves grunting loudly as they jumped across the stage.

''What would you do differently then? Would you let the war continue unabated instead?'' Tife said indignantly.

''I would end the root cause of the war itself, '' Zala said looking up to the gallery once more.

''You would suggest that our Queen is to blame for the wars raging on around the world?'' Tife asked incredulously. Zala put down her glass and looked her straight in the eyes.

''Not the Queen herself but the very institution of regal authority is at the heart of blame. Kings and Queens amass so much wealth and power that they only logical option is to misuse that power to expand their interests. They order common people to wage war on their behalf while they sit safe in their fortified castles. Their power slowly corrupts them until it consumes them. Power corrupts and absolute power corrupts absolutely after all.''

The performance on stage reached a crescendo with one dancer lunging forward with sword in hand striking another in the chest. The dancer who was struck slumped to the ground as the other dancers rushed forward to take a bow on the stage.

''You sound just like one of those Red Dawn terrorists,'' Tife said as she stood up angrily from the table and proceeded to the frozen, reflecting pools outside amphitheater. She sat on one of the benches beside the frozen reflecting pool watching as large sheets of broken ice floated across its surface.

Zala had enraged her with the suggestion linking the violence to the Queen. The authority behind the monarchy was necessary for peace and unity in the AU. Its position had ensured warring factions in the region remained unified towards a singular goal aimed at the prosperity of its people.

The crown had equally ensured its people remained taken care of even in the face of a global crisis. The blame for constant war lay solely on terrorist elements like the Red Dawn and the Slovian militia seeking greater expansion of their empire. Both these antagonizing forces had sent the entire world at the brink of disaster. Only through the leadership of the Queen did a de- escalation begin to take shape.

She pondered on these things as a figure approached her from across the pool. It was one of the boys she had seen on the side of the road. He was ghostly pale; his body still covered in snow and dirt. He made a feeding motion with his hand bringing them both up to his mouth. Tife tensed up as she stared down the boy. She broke her gaze as a figure touched her shoulder from behind. She turned around to meet a woman with garden shears in her hands. She was dressed in a plain gray robe which ran the length of her body.

''Madam, are you alright?'' the woman asked in mandarin. ''I saw you staring into the bushes.'' Tife turned back to see the boy had disappeared from sight.

''I thought I saw a child behind those bushes there,'' Tife replied, pointing in the direction she had seen the boy.

''Street urchins occasionally sneak into the grounds at night, '' she explained with a wide smile, ''They scavenge what they can find from our dumpsters nearby. I'll have a security guard do a sweep of the area.'' The woman returned to trimming the bushes as the pale moonlight washed over the snow-covered garden.

A few hours later Tife, alongside the royal delegation comprising of the Queen, the General and a few soldiers departed to the waiting plane on the runway. General Sumaina had ordered a contingent of troops to remain with the boat vessel while a smaller group traveled with the Queen. He had already arranged for a troop regiment to rendezvous with them the moment they landed in the demilitarized zone.

Tife grew to understand the General as a meticulous man who left nothing to chance. His organizational prowess had seen him rise to the level of commander of the allied forces. Despite his successful track record, Tife found the man to be humble, never seeking fame or glory for himself. He clearly displayed a devotion to the Queen which won him great favor with her. The Queen in turn seemed the most relaxed when she was around him and entrusted him with greater responsibility for her safety.

Despite their vastly different portfolios, Tife was made to maintain close communication with General Sumaina. One of her duties involved keeping him apprised with the diplomatic effort happening behind the scenes. He would always listen patiently as Tife briefed him on the resolutions from the many meetings she had with her counterparts across the world. After which he would ask her for counsel on the necessity for greater or less military involvement in the war effort. Tife was flattered that a man with his many years of experience would ask her for advice on subjects of military engagement.

The journey would take no less than two hours to arrive at the airport runway. Tife had never flown in a plane before now and her apprehension to the idea of flying was written across her face. Increasing her concerns were the frequent reports she had received from the frontlines of war planes malfunctioning and crashing into enemy territory. Grim reports like those did not inspire confidence on the safety of flying.

The plane taxied down the runway before picking up speed and ascending off the ground. Tife gripped her chair tightly as an uncomfortable sinking feeling began to tug in her belly. She looked out the window to see the plains descend from sight and be replaced by an expansive view of the terrain from above.

From this vantage point, Tife had a bird's eye view of the city landscape. Each building in the Chinese colonies shared the same characteristics with wide ceramic roofing eaves and walls made from wood. Buildings in the center of the city were typically larger than others on the periphery with one in particular standing out from the rest. It covered a vast area and was several stories high. The yellow paint from the roofing reflected the diffuse autumn sunlight making it shine bright in the rich canvass.

''I'm told that building is the Emperor's residence,'' said Zala who had moved closer to Tife's seat, ''He stays there when he visits the colonies,'' and after a brief pause she added, ''I would like to apologize for my remarks earlier. When I have too much to drink, I say foolish things.'' Tife turned to her as she sat down beside her, meeting her gaze.

''Your comments could have been easily misconstrued as high treason if they rose to the Queen's ears,'' said Tife lowering her voice to a whisper. ''Your loyalty should be to your Queen.''

Zala nodded her head in agreement, ''and it is, no question about that. As a reporter, I am made to ask the tough questions. Sometimes these may be upsetting to people's sensibilities, but I must do my job, '' she said with a wide smile across her face.

The aircraft continued to skirt through the sky as it neared closer to the demilitarized zone between the colonies. It flew under the clouds giving Tife a view of the changing terrain as they proceeded west through the region. Clear signs of the devastating conflict dotted the landscape. Smoldering buildings marked the ground where heavy mortar fire had struck.

The effects of her diplomatic efforts or failures became strikingly clear in that moment. The raging war had destroyed people's lives and caused untold hardship on the colonies. The fortified cities on the coast housing various leaders in the region were far removed from the chaos which the conflict had spurred.

The aircraft descended lower until it landed on a runway in a joint military base owned by the AU and Chinese empire. Several military vehicles moved into position as the plane taxied across the runway.

A man dressed in full military fatigue and thick black boots approached the plane as they disembarked. He gave a generous bow to the Queen followed by hard salute to General Sumaina.

''My Queen, this is Lieutenant General Mao Feng Li. He co-ordinates the military effort on the ground. We have been in constant communication since the war began.

''It is a pleasure to meet you, your highness,'' Mao said offering another curt bow. ''Your leadership has been instrumental in our many victories against the tyrants in the west. Forgive the less than agreeable surroundings. The constant barrage of mortar fire only recently seized with the armistice in place.'' The pungent smell of sulfur filled the air as they made their way to a wire-net fencing which stretched across in either direction. Sandbag barricades and spikes lined the entrance leading across into the demilitarized zone.

''The meeting venue is several kilometers in that direction,'' Mao explained, pointing in the direction of the mountains which peaked in the distance. ''The temporary seize fire has allowed for the construction of a conference venue to the North of those hills.

''Do we have a unit patrolling the venue for any signs of sabotage, '' General Sumaina inquired.

''Absolutely,'' Mao responded quickly. ''The seize fire allows for ten units of twenty soldiers each patrolling the territory. A reconnaissance helicopter was also permitted in the arrangements. In the event of any foul play, we will detect it fairly quickly.'' Tife had been part of the team negotiating the terms of the seize fire and was familiar with all the guidelines listed for the historic meeting to take place. She also knew the demands listed by each side of the conflict.

The Allied troops under the leadership of Queen Yaa-Yaa sought the full dismantling of bases dedicated to the development and deployment of biological weapons currently being pursued by the Slovians. An additional demand would see large chunks of the demilitarized zone falling into Chinese hands.

The Axis troops led by the Slovians demanded a full de-escalation of war on their borders in Europe and the Americas and the forfeit of disputed territories in Antarctica, a demand vehemently refused by the Chinese Emperor. With no side willing to budge, Tife could only hope for a reasonable compromise at the summit.

With only hours leading up to the event, the Queen saw it necessary to have a final debriefing with her accompanying entourage for the event. As it was her first time in the Americas as well, she would have unfiltered access to news from the frontlines.

Lieutenant General Mao, General Sumaina and Tife were called in to a small conference room on the military base. Once there, the Lieutenant General proceeded to provide up to date information on the progress of the war campaign. They had a detailed map showing the entire world map laid out on the table. Troops were represented with small wooden blocks like chess pieces on a board. The blocks were spread sparsely in multiple places around the map with a large number placed on the North American side of the board.

''We have lost a significant number of troops in our skirmishes with the Slovians,'' said General Sumaina. ''In the event that talks break down and tensions flare up in the region, our forces may become overwhelmed very quickly.''

''How soon can we deploy another troop contingent stationed in Luanda to the frontlines?'' the Queen posed to General Sumaina.

''All other troop reserves have been moved to aid Queen Salma in her defense against the combined British and French armies in Zaragoza,'' General Sumaina explained pointing to the blocks positioned at the Northern tip of Africa. ''There are fears that they will use this summit to launch a surprise attack and reclaim those territories leaving us vulnerable on our Northern borders.''

''And what do you recommendation as a course of action then, General? ''the Queen demanded.

''Approach the Qur'anic Alliance for an injection of mercenary troops on the frontline,'' he replied finally.

''I seek a de-escalation of war with this peace summit. I have no intention to prolong this war effort any further.'' As they spoke, Tife's mind wandered to the attack on the Capital five years ago that started this conflict in the first place.

She could still remember the overwhelming smell of blood and smoke which filled the air, the haunting sight of the Queen screaming as she was drenched in blood and of course the lifeless body of her father which lay crumpled in the distance. She involuntarily scratched the scar on her leg as the reverie played out in her mind with vivid quality. She had become so lost in thought that she did not hear General Sumaina calling her name.

''...Tife, we asked for your expert opinion on the negotiations. Do you believe the Slovians will honor their side of the truce if we sign the treaty?'' The room was silent as everyone turned their full attention to Tife. She cleared her throat before addressing the room.

''The Slovians have not shown forthrightness in previous signed agreements. Even with a reasonable compromise in place, they may not accept the terms of the treaty. A strong military deterrent in place would provide a stronger position for establishing a longer lasting agreement. A short injection of funds to ensure a successful summit would prevent future spending on any long- term conflict.'' Her response was met by a wide grin from the Queen, a grunt of affirmation from General Sumaina and a respectful bow from Lieutenant General Mao.

''Wise words we can act on, don't you agree, General?'' The Queen said as she reclined in her seat. General Sumaina stroked his beard pensively as he gazed at the map.

''I'll have word sent to my proxies in the field. If we expedite the troop deployment, we can have several contingents sent to the frontlines within weeks,'' General Sumaina added several blocks to the border positions in mainland Europe.

''Excellent! Lieutenant General Mao, have the convoy prepared for our trip to the summit,'' as they made their way out the door, the Queen added, ''Tife, I would like to have a private word alone with you.'' As the two military generals made their way to the tents to finalize preparations, the Queen motioned for Tife to take a walk with her around the base.

As Emissary for the crown, Tife had the audience of the Queen on many occasions, however these were more of a formal nature in the interest of discussing matters of state with her. She had also shared many of these engagements flanked by General Sumaina or another dignitary within the empire. Never had she enjoyed a private meeting in the presence of the Queen before, a privilege considered rare for many in the kingdom.

They passed by several service men busy in the base. A joint military drill was underway as they passed by a large tent. The drill sergeant barked orders for the troops holding identical rifles in their hands. They turned and marched in perfect synchronization to each command.

The drill sergeant shouted another command as the Queen and Tife drew near prompting a harmonized acrobatic throw of their rifles in the air and various cries of deference directed at the monarch. Waving them down as she passed by, the service men drew hard salutes until she walked by.

''Oh my, they are putting on quite the show in my honor, don't you think Tife?'' she asked curiously. When Tife looked away nervously, the Queen met her momentary gaze with a smile adding, ''you are permitted to speak freely around me.''

''A strong military is always required in times of war,'' Tife began saying. ''They must always be prepared in case of another attack. However, they do seem to be putting a great deal of effort into impressing you.'' The Queen let out a hearty laugh at those remarks. The chilling winter winds whisked across their bodies as they strolled across the base. Tife wondered internally why anyone would want to live in such inclement weather. She longed for the tropical sun which shun brightly in the sky as it regularly did in Luanda.

''I do appreciate candid remarks for a change. Everyone is usually so careful when they speak to me.'' She paused as they reached the edge of the demilitarized zone again. The wire edge fencing and spike blocks were not the only deterrent to an attack. Mounted machine guns were arranged in strategic locations around the fence. Any would-be attacker would risk staring down the muzzle of these rapid-fire machines.

''You remind me very much of the daughter I never had, Tife. If not for the royal succession of blood, you may have made an excellent Queen yourself someday,'' Queen Yaa-Yaa said finally. Tife turned in shock to the Queen who responded with a wide grin. Tife's feet remained rooted to the spot as drill cries boomed in the distance.

THE SUMMIT

A military convoy sat parked near the entrance into the demilitarized zone. General Sumaina had a reconnaissance unit dispatched hours prior to the meeting to scan the area for any suspicious activity. He possessed little faith in the Slovian assurance for a conflict-free summit. Their duplicitous nature and aggressive stance in the region made trusting them difficult.

Adding to his concerns were reports of large army mobilizations on the Slovian side; an activity which could easily be misconstrued as a renewing of tensions and a prelude to war in the event talks broke down. In response, General Sumaina with the permission of the Queen ordered a standing force at the ready in the military base and outposts. He would ensure they had an adequate response plan available in the face of renewed aggression.

In the event of a violent break in talks, the General discussed emergency escape plans with the Queen before they departed the base. A helicopter was on standby at the base ready to deploy and airlift the Queen from the summit if needed. Several units also stood at the ready in the military base ready to provide cover fire if required. The General made sure to honor every part of the armistice while preparing for every available contingency he could imagine. He vowed not to be caught off-guard.

The convoy departed the base making its way to the conference venue deep within the mountain terrain. General Sumaina rode in the same car with the Queen and Tife. He instinctively touched his side arm at each bump they hit in the road. Fortunately for them, a route had been cleared and secured by an advance unit before they travelled along the path. A service man would greet them with a hard salute as they cleared another checkpoint in the road. Several of these were posted to safeguard the lives of the delegation proceeding to the summit grounds.

The General pledged to protect the Queen and would honor that promise with his life if required. He had been duly informed of the Chinese Emperor's wish to make separate security arrangements to arrive at the summit venue. General Sumaina knew the man to be overly cautious with reports circulating that he never actually slept in his palace and instead opted to sleep in secret bunkers spread out through the area. As a man who had made many enemies in his lust for power, the Emperor was wise to keep his movements secret, Sumaina thought.

The snowy peaks of the mountains came into focus as they forged deeper into the icy terrain. The General peered uneasily out the window of the armored vehicle as they made their way past. An ambush could easily occur in these mountainous regions and for that, he would be especially cautious as they made their way through.

The gray façade of the summit venue came into view as they journeyed past the last of the imposing hills. The building was the only one present built in the center of several tall mountains. Parked beside the building were several helicopters which General Sumaina assumed were owned by world leaders already present at the event many of whom he had never met before.

Dignitaries expected to be present at the venue was the Czar of Slovia, Nicholas Romanov VI, the Prussian Premiere Sophia Schulze, the Austria-Hungarian King Zoltan Verdes, the Sovereign of the African Union Queen Yaa-Yaa and the Chinese Emperor Mo

Xuefang. Representatives from the Qur'anic Alliance and the British and French monarchies were also expected at the event. As they refused to send their monarchs to the summit, they would be barred from ratifying any treaties and would not be direct participants.

The summit was hailed as the first of its kind, attracting powerful rulers of diverse territories across the planet to one venue. With so many strong personalities present, the risk of the event devolving into chaos was highly probable. As the highest-ranking General in the army, General Sumaina was tasked with knowing his adversaries completely in order to craft out an effective strategy to best them. He had thus learned of several strange facts regarding each of the monarchs.

The Austria-Hungarian King for instance was rumored to exhibit borderline insanity from time to time. It was gathered that he would actively participate in torturing suspected dissidents in his kingdom by cutting of their fingers and ears himself in his throne room. His strict policy against opposing views made his grip on power absolute.

The Prussian Premiere was rumored to be a cannibal, consuming the flesh from the prettiest women she could find in her empire. She credited this practice to the youthful look she maintained over the years.

The Slovian Czar was said to maintain a secret prison for rebels and dissidents who worked endlessly till they succumbed to starvation, exhaustion, or disease. Reports of dead bodies lying exposed in these labor camps for days were rampant. Whether it was a by-product of the massive power to which they wielded, each ruler exhibited an instability which made working with them difficult. General Sumaina would remain at high alert as he engaged with each of them.

The venue itself was policed by several armed guards wearing different uniforms. Each monarch was allowed one unit comprising ten soldiers to be present at the event. Many journalists present jockeyed around dignitaries loitering outside the hall hoping to scoop the next big headline which would boost their newspaper sales.

A large bell rang signaling the start of the proceedings. General Sumaina's military unit greeted them at the entrance of the large building and proceeded to escort his entourage into a large semi-circular venue hall with a large screen hanging in front. A plump, rotund man with a handle-bar moustache announced their arrival to the room filled with seated dignitaries and journalists from across the world.

''Presenting the Sovereign of the African Union and Queen of Luanda, her excellency Queen Yaa-Yaa,'' he declared, his voice booming across the hall. He repeated his greeting in several languages for the benefit of everyone seated. General Sumaina walked closely behind as Queen Yaa-Yaa made her way elegantly down the aisle and into a circular seating arrangement in the front of the room. He ordered his military escort to have a seat in one of the first aisles in the large auditorium alongside himself. He was determined to maintain a close eye of the proceedings.

Already seated at the table was Premiere Sophia, a woman with long, blond hair and ocean blue eyes. Adorning her head was a diamond crown with a matching shawl which ran down to her shoulders. Queen Yaa-Yaa gave a courteous bow of acknowledgement which the woman returned with one of her own. Standing behind her was a severe looking woman in a plain green uniform who had her eyes affixed forward, never blinking once.

''Next, it is my honor to present King Zoltan Verdes, ruler of the Austria-Hungarian empire to this summit.'' Entering through the doors and walking with swift strides was a bald man with an impressive white beard. He sported a finely embroidered grey tunic and a red cape which fell to his ankles. Following briskly behind him were five seemingly identical women with jet black hair tied back behind their heads. They took a seat in the aisles provided for them with the rest of the dignitaries while the King took his place on the seat beside Sophia.

''I have the pleasure of welcoming the Czar of Slovia, his excellency Nicholas Romanov VI to this auspicious occasion.'' Walking slowly into the room was a bullish man wearing a blood- red uniform with a blue sash draped across his rotund belly. Accompanying him were several soldiers wearing thick fur hats. The Czar sat heavily into the seat beside the Austria-Hungarian king.

''And lastly, I would like to welcome Emperor Mo Xuefang, leader of the Chinese Empire to this gathering.'' A man wearing flowing black robes topped off with a flat, rectangular hat walked down the aisle and into the seat across from the Slovian Czar. The Czar stood up and fumed as the Emperor took his seat and ran his fingers down his long, white beard.

The air remained tense as the summit began. General Sumaina instinctively touched his side arm hidden inside his breast pocket. Standard protocols dictated no firearms be allowed into the venue but that would not prevent him from having one close to his person. The announcer walked up to table seating the various monarchs. Offering a respectful bow, he turned his attention back to the audience.

''We shall now begin the peace summit. I invite the Prussian Premiere, her Excellency Sophia Schulze to moderate this event.''

''Thank you for the kind introduction,'' she began in her own language as she rose from her seat. Emissaries behind each of the monarchs stood at the ready to translate her words in real time into their own.

''I was chosen to be the moderator at this event since the Prussian people have decided to remain neutral in this conflict. We all desire one thing, for peace to return to our lands. This war between our empires will tear this earth asunder. It is time we set our grievances aside and embrace-.''

''- I did not come here to share nice words with any of you,'' The Czar interjected, shooting up from his seat and slamming his fists on the table, ''I came here to demand an end to your siege on our military installations both here and near the seat of my kingdom. I also demand an end to the harassment of my people living peacefully in the borderlands of my colonies.''

''You speak of harassment when you send your assassins to murder me in cold blood?'' Queen Yaa-Yaa stood up to face the Czar, ''your insatiable expansionist agenda is what prompted my people to war.''

''I am not responsible for the actions of a rogue terrorist group in my empire. Your grouse is with the Red Dawn cell and not with me. Desist from further action or we will ramp up our attacks on your bases.'' The tense exchange prompted the military service men and women in the audience to stand up from their seats. General Sumaina began to pull out the pistol from his breast pocket. He signaled to his unit to be on the ready for his command.

''There will be plenty of time to make your demands,'' Premiere Sophia interjected, seeking to maintain control of the proceedings, ''the goal of this summit is to reach a reasonable compromise between warring sides. Let us not get ahead of ourselves. Please resume your seats.''

The Czar angrily slumped back into his seat and fumed silently. Queen Yaa-Yaa glared heavily at him as she sat back down as well. Satisfied with the easing of tensions in the room, General Sumaina returned his pistol back to its holster. He watched the rest of the proceedings at high alert from his vantage point in the front row occasionally standing up to survey the outer perimeter of the auditorium.

The peace summit was heralded as a beacon to the importance of open dialogue between opposing sides. Sumaina saw it only as a monument of capitulation and weakness. The precipitation of war stemmed from a stubbornness exhibited from the Slovian Czar to maintain his biological weapons stockpile, a main source of contention in the talks. The diplomatic efforts led by their foreign delegation had ironed out many of these details but the capricious nature of the monarchs placed considerable doubt whether they would agree to the terms.

It was important for each of the warring sides to see their figure heads accept the terms of a treaty giving an even greater breath of importance to the peace summit. The General continued to give voice to the significance of military superiority, a sentiment appreciated by Queen Yaa- Yaa. Maintaining a strong and robust military force was key to maintaining peace and not signatures on a paper. Sumaina would not see the military strength of the African Union wane from an inconsequential agreement between monarchs.

The summit itself was expected to last no longer than a day. The monarchs would read the terms of the peace agreement alongside their diplomatic counterparts. Once they were satisfied, they would all sign the treaty in a big press event held in the evening.

Several items of discussion were still left up for debate including claims to the territory in the upper provinces of North America. Slovia and Chinese powers drew strong claims to the region seeking greater control of the remote lands.

Slovia also demanded troop withdrawals from several of its occupied territories in Europe. Aided by AU forces, the Chinese Emperor had successfully seized several border cities owned by their adversaries in Eurasia. The treaty would see many of these cities returned to them.

A key area of contention was the biological stockpile held by the Slovians. The treaty would see a total dismantling of all biological sites they owned; a move they vehemently resisted. They argued that they were not signatories to the previous treaty and were not obliged to give up their weapons arsenal. Sumaina was insistent that they not back down from this demand. The Slovians must give up their stockpile for a peace treaty to be agreed upon. Any compromise to the contrary would be strongly opposed by him and the military.

A break in the negotiation allowed for the monarchs to meet with their respective advisors who would provide guidance to their leaders regarding tendered proposals. Whilst other leaders convened with large sets of accompanying personnel, Queen Yaa-Yaa met in a private room with General Sumaina and Tife to discuss the proceedings.

The Queen explained the compromise she had agreed to: a full withdrawal of her forces from the territories in North America and Europe for the dismantling of all biological weapons depot owned by the Slovians. The Chinese Emperor had also demanded full access to the resource belt in the demilitarized zone. The distribution of territories in the upper North American provinces, the 'Terra Incognita' as it was known, had not been agreed upon and would still remain a subject of debate in the coming months.

''And your opinion in all of this, General? Do you believe we should proceed?'' Queen Yaa-Yaa probed.

''The Slovians cannot be fully trusted,'' General Sumaina countered, ''We would have to guarantee that they complied with the treaty.''

''The proposal requires outside observers to witness the systematic decommissioning of their bases as well as routine inspections to ensure compliance,'' Tife explained, ''We will be on the ground to verify any claims they make throughout the process.''

''I would like to see an end to this war, General. My people have paid the price of war for long enough,'' the Queen added.

The terms were agreed upon. General Sumaina however had no faith in the Slovians and their commitment to an agreement. His many years of military experience also told him that a long drawn out conflict between their warring empires would only spell ruin for both sides. He would have much rather preferred settling this conflict by taking over these installations through direct military force. The biological arsenal being developed by the Slovians put their kingdom in grave jeopardy. His role as an advisor to the Queen precluded his ability to make such drastic decisions.

The proceedings resumed in the evening with the delegates arranging themselves in their seats. The monarchs took their positions at the forefront of the large hall. Velvet curtains with a dove insignia had been hung up on the walls of the venue. Several journalists jostled to the front of the room to have pictures taken of the historic signing to take place. Premiere Sophia Shulze stood up to face the delegation once the room had settled down.

''I believe we have arrived at a fair compromise which each side can agree on,'' she declared. ''After much deliberation, each side has agreed to a full cease fire and an end to all military aggression. This momentous day will be marked in celebration of this agreement aptly called the 'Americas Peace Accords'.'' The air was filled with furious scribbling from the journalists occupying the front. Queen Yaa-Yaa stood up to address the crowd. Her gold crown radiated with the reflection from the yellow lights in the room.

''We the people of the African Union herald the arrival of this peace agreement and an end to this senseless war perpetuated by unnecessary aggression, '' she said while offering a side-eye glance to the Czar. ''We fully agree to commit to the terms outlined in the framework.'' The Czar quickly rose up as Queen Yaa-Yaa resumed her seat at the table.

''As do my people, ''the Czar replied. ''We were nothing but helpless bystanders in this war. My only interest was the defense of my people and I was attacked for doing so. We are equally glad to put this war behind us. As a gesture of peace between our empires, we would like to extend an invitation to witness the public execution of Red Dawn terrorists in our largest district city of Krepost. We have plans to adequately care for any delegation you send.''

After the few closing remarks from the monarchs, The ceremonial signing of the peace agreement quickly followed suit. Each monarch took turns scribbling their unique signatures on the agreement which was accompanied with a photo taken of them together.

The summit was heralded as a massive success for all those who attended the event. General Sumaina on the other hand brooded in silence. They had given up considerable leverage in the negotiations on a promise by the Slovians. He had not expected the Queen to accept terms which would weaken their position in the war effort. This miscalculation could only harm the security of their empire in the long run. Compromise only showed weakness to your enemy.

''Your Highness, our transport back to the Chinese colonies is ready, '' he whispered to the Queen who was taking questions from reporters circling her.

''Thank you all for being here for this historic event. May peace reign in our lands once more,'' the Queen declared before walking outside to the waiting convoy in front. She turned her attention to Tife who followed closely behind.

''Tife as my Emissary, I would like you to represent me at the public execution in Krepost. The Czar has given his word that you will be safe but I will have the General arrange an escort of soldiers to accompany you as an added precaution,'' the Queen directed.

General Sumaina ordered several members of the advance unit into the convoy escorting Tife while he made it back to the base with the Queen's escort. The area was quickly overwhelmed with the sound of vehicles and helicopters taking off. The grey façade of the peace venue quickly disappeared from site as they passed the last of the surrounding mountains.

Tife was accompanied by Zala and two other Chinese representatives as they joined the military convoy back to the Slovian side of the demilitarized zone. She fully understood the risks of travelling to enemy territory and was glad the Queen had ordered a military troop to accompany her on the visit.

She understood her responsibility as Emissary would necessarily put her in perilous situations requiring diplomacy. The privilege of representing the Queen however on such an auspicious assignment was not lost on her. It meant she would enjoy much of the same privileges extended to a monarch on her visit to a foreign empire, a fact which filled her with nervous delight.

The gates leading into the Slovian base slid open as their car quickly made its way past the last of the military checkpoints of the demilitarised zone. Much like their Chinese counterparts, a heavily guarded military outpost secured the entrance into Slovian territory. Several units of soldiers sporting auburn-colored uniforms and fluffy hats littered the military base. The base was covered in a white veil of snow as it began pouring from the sky.

Escorting them into the city was a pale, gaunt man in his late sixties. He introduced himself as Igor Smirnov, the Councilor in charge of the district of Krepost. He informed the delegation that he would be directly responsible for their care during their brief stay in Krepost. Tife however was struck by the rigidness of the man. The mechanical motion of his movements reminded Tife of a puppet being controlled by the strings of their puppeteer.

A helicopter took them across the territory to a helipad on the far east side of the region. A combination of sleet and snow fell in large plumes obstructing their view as they travelled through the sky. The helicopter arrived at a landing base not far from the city gates. Igor explained that security reasons prevented they land within Krepost and would take a car into the city limits instead. Several red flags with the symbol of two eagles facing opposite directions waved in the air on mounted poles as they reached the tall gates leading into the city.

''As you can see, the people in Krepost enjoy unparallel peace and security, something our noble Czar would like to extend to every region willing to accept his glorious leadership,'' Igor declared with a toothy smile as they made their way down the streets deeper into the city. Both Tife and Zala could understand his language so he addressed them in his native tongue.

The car slowly made its way through the snowy mist covering the streets of the city. They passed street after street of identical, rectangular buildings with chimneys that billowed with thick plumes of black soot. The combination of snow and ash matted the windows of the vehicle making it increasingly hard to see outside.

Through the hazy mist of the windows, Tife spotted several people walking about in the streets. Despite the chilly weather outside, many wore the same bland light blue attire; a far cry from the colorful outfits adorned by the people in Luanda. The men sported long-sleeved tee shirts and trousers while all the women wore flowing dresses that reached down past their ankles. Many walked huddled in pairs to warm themselves as they hurried down the streets.

Soldiers dressed in the same auburn uniforms as seen on the military base were posted sporadically on various street corners. Draped across their backs were intimidating bayonets with sharp spiked tips.

Tife peered out the window as a soldier accosted a couple striding down the street. The couple froze in terror as the soldier shouted several commands to them. Apparently unsatisfied with their response, the soldier called upon several of his colleagues to his aid. One soldier struck the man from behind with the hilt of his gun and dragged him into a nearby car. The woman accompanying him cried in anguish as he was whisked away in the vehicle.

''We have a strict curfew after six o'clock here in my city, '' Igor explained as he noticed Tife's interest in the scene happening outside, ''you must have permission to walk the streets after this hour. My people know of these rules but unfortunately some choose to flaunt them,'' he finished with another toothy grin.

They arrived at a heavily guarded compound in the center of town. Igor explained it was the state house reserved for foreign delegations. The interior was bedecked with painted symbols of the Czar and the state flag, a constant reminder of the absolute power wielded by the monarch.

Despite the many similarities of the power matrix in the Slovian colonies, Tife could not help but draw a clear distinction between theirs and the one practiced back in her homeland. Whereas Queen Yaa-Yaa strived to take care of her subjects, the Czar had shown neglect for his own. The war-mongering posture of its ruler had bankrupted the expansive empire and impoverished the kingdom.

The people clearly lived in fear of their rulers, a fact on full display in the city. Her job as Emissary however was not to judge the actions of a people's rulers but to find ways of cooperating with them. She was saddened however that the people would have to suffer for the poor choices of their rulers. Igor addressed the delegation as they settled into the posh accommodation provided for them. The contingent of soldiers posted to guard them were housed in a separate block beside the house.

''I have other functions to attend to but if you require any assistance, the men posted outside your door will be happy to help you, '' he gestured to the two soldiers guarding the entrance. He informed them of the time for the execution as he stepped outside the door into the frosty air. The pale moonlight glowed ominously above in the distance.

''You are guests of the Czar and are fully entitled to explore the city,'' he added as he handed them red strips of paper each marked with a gold crest in the shape of two eagles.

''We ask that you keep these on you at all times in case you are accosted by our soldiers. It signifies that you are our guests for the duration of your stay. We do ask that you not speak to any of the locals in my city. They are all well aware of the rules against interacting with foreigners and will be met with harsh punishments if they are caught.'' He gave a curt bow as he left them alone in the sprawling estate.

The bitter cold winds from outside wafted occasionally into the poorly insulated building. Tife made her way upstairs from her room to the living room below to find Zala curled up in a ball beside a lit fireplace; her journal notes spread out beside her.

The flames from the fire crackled and danced across her ebony face. Tife picked up the notes and found a seat beside the fireplace. The warmth soothed her bones which ached from the cold. She longed for the warm, sunny daylit skies back in Luanda. She would be glad for this assignment to be over.

Much of Zala's notes were dictations from the summit that had held the day before. It detailed the conversations from the leaders who attended the conference as well as individual interviews she had received from some of them.

She had made several notes from the interview she had with the Slovian Czar. Zala had pressed him numerous times on the reports of the leader's connections with the Red Dawn terrorist leader said to be hiding somewhere in the colonies. The Czar had vehemently denied any knowledge of his whereabouts and pivoted to what he described as his success in delivering a steady supply of food to his people both in the colonies and the mainland.

Zala made many notes on the conditions of the people she had seen during their visit thus far writing, 'the Czar's comments on constant market supply lines is in direct opposition the current realities experienced in the colonies. Many of the residents in Slovia's largest colony of Krepost seem malnourished and underfed.'

'Strict curfews in place seek to curb the activities of dissident groups like the Red Dawn from operating unnoticed in the city. Soldiers constantly patrol the streets searching for members of the terrorist group.' Tife quickly returned the notes beside Zala as she stirred in her sleep. She sat back and watched the flames cast shadows across the walls of the decorated living room space.

Zala's notes reflected many of her personal thoughts on the matter. Her father had sat her down many times to discuss politics and would always re-echo a strong sentiment of his: that leaders are responsible for their people. If a leader cannot take care of their people, then it was the duty of the people to revolt against their rulers. He shared these strong views in confidence with Tife and asked her never to repeat them to another person. Opinions such as those would easily be misconstrued to be treasonous against the crown.

Sentiments such as those surely would not apply to the rulership displayed by their Queen, she thought. Queen Yaa-Yaa offered peace that many empires could only dream of. Like the Queens before her, she had demonstrated a unique acumen to manage a diverse kingdom and weigh out the expectations of her subjects.

As Sovereign, she had maintained the territorial boundaries of the empire and fought back against its most dangerous enemies. The Czar could learn many things from Queen Yaa-Yaa on what true leadership looks like. As she mused to herself, her eyes fell heavy under the burning embers of the crackling fireplace, allowing her mind to drift into the cool darkness.

Tife awoke alone in the sprawling living room of the building. The diffuse light from outside washed into the concrete interior of the state house. She quickly rushed upstairs, got ready and returned downstairs to find Zala and the other two Chinese delegates seated by the glowing fireplace. She had barely spoken to either one of them and took the opportunity to formally introduce herself to them.

The woman introduced herself as Chen, the newly appointed Chinese foreign Emissary to the Slovian empire. Now that formal diplomatic ties were established between the two kingdoms, she was charged with communicating with Slovian delegates in matters of state.

The man who accompanied her was named Han, a reporter for the Tiantang newspaper. Beside him was a large case with his camera rig inside. Zala in her usual colourful fashion sported a Kente print hair-tie with a matching dress under a thick sweater. Attending to them was a pale woman wearing a white maid gown. Thick swathes of steam rose up as she poured a generous amount of coffee into a cup and handed it to everyone seated.

Zala took a huge whiff of the white, hot steam flowing from the cup before remarking, ''there is nothing like a nice cup of coffee in the morning, don't you agree? Too bad it's not as good as the coffee we get back home.''

''Has the councilor arrived to take us to the execution grounds?'' Tife inquired.

''One of the guards told me he will be here momenta…I believe he is here right now,'' she said as several knocks echoed through the room. The maid shuffled to the door to welcome in the Councilor.

The chilly air from outside greeted them in the warm living room.

Igor escorted them to a waiting car parked outside the estate. Following closely behind were several armed guards who cautiously scanned the area every so often. In stark contrast to the activity she had seen the day prior, the streets were completely empty save for a few soldiers who still patrolled the area. Igor explained that a mandatory gathering had been called expressly for the public execution. Commercial activities would be suspended until the end of the event.

The arrived at an expansive plaza with ornate buildings several meters high framing the massive square. Crowded inside were several thousand residents from the city. Five units of soldiers stood behind them in close formation alongside three imposing military tanks.

Two large bronze statues in the image of the Slovian ruler stood on either side of the large stage erected on the steps of the state building. A large, red banner hung from the front of the building with their recognizable eagle insignia printed boldly in its center.

They all stepped out of the vehicle and made their way up the state building steps to the top where they could be in full view of the crowd. Igor stepped up to the podium in front. With a loud cry, he pressed a balled fist to his chest and turned to one of the brass statues of the Slovian Czar. The people in the crowd followed suit, pressing their hands to their chest in salute to their leader.

Tife was momentarily jolted at the sound of gunshots which rang from the back. The soldiers had shot their rifles to salute their Czar. Tife had witnessed first-hand the absolute power the Slovian Czar exerted over his people. Igor turned his attention back to the crowd addressing them in his local tongue.

''On behalf of our noble Czar, his Excellency Nicholas Romanov VI, I welcome our guests from the Chinese and African empires.

With the signing of the America Peace Accords that our noble leader negotiated against his rivals, we have recorded a huge victory for the people of Slovia.'' The crowd of people gathered cheered in delight at these words. Igor outstretched his hands and with starry eyes, gazed into the distance.

''Despite the unprecedented peace our noble leader has ushered in, there are those amongst you who seek to destroy this for selfish gain. We will not let these agents of perdition destroy what our visionary monarchs have fought so long to achieve. Subversion of the state will not be tolerated.'' This remark was met with hisses and boos from the crowds. As he spoke, large gallows several meters high were wheeled unto the stage. On it were arranged three nooses which hung from its highest horizontal beam.

''Patriots amongst you duly alerted my soldiers of the whereabouts of these so called 'Red Dawn' rebels in the city. They were generously compensated for offering up this information. Bring out these rogues for all the people to see,'' Igor commanded. Armed soldiers pushed three men unto the stage. Their clothes hung in filthy rags from their body. Their hair was unkempt and paired with their scruffy beards gave them the resemblance of wild animals.

Strapped to their ankles and wrists were thick, rusted iron chains which dangled and scrapped across the concrete flooring. The soldiers roughly took them by the arms and thrust them beside the podium. Igor grimaced and spat on one of them as they looked on at the heckling crowd.

''These men deserve nothing less than death for plotting and scheming against the empire,'' Igor declared. ''They are also responsible for putting our nations sovereignty in danger by plotting to overthrow the leaders of our now friendly kingdoms. They put all our lives in jeopardy and will forfeit their lives!'' The people raged in reply, shouting and screaming in agreement.

Tife looked upon the faces of the three men gathered. The attack at the Royal March filled her mind once more. These men represented an organization which took the lives of several people, including her father's.

The images of bodies strewn across the floor came back in vivid detail. She recalled her father's face contorted in pain as his life evaporated from his body. Tife, determined to keep her composure, balled her fists as the white-hot anger began to well up inside her.

Igor gave a nod to the soldiers who responded by dragging the men to the suspended board atop the wooden gallows. Each one had a noose placed over their heads and tightened around their necks. The people's voices thundered in reply. Zala and Han moved in position to get a better view of the execution. Han set up his camera while Zala vigorously scribbled notes on her pen pad. Igor moved over to the large structure and motioned his hand to a lever to its side.

The crowd chanted repeatedly, ''DEATH TO THE TERRORISTS!'' whilst jostling frantically in place. Tife watched closely as the tension built up in the air. The men in the gallows stood motionless, accepting their deaths before a hungry crowd. Each one closed their eyes, waiting for their ends to come.

Igor pulled down the lever and immediately, the board underneath the men gave way. The nooses caught their bodies and suspended them above the ground. The men thrashed their legs as the noose tightened around their necks. Their faces turned bright red as blood vessels exploded across their body. Foam began to pour out of their mouths as their lives slowly faded away.

One man had stopped kicking and hung lifelessly from the noose. The others held on a little longer until the kicks from their legs became twitches and spasms. All the men now hung limply from their nooses; bloodshot eyes open in painful agony.

The screams from the crowd now grew to a fever pitch as the execution drew to an end. Zala continued to take notes as the bright shutter from Han's camera lit up the lifeless corpses. The soldiers standing beside the gallows waited several minutes before they took down the bodies and wrapped them in plastic bags. Tife however remained rooted in shock at the barbaric act she had witnessed.

This would be the second time she would watch a person die in front of her. She knew the men deserved their punishment but that did not quell the feeling of unease which gripped her body. The image of their lifeless faces was seared into her head. She tried to steady herself as the ground spun underneath her but to no avail. She doubled down on the ground and threw up on the interlocking concrete steps of the plaza staircase.

''My apologies for the gory scenes you had to witness at the execution today, my Emissary, '' Igor said in his thick accent as he conveyed them back to the state house. ''I did not realize how distressing those images would be to you. Are you sure you will be alright?''

''I will be fine Councilor, thank you for your concern,'' she replied as the feeling of nausea still weighed down on her.

''Well, we do thank you for gracing us with your presence today and thank your Queen for sending such able representation to our humble city,'' Igor continued. ''May this mark the start of a beautiful relationship between our two empires. ''

They all disembarked as the convoy came to a halt at the gates of the state house. Igor explained he had pending duties to handle and could not entertain them any longer in person. He however assured Tife that their transport back to the airfield and to the Chinese territories will be made available in the early hours of the morning.

Zala spent the rest of the evening going through notes and pictures taken with Han at the execution. It was agreed that all the images and reports would be shared between them prior to departing the next morning.

Tife adjourned early to her room in the upper floors of the state house. She looked forward to returning home and putting the events of the past few days behind her. She however was glad the peace summit had gone well. Endless work poured in by diplomats across the world were to thank for convincing their rulers to sign the agreement. It was the first step towards peaceful co- habitation between many of the world powers. Any press towards further aggression could only have deadly repercussions for all people involved.

Of even greater concern was the stockpiling of greater biological arsenals by these monarchs. Tife always found it hypocritical that the African Union held a considerable cache of their own in several military bunkers spread out across the continent.

Although many of these weapons were supposed to be decommissioned, Queen Yaa-Yaa and Queens before her strictly opposed the total destruction of their arsenal. They drew from a legacy which began from Queen Nzinga. Those weapons were instrumental in the success of early wars against European invaders and there was a long-held belief that those weapons served as a deterrent against future attempts at invading their shores.

The treaty signing banning their use in military conflict did have an effect of curbing further development of these weapons but did little to allay the concerns of many of her diplomatic counterparts who feared increasing tensions could spark their use one more. The new peace treaty was critical to ensuring this never came to pass.

Tife was awoken to the sound of loud gunshots emanating from the soldier's quarters nearby with painful screams and quick movements following. Tife rushed to the nearby window to see several dark figures running across the compound towards the state house. She ran outside into the hallway to find Zala crouched down near the staircase banister; her face lit up in terror.

''What's happening?'' Tife queried in anxious breaths. Zala shook her head in response, raising her arms in panic as several more gunshots rang through the house. The Chinese delegation was on the other side of the hall. They too had been awoken by the loud noises and looked down the bannister into the living room downstairs. The entire compound was lit up with activity as more gunshots rang through the house. Several bullets struck the concrete walls of the state house with some piercing through the door.

Silence now dominated the empty space as the barrage of shooting momentarily paused. Several bodies could still be heard moving across the snow outside with each footstep becoming more pronounced as they neared the entrance into the house.

Several loud kicks to the door rend the fragile frame of the front door open; its ends hanging loosely from its bronze hinges. Over a dozen armed men came storming through accompanied by the cold wash of the outside air. They poured into the living room and spread out across the first floor with guns in hand.

Tife, followed closely behind by Zala, crouched back into her room and locked the door behind her. Grabbing a nearby chair, Tife braced the handle of the door. They both rushed to the safety of the bathroom, locked the door behind them and crouched down behind the shower curtain as they listened to the ensuing activity downstairs.

More shuffling could be heard through the kitchen as the armed men rushed further into the house. Suddenly, several raps struck the door into her room followed by the sound of fast footsteps into the small space. The sound of closet doors and cupboards opening quickly followed as the armed men searched the room for them. Tife shut her eyes tightly and held her breath, praying for the men to leave the room.

A loud bang ripped the bathroom door free. Zala screamed in terror as the men opened the shower curtain and pulled her out of the bathtub. Tife was dragged out by her hair and into the living room downstairs by the armed intruders.

The armed men shouted random instructions to them in their language. Each was dressed in black clothing with their heads concealed in a matching black mask. They shoved them to the ground and forced them to kneel on the hardwood floor. Cold air from outside flitted into the room. The dying embers of the fireplace did little to suppress the overriding frigid air which filled the space.

One of the armed men turned his attention to Tife. He menaced with his gun as he questioned her aggressively, demanding her name and job title. He did the same for the other three delegates kneeling on the hardwood floor.

''Is there anyone else with you in the building? Do not lie to me'' he demanded further, raising his gun to Tife's eye level once more. Tife promptly shook her head swiftly, her body shaking violently in terror as she stared down the muzzle of the gun. Another armed man marched into the room, nodding his head to confirm Tife's statement. The masked man interrogating Tife returned his attention back to her.

''Co-operate with us and you will not be harmed. Resist in anyway and this will be your fate,'' he motioned to one of the men standing behind them. Instantly, he grabbed Zala roughly up by the arm and brought her outside. Zala screamed in terror as she was dragged into cold night. Tife flinched as the sound of a singular shot echoed through the house and the surroundings. She stared down at the floor, eyes wide open in terror. Large tears began to stream down her face.

''Comrade, we must hurry. Reinforcements will be here any moment now. We must take our leave now or risk encountering resistance during our escape,'' another armed man advised.

''Strip the rest of the guards of their uniforms and take these prisoners to the trucks. We depart immediately,'' the man ordered. Tife and the Chinese delegation were each handed a pair of clean clothes and a thick sweater to wear. They were swiftly taken outside to two army-style green military vehicles parked outside.

As she walked towards the car, Tife spotted several naked corpses lying on the ground. Sprinkles of snow falling from above had already begun to conceal the bodies in a white haze. She turned around to see many of the armed men now sporting the military uniforms they had taken from the bodies.

Tife was placed in the front of the vehicle alongside the man who had initially interrogated her. She recognized him by the throaty sound of his voice as he began to address her. He was now wearing one of the uniforms retrieved from the dead guards along with a thick sweater and furry hat.

''Here, take this. My men found it in your room, '' he handed her the red strip of paper the Councilor had handed to her when they had arrived at the state house manor.

''We will be passing through a military checkpoint soon. Once we arrive there, you will confirm that we rescued you from an attack organized by the Red Dawn at the state house. Say anything to the contrary and you will end up like your friend back there, understood?'' he said menacingly. Tife quickly nodded her head in agreement. The man shouted several more orders to his colleagues before they loaded into the back of the two cars and drove off, leaving the state manor behind in their wake.

They proceeded down the road guided by the yellow haze of the car's headlights. The vehicle bounced intermittently through the icy streets and growing snow which filled the motorways.

Tife remained fixed to her seat, her mouth dry from shee terror. Part of her training as an Emissary had covered instances where she became a prisoner to a foreign entity. In situations like that, she was trained on how to remain calm in the moment. She was instructed that it was more important to cooperate with her captors, giving them any information they requested of her.

Equally important was paying attention to her immediate surroundings. An opportunity to escape may present itself and knowledge of her environs was crucial in finding assistance.

Her mind however returned to the fate of Zala. The singular bullet which took her life still rang in her head. Tife still made the effort to clear her mind. Her life depended on her remaining calm and collected.

She looked outside the window trying to gauge how far they had travelled so far. The car had gone several minutes down the snow-covered roads. It suddenly veered down an icy road bordered by a sheer mountain top and icy lake which reflected the moonlight on its surface. She turned her attention back to the man driving the vehicle. His eyes were fixed intently on the road, peering through the haze of the falling snow.

He suddenly grew concerned as headlights approached them down the road. He ordered Tife to remain stationary and quiet as the glowing lights grew closer to them. A military vehicle whisked past their vehicle and was closely followed by two more behind. The soldier driving the vehicle paid little attention to their trucks as they drove by.

Once the military vehicles had disappeared out of sight, the man driving Tife's vehicle signaled behind to the other car following them. Both vehicles now increased their speeds and proceeded hastily down the poorly lit roads.

They travelled several kilometers till they arrived at a blockade in the center of the road. Several spike strips and barricades ran across the road. Mounted machine guns could be seen camouflaged in the hazy snow fall. A man dressed in full military fatigue walked up to the center of the road. Draped across his chest was a rifle which he held firmly as he accosted them. The man driving Tife's vehicle turned his gaze to her once more. His eyes grew tense and fierce once more.

''Remember to say exactly what I told you before,'' he warned, touching his gun as he spoke. ''Your life and the lives of your colleagues depend on it, do you understand?'' Tife swallowed hard before replying, ''I understand.''

They came to a stop a short distance from the man in the road. He walked to the side of the window accompanied by another soldier who approached the passenger window.

''Name and badge number,'' the man demanded. The driver of Tife's vehicle turned his chest to show the name tag sewn into the uniform of the dead man he had taken it from. The man at the window peered into the vehicle to see it, reading it aloud.

''Yerkov Andreevich, B1909. Your unit was stationed in the capital. We have no instruction that you would be travelling past this checkpoint tonight,'' the man informed them. The man wearing Yerkov's uniform now grew anxious as he addressed the soldier at the window.

''We had an incident at the State Manor,'' he began frantically, ''terrorists attacked and killed many of my men stationed there. We managed to rescue the diplomats staying at the residence and are taking them to the military base at Stena.'' The soldier at the window looked at him intently before turning his attention to Tife in the passenger seat.

''Is this true, Madam?'' he asked in his thick voice. 'Yerkov' turned his head to Tife. He slowly touched the muzzle of his gun as he waited for her response.

''Yes, these men came to our rescue when Red Dawn rebels attacked the Manor,'' she replied in a measured tone. She pulled out the red slip Igor had given her and passed it to the man by her window. He turned it over and then showed it to his colleague on the driver's side. The man inspected it before returning it back to her.

''We have received no distress call from that sector of the capital. On whose authority do you transfer these people with?'' the soldier inquired.

''The Councilor gave us emergency instructions to take them to a secure location, '' Yerkov replied swiftly. ''You would not want to stand in the way of his orders, would you?'' The soldier considered it before nodding in agreement. He shouted instructions to the other soldiers at the checkpoint. The spikes mounted in the road were dragged off to the side and several of the barricades were moved away.

They began to drive their vehicles through as the soldier shouted several more orders to the troops at the base. Many began to pile into vehicles and race down in the opposite direction they had come from. The checkpoint disappeared from view as they made their way through the snow. Once they were clear, the vehicles pulled over to the side of the highway and parked on the side of the road.

''Well done. You played your part well, '' Yerkov said to Tife. He shouted orders to the men who had disembarked from the vehicle. One man ripped open the passenger side of the truck and slipped a black bag over Tife's head. He proceeded to lead her to the back of the truck and placed her on a seat in the small space. Tife sat helplessly in the truck as it started down the path once more, cutting through the endless deluge of the snowy filled roads.

DEADLY ALLIANCES

Czar Nicholas believed himself a man cursed from birth. Being the only son of his father, he was first in the line of succession after his father's mysterious passing. At the tender age of fifteen, he was pronounced the new king regent and was henceforth constantly surrounded by people who bowed and scraped for his attention.

Memories of growing up surrounded by pompous princess and princesses of noble birth still lingered in his mind. He remembered how that they only showed a vain interest in themselves and the wealth of their families. They showed no interest in exercising youthful passions and acting like the children they were.

His childhood was spent in the company of courtiers called the Koren who advised him on a wide range of topics from war stratagem to food distribution in their territories. They handled matters of state he was told were too sensitive for him to deal with at his age. The Koren would make sure he was apprised of their decisions but still remained in steadfast control of all aspects of his life.

When proclamations were to be issued to the people and the military elite, they invoked the power of his seat to give legitimate backing to their decisions. He remained no more than a figurehead to his own royal court, metting out hollow royal decrees to his people. In time, he grew detached from his royal upbringing, preferring to occupy himself with solitary passions which he enjoyed.

He grew deeply interested in outdoor sports like hunting and horseback riding. In the company of his personal guardsmen, he would wander the forests alone looking for small prey he could practice his shots on. On many of his hunts, he managed to score several kills, taking their carcasses back to the palace and mounting them on his trophy walls.

On one particular outing, he met a young girl also hunting small game in the forest. She introduced herself as Alyona Petrov, princess to one of the most powerful families in his court. He quickly developed a deep interest in her and they spent most of their time together from that day onwards.

Their relationship quickly accelerated into marriage; a move highly supported by the Koren. The union of the Romanov and Petrov families would only bolster the strength of the crown and offer greater stability in the kingdom. These points did not matter to Nicholas. Instead, he was happy that he had found someone that could be his confidant and lover.

Alyona would subtly offer council to her new husband. Her soothing voice of reason was always appreciated by Nicholas who welcomed her advice and acted accordingly. The Koren believed in expanding the territories mustered by Slovia even if that brought them in direct conflict with nearby empires. Their stockpile of biological weapons was crucial in pursuing such lofty ambitions.

Alyona would whisper to her husband of the need to keep these weapons at their disposal. Treaty signatures like the one in Vienna could only weaken the power base of their great empire and she promptly persuaded him against signing it. Nicholas assiduously listened to his wife, prompting him to call for even more advanced weapons development in pursuit of their expansionist agenda.

Nicholas' wife would regularly leave the royal residence to meet with members of her family scattered around the kingdom. Nicholas saw no reason to doubt her and would offer to send a company of courtiers to accompany her, a gesture she would routinely refused.

These visits became more regular, prompting him to become more suspicious. He could not bear the idea that she was having an affair behind his back, a thought which deeply enraged him. Nicholas was determined to discover the true nature of her visits and employed the services of his most trusted guardsmen to follow her the next time she visited her relatives.

The guardsmen returned with shocking information. His wife was not engaged in any sort of affair but was involved in something more sinister. She had ventured to a small island off the Eastern coast to meet with a small group of people. They held several talks behind closed doors and would make considerable attempts to conceal their identities. The guardsmen had managed to take pictures of some of the participants and handed them to the Czar.

Nicholas instantly recognized many of the individuals in the picture. It was several members of the Koren themselves. They had no need to meet with the Queen for matters pertaining to the empire. More so, the effort to conceal their meetings brought their actions into greater question.

Nicholas could only arrive at one conclusion: the Koren were conspiring against him and using the Queen as a proxy to assert their influence over him. Her actions called into question their accidental meeting in the forest that day. Did the Koren have a role to play in their union? Did her advice to the Czar genuinely come from her or was she being used as a pawn to control him further?

Nicholas felt betrayed and would take action swiftly. As Alyona was still a member of a powerful family within his court, he would have to be careful in exacting his vengeance against her and the Koren. This resolution would bring in close contact with members of the Red Dawn, the rebel group operating within his borders. Their self-proclaimed mandate was an end to the oppression of the monarchy and a move to more democratic institutions.

Many of their members were hunted down or captured, occupying their prison cells within secret bunkers. Nicholas would enlist their services to bring an end to the Koren once and for all. He personified the monarchy and all it stood for but would convince the Red Dawn and their leaders that he was not their enemy. The Koren, he would declare, were in fact responsible for the tyranny in the kingdom and with their combined effort could be eliminated.

In public, he would denounce the terrorist sect but in secret, he would work with them to dislodge the influence the Koren had in his kingdom. Ridding them of their power he proposed would usher in opportunity for reform within his kingdom. Nicholas however had no intention of reforming his empire. Once he got rid of the Koren, he would swiftly restore his power base and clamp down on the Red Dawn.

In concert with their members in prison, Nicholas schemed and plotted with the Red Dawn leadership for months. He would start by taking the life of the woman he had loved for so many years, a woman who had gone on to betray him. He would wait patiently to exact his vengeance on her. Alyona informed him that she would be making one of her regular trips to her relatives. She would only be gone for a few days and would return as soon as she could.

This was the moment Nicholas would seize to get rid of her. He duly passed her travel information to the Red Dawn urging them to strike her transport on her way back from meeting with the Koren. This was crucial to throw off any suspicion of his involvement into her murder.

Many days passed with no word until an urgent message came

through to the kingdom. The Queen's convoy was attacked on the outskirts of town. The car carrying her had been destroyed beyond repair. The Queen's body was found mutilated in the field.

News of the Queen's death threw the entire kingdom into sadness and mourning. Czar Nicholas ordered his people to wear black for seven days to honor the memory of the Queen. The flag symbolizing the empire would fly at half-mast and all non-critical events within the kingdom would be suspended. He publicly denounced the Red Dawn, promising swift justice, and their eventual demise.

To demonstrate his resolve, he publicly executed ten of their members locked up in his prisons. He had communicated with the Red Dawn high commander through his proxies before making the decision public. They both agreed it would be wise to make his contempt for the rebel group public and on full display.

The high commander offered ten of his men whom he deemed martyrs for the cause of democracy which they sought to achieve after their deaths. They would be remembered as heroes in the new republic and would be immortalized once victory was achieved.

Members of the Koren visited him over the next couple of days to express their deepest sympathies and offer their condolence for his loss. Nicholas silently seethed in anger at their disingenuous shows of grief. Left up to him, he would have them swinging from their necks in the gallows.

He exercised restraint because he understood the full weight of the power the Koren wielded over the kingdom. They had managed to maintain their position as counsel to the crown for many centuries, advising the Czars who occupied the throne before him. Many of the members were descendants of the first individuals to serve in the council. Their network of power ran deep, cutting across the entire spectrum of power in his kingdom from the noble families to the military. Any direct attack on them would be followed by swift retaliation.

He remembered witnessing many verbal disagreements between his father and the Koren during their weekly briefings together. Nicholas now strongly believed the Koren had a hand to play in his sudden death.

Dislodging them from their seat of control would require destroying the very foundations of their power base. The Red Dawn with their twisted ideology of democracy would form useful allies in his campaign against this rogue organization. Never had the words, 'the enemy of my enemy is my friend,'' rung truer for Nicholas.

His efforts to destroy the Koren competed with external troubles outside his borders. A violent push from Prussia to regain much of its lost territory to his kingdom was underway, placing significant stress on his food supplies. Bad harvests had also beset the farmers in many of their farmlands. Famine had broken out in many parts of the countryside and beyond. The colonies complained of food shortages which wreaked havoc on their people. Talks of revolt in these territories begun to spread though the population.

The Czar would not allow another insurrection to take hold and prevent him from attaining his goals. He ordered a violent crackdown on any group promoting such dangerous action. He pushed for greater military presence in the streets to quell any notion of rebellion, both in Europe and the colonies. Those who still insisted on pushing these dangerous thoughts were sent to his gulags. Their labor would be useful in boosting agricultural production to feed the military still fighting invaders at their borders.

The Koren waited a respectable few months before pushing Nicholas to remarry. 'A Czar needs his Queen to govern properly,' they would say. Nicholas knew better than to trust them now. They had lost their unique leverage in making him comply to their will. He vowed never to be used again in that matter and instead thrust himself into building his weapons reserves.

His war stance was met with stiff resistance from several neighboring nations who saw it as a preemption to a full-scale invasion. Nicholas would not back down from his mission to reclaim the power which was slowly eroding from underneath him. He pressed for expanding his military fleet, conscripting able-bodied members of the public into service. They would defend their country with their lives or be sent to the gulags for insubordination to their Czar.

The Czar had been perceptive to threats within his own borders. He had heard reports of men and women refusing to engage in military service to their empire citing their religious background as grounds of refusal. Acts of defiance such as these would be met with a swift response. He threw many of these individuals in the gulags or hung them from the gallows in public as a warning to others on what would happen when they disobeyed their Czar. Many managed to escape to other nations more accepting of their treachery.

Their colonies in North America offered them significant resources in their fight against their enemies in Europe. Competing interests with the Chinese Emperor put their empires well at odds. Crushing him and his armies remained Nicholas' only chance of securing his empire's resource flow from the continent. However, even Nicholas could perceive victory slowly tipping in the favor of the Chinese Emperor. With a struggling military front and waning reserves, he took the only option available to him.

Despite the firm opposition expressed by the Koren, he would agree to a temporary seize fire between himself and the Chinese Emperor. He would simply agree to an easing of tensions but would not agree to relinquish territories he had conquered. Nicholas saw this an opportunity to replenish his already waning resources and further his development of biological weapons. Only when he was ready would he then push for a final assault which would firmly entrench his control of disputed territories both in the colonies and in Europe.

The Red Dawn had been successful in eliminating several members of the Koren council over the course of their partnership. His informal agreement with them allowed a certain degree of protection to act within his borders with the understanding that they would work to erode the power base that the Koren enjoyed. This included taking out members of royal families and service men in the military who were loyal to them.

Disappearances and killings of high-ranking members of society became daily occurrences and a heightened fear within the elite quickly took hold. The Koren and royal family members alike approached Nicholas demanding for greater protection for themselves and urged him to crack down harder on the group. The Czar listened to their demands and vowed to take greater action against the rebel group. His involvement in the attacks were largely concealed from them.

The attack on the new Sovereign of the African Union soil allegedly masterminded by the Red Dawn made Nicholas question his relationship with them. The killing of their leader had sparked a wave of renewed tensions and brought the AU in direct conflict with his empire. Their powerful block of distinct kingdoms had been reluctant to take sides in the unending conflict over territory in the West and across Europe.

Queen Yaa-Yaa of the AU grew livid and blamed the Czar for allowing this criminal organisation to grow in strength within his borders. Rumors had swirled for many years that he enjoyed a close relationship with them. The attack on Queen Yaa-Yaa only confirmed these suspicions. The inevitable conflict between his empire and the AU quickly escalated into a full- fledged war between the two sides. With the aid of the Chinese Emperor, their combined forces quickly overwhelmed Czar Nicholas' recovering forces.

Czar Nicholas would risk defeat if he did not call support from another nation in the war effort. Despite reservations expressed by the Koren, he requested support from the Austria- Hungarian King,

Zoltan Verdes. The man was widely known to exhibit strange behavior and bouts of insanity, but Nicholas had no choice. He had to enlist his help if he hoped to survive the ensuing war.

King Zoltan agreed to his proposal but only on the grounds that he would have claims to large portions of the conquered lands. Czar Nicholas begrudgingly agreed to his request. He would relinquish much of the territories they claimed from the Chinese Emperor in exchange for the Austria-Hungarian King's support. It was the only way to secure victory.

Meanwhile, the Czar had to face the backlash from the attack by the Red Dawn a continent away. He was furious that they risked precipitating war between his empire and a largely neutral one in a senseless attack. Whatever motivation they had in carrying out the attack was irrelevant as he would now suffer the stiff consequences.

The Koren and royal elite alike became increasingly suspicious of Czar Nicholas. The attack on the AU made them suspect his involvement even more in the attacks perpetrated by the Red Dawn terrorist group. If he did not act quickly, they would use their political weight to usurp his power and take over his throne. Seemingly pressed from every side, he mulled over the best course of action given the circumstances.

His emissaries and diplomatic personnel informed him of ongoing peace negotiations happening to de-escalate the mounting crisis. A meeting was scheduled to hold in the neutral territory between his colonies in North America and those of the Chinese Emperor.

Leaders from other kingdoms would also be in attendance. It offered him the perfect opportunity to denounce the actions of the Red Dawn, absolve himself of any involvement in the events which precipitated the war and demand for a secession to the endless suffering being inflicted on his kingdom.

His diplomats spoke of compromises being drawn up to ensure a peaceful negotiation. One issue of contention was the dismantling of the biological stockpile of weapons he owned in several military bunkers scattered across his territories. He repeatedly refused to accept any compromise which would make him surrender those weapons. He vowed to resist the agreement at the peace summit scheduled to hold in a few days.

He arrived well enough at the venue to see many of the monarchs to the various world empires present. At the beginning of the proceedings, he made his stance clear. He pushed back on the unwarranted aggression being shown to his people and his empire and demanded a halt to the attacks. Nicholas made it clear that the Red Dawn were responsible for the attacks and not his court. A strong public condemnation of the group on the world stage was vital in his pursuit to reclaim control of his kingdom.

During one of the breakout sessions, a man from the AU delegation approached him. He was a stern looking military man of middle age. He was well groomed and had a visible black scar running down his cheek. He spoke the Czar's tongue fluently and promptly introduced himself as General Sumaina, Commander of the allied AU military forces. He requested to speak in private with Nicholas, a request he initially refused. What business could he have with a military war general to his adversary?

''I have proof you have been working with the Red Dawn,'' General Sumaina whispered to him. The Czar's eyes grew wide in fright at these words. He excused himself and followed the General upstairs where they could speak in private.

General Sumaina ushered him into a solitary room on the upper floors of the building. The voices in the halls downstairs could still be heard on this floor. General Sumaina shut the doors behind him leaving Nicholas' personal guard outside. General Sumaina was an intimidating man. His tall stature accompanied with the grim expression on his face made him an imposing figure.

''What is the meaning of this, '' Czar Nicholas demanded. The General sauntered across the room and found a seat in the corner. Nicholas felt instantly uncomfortable as his piercing gaze fell on him.

''I have learned of a very interesting relationship you share with certain rebel groups within your empire, Czar Nicholas,'' General Sumaina began as he pulled out several photos from his breast pocket. He laid them on the table beside him and urged the Czar to take them. Nicholas hesitantly motioned to the desk and picked up the photos.

His eyes opened wide in shock as he saw himself in several of the photos. They had been taken during several of his rendezvous with the 'Bear', leader to the Red Dawn faction. The Bear would on occasion request he meet in random locations, mostly in woody areas located in the countryside. The Czar would leave to these areas on the pretence that he was going hunting alone. Once there, he would venture deep into the woods following the directions he had received from the rebel leader.

He would arrive at the location to find a man wearing a bear-shaped mask. The rest of his body was shrouded in thick, military style camouflage. Two other people wearing the same mask would appear and search him thoroughly before allowing him to approach the man.

They would proceed to place a bag over his head and take him to a second location through the woods. Only there would they agree to speak to him. The masked men would always insist he was not the rebel leader but merely a proxy on his behalf. The real leader was careful never to reveal himself to the Czar.

Nicholas remain non-plussed that any such evidence of his involvement with the Red Dawn existed. He turned his attention back at General Sumaina who remained calmly seated in the corner. The Czar angrily tossed the photos back on the table and glared at Sumaina.

''How dare you accuse me of working with those rebels with doctored photographs?'' Czar Nicholas replied, raising his voice now.

''I think you and I both know those photographs are not fake, your Excellency. And if you would like them to remain hidden from the public's eye, I suggest you listen to what I have to say. I am sure members of royal families back home and your Koren council would be enraged to finally have proof that their leader was conspiring against them.''

Nicholas gritted his teeth in anger and shouted several obscenities before facing Sumaina again. His hands were balled into tight fists.

''What do you want?'' Nicholas demanded angrily. The General stood up slowly from his seat, brushing off the particles of dust which had clung on to the front of his uniform.

''You will immediately halt the production of any more biological weapons in your borders. You will also pledge to dismantle all of your production facilities by winter's end. My Queen will pledge a delegation to ensure you comply with all the terms of the peace agreement. Any further aggression from your military will force me to release the evidence I have against you. Do we have an understanding?''

The Czar felt trapped like a rat in the corner. He could not risk evidence of his relationship with the Red Dawn being exposed to the public. It would spell doom for his rule. The Koren still remained strong with several active members. He needed more time to plan his revenge against them all.

''I cannot give up my entire negotiating hand at this summit, '' the Czar said finally. ''If I completely withdraw my objections, I will be seen as weak in front of my generals and to the Koren. It would spark just as much unrest.'' General Sumaina considered this deeply before turning his attention back to the monarch.

''We will say you made a compromise,'' General Sumaina responded. ''As commander of the AU's troops, I can arrange a withdrawal of our forces from many of your territories. I am sure the Koren will be more than satisfied by this agreement,'' as he walked to the door, the General whispered in a menacing tone, ''It would be in your best interest to accept this proposal, Czar.'' With that, the General made his way out the room, leaving Nicholas alone in the small office.

Nicholas ventured back down into the conference hall where several delegates were still in deep conversation with themselves. He summoned his emissary to his side and explained his new stance with him. He would communicate his position to the other emissary's who in turn would inform their respective monarchs.

Many expressed shock over his sudden change in position. The group of allied nations would nonetheless celebrate his choice to de-escalate tensions and sign the peace accord, marking their victory in bringing Czar Nicholas to his knees.

Under the watchful gaze of General Sumaina, the Czar pledged his empire's resolve to dismantle any or all biological weapons depot currently active or in development. In exchange, he wanted troops stationed at his borders removed from the battlefield. He would not entertain their presence once the agreement was signed.

With a compromise in place, both parties signed the peace accord. As an additional gesture of goodwill, he would hold a ceremony to execute members of the Red Dawn who infiltrated the colonies. A public show would fully distance himself from the rebel group.

He would return home on the back of mixed fortunes. On one hand, he had secured a commitment to ease the aggression being shown at their borders by the Allied enemy troops. On the other hand, he would be seen as weak for agreeing to destroy their arsenal of biological weapons which gave them respect in the eyes of the world.

Of greater concern to the Czar was how the General found out about his former ties to the Red Dawn. How did he get a hold of those pictures showing his meetings with their leader? Was he the Red Dawn leader himself? The Czar would have to be more careful in his dealings from now on. Having reached an agreement with the external aggressors terrorising his borders, he could focus inward to the enemies at his doorstep.

The Koren still remained a powerful block within his kingdom and now that he could no longer rely on the support of the Red Dawn to curtail their influence, he needed to find ways to halt their sway in his court. In the meantime, he would use this cessation of violence to reassess his strategy against them.

He arrived at his official residence in the colonies the same day. He opted to rest a day there before embarking on the long trip back home to his kingdom in Europe. He could not afford to be away from the heart of his empire for too long lest the Koren use it as an opportunity to usurp his throne.

The outpost at Krepost housed several leaders in the colony and therefore retained many comforts he was used to. An expansive villa built specifically to house him during his visits was bedecked with lavish royal décor. It was largely unoccupied save for the rare occasions he visited the colonies.

He spent the rest of the evening relaxing in the heated water baths in the lower floors. He melted in the water as several female attendants massaged the length of his body releasing days of tension he had accumulated. He let his mind go blank from all the worries he had been dealing with these past couple of years. Nicholas hoped he would not have to deal with the pressures of war for a long time.

The Czar was making plans to leave back for Europe when news of the attack on the state manor reached his ears early the next morning. The Councilor, Igor Smirnov, arrived at the Czar's residence accompanied by two guards. He bowed low as he approached the Czar in his meeting room. He went on to make a report on the events which transpired at the state manor.

Igor reported how reinforcements swarmed the base after a military truck conveying the emissary to Queen Yaa-Yaa had ran past a nearby checkpoint. The men in the vehicle apparently tipped off the soldiers at the checkpoint of the attack by the Red Dawn on the State Manor.

When they arrived there, they found the naked remains of their fellow soldiers buried in the snow. Only then did they suspect that convoy which had passed the checkpoint was in fact the Red Dawn rebels disguised in military fatigue. The Czar rose up from his seat and approached the side wall with several swords adorning the face of it. Igor looked on tensely at the Czar as he took one of them down.

''You oversaw security for the state manor, did you not Igor?'' Nicholas asked. Igor fell down to one knee and bent his head low in deference.

''I did, my liege. I am responsible for this failure to secure our guests. But I suspect the delegates at the manor of working with the terrorists to escape. These soldiers can collaborate my suspicions, '' Igor said as he turned to the two guards beside him.

''Who else knows about the rebel attack at the state manor?'' Nicholas asked as he inspected the sword he had taken down. Its sharp edge glinted in the early morning rays which streamed through the window.

''Only the units stationed at the checkpoint. We thought it best to report to you before we took any action,'' Igor replied.

''Good, good. Men, hold the councilor down for me, '' the Czar ordered. Immediately, the two soldiers responded by grabbing Igor and splaying him across a nearby table.

''Do you understand the severity of the repercussions of your failure, Councilor? Do you realize what will happen when our enemies hear of the abduction of one of their own?'' the Czar said as he approached the councilor with sword in hand. ''Your failure has put all of us in danger and you must be punished for it.'' He motioned to one of the guards to extend the Councilor's right hand over the table.

In one swoop, the Czar brought the sword down slicing through the wrist of the councilor. Igor screamed in pain as thick streams of blood came flowing from his hand. His severed hand lay in the middle of a growing pool of blood. Igor clutched his arm as he writhed in anguish on the ground. Nicholas looked on at him with dispassion and apathy. He wiped the blood of his blade and placed it back on the wall.

''Be glad that you will leave here with your life and not just without a body part, Councilor,'' Czar Nicholas menaced through gritted teeth. ''Make it your top priority to find the missing delegates and investigate their ties if any with the Red Dawn.'' The councilor still wailed in pain as he cradled his blood-soaked hand.

''Get out of my sight! And find someone to clean up this mess,'' Nicholas ordered. Through bleary eyes, Igor trudged out of the room. The soldiers who had accompanied him followed closely behind. Nicholas grabbed a chair from the corner and threw it across the room. It came crashing on a nearby wall on the far end. He breathed and fumed in the room which now admitted more sunshine from outside.

The Red Dawn was determined to destabilize his empire with their overt attacks on delegates from their rival empires. The abduction of their emissaries could reignite tensions between the two warring kingdoms further taking his attention from more pressing concerns back in his court. He had hoped to replenish his forces with the momentary suspension of military aggression against his troops.

His priority now would be to find the missing emissaries and discover if they were working with the terrorists in any way. He had to make sure he stayed ahead of the narrative or risk losing more ground to his foes. Nicholas resolved that he would delay his trip back to his kingdom until he had this matter sorted out.

Three days had passed and no news of the whereabouts of the delegates had reached his ears. Nicholas sent out a district-wide alert to all the military units stationed at Krepost to focus their efforts in finding the missing delegates. He already made the decision to order the shutdown of any communication towers in the area to prevent the leaking of any news of the delegates abduction to the foreign press. Nicholas was determined to stop a possible international incident from developing, an objective the Red Dawn were undoubtably attempting to achieve.

His soldiers scoured the streets and searched houses across the district. They resorted to brutal questioning to gather information on the location of the emissaries. Any attempt at withholding information from them was met with brutal force. Many residents suspected of working with the terrorists were sent off to the labor camps in the North-Western region of the colonies, a punishment many considered worse than death.

Nicholas sent for senior members of the military leading the search for the missing delegates. He was determined to stay up to date on the status of the search. He knew he could not prevent news of their abduction from leaking for too long as their counterparts back home would expect their return.

The Czar needed to speed up the process of finding them so he ordered several more troops from the surrounding districts to aid in the expanded search. If the rebels were no longer in the town of Krepost, they would set up a base camp somewhere far out of the reach of the military. The only location nearby without heavy military presence were the thick forests just outside the perimeter of the city. If they made it out there, it would be difficult to track them down.

To urge the public to volunteer any information leading to the capture of the rebels, Nicholas announced a handsome reward to the citizens in Krepost. He hoped to appeal to people's greed to find the location of the rebel base.

It was not long before someone came forward and was immediately brought before him at his castle. The soldiers brought in a fidgety old man to his meeting room. The man had greying hair and a thick white beard. He wore a long, threadbare coat and thick black gloves. He looked around nervously as he was brought before the Czar. He immediately fell to his knees at the sight of Nicholas on his throne.

''I was told that you have information on the whereabouts of the terrorists, '' Czar Nicholas inquired. The man looked up at the Czar with beady eyes.

''Your Excellency, I am part of a hunting party which looks for wild game in the forest. We all have permits to leave the city to forage for food from the nearby forests. A good portion of all our hunts is given to the city council while we keep the rest. It was during our regular hunts that I was approached by two men in military uniforms. They asked me several questions before disappearing once more back into the trees.''

''What did they want to know from you?'' the Czar demanded.

''They wanted to know the hunting routes in the area where they too could find wild game. They also asked if I had seen anyone else patrolling the area in the same uniform.''

''And what did you tell them?'' the Czar inquired further.

''I had not seen any other soldier in the area apart from those within the city. I found the entire encounter very strange, so I reported it to the guards at the city gates.''

''You did very well to report the incident to the guards,'' the Czar said before addressing the soldiers. ''Have my men search the area around where he saw the two imposters. Their base camp must be somewhere nearby.'' Nicholas motioned for the man to be let out but he hesitated.

''My liege, I was told there would be a handsome reward for anyone who had information on the rebels?'' the man said nervously, ''My family is very poor and would appreciate the money.'' The man tensed up as Nicholas' piercing gaze fell on him. He gave a long pause before addressing the soldier to the left of him, ''Give him what he is owed,'' he ordered before dismissing the man from his chamber.

Nicholas felt a ray of hope from the news brought to him about the rebel's possible location. He could not help feeling a twinge of responsibility for the current influence the terrorist group wielded both in Slovia, the very seat of his power, and here in the colonies. During his long partnership with them, he had provided them with a constant source of weaponry from his private arsenal.

He could not risk anyone discovering his relationship with them so he had secret tunnels built under several bunkers where their agents could move in and out to collect them freely. Nicholas made sure to have those hideouts were destroyed once their partnership fell apart but his actions had emboldened the group and their current ambition to destroy his kingdom. With no other allies in his fight to restore order in his court, Nicholas felt alone and confused.

With each passing day Nicholas, became more anxious to put an end to this matter. He began receiving daily communications from Jinhai Wen, the Chinese Emissary to the Slovian kingdom. The Chinese Emperor was livid that two of their Emissaries were being held captive by terrorist groups operating in his territory. He demanded their immediate release and return to them else they take matters into their own hands through forceful means.

The Sovereign of the AU had also become aware of their delegates capture and sent similar warnings to the Czar, ''your irresponsibility to our diplomatic envoys will re-ignite war between our empires. I demand you do everything in your power to return our people to us or risk renewed military attacks on your bases,'' the Queen threatened in a new message to the Slovian Czar.

With pressures mounting on him to take action, Nicholas dedicated his entire military force to finding the missing delegates. More aggressive searches and arrests were made in the surrounding provinces now. He could not risk war precipitating once more on his territory and was determined to forestall it at any costs.

He sent several more envoys to the Chinese side asking for more time to find their people. Nicholas received reports that the AU was amassing forces to invade their colonies prompting him to initiate direct contact with Queen Yaa-Yaa urging her to stand down. Attempts to accelerate the resumption of war was exactly what the Red Dawn wanted, he told her. He was doing everything in his power to bring the prisoners back home safely.

But Nicholas feared the worst now. The search for the missing delegates had turned up nothing leaving many to speculate that they had managed to escape from the territories. Worse still, he feared the prisoners had been executed in retaliation for the killing of their members.

His fears where allayed when soldiers reported a message they had found in the woods. One of their colleagues went missing many days ago and was found several days later in the woods beaten and tied up to a tree. He had several cuts and bruises across his body but was alive. He said they captured him and interrogated him for several days before releasing him. He said he never saw the abducted envoys during his capture.

''They also gave him a message to deliver personally to you, my Czar, '' the soldier said. ''They said they were willing to release the hostages in exchange for the release of all their people being held in prisons here and in Europe. They also demanded that you publicly abdicate your crown to the Koren and step down.''

''Abdicate my crown??!'' the Czar bellowed at the top of his voice. He grabbed a seat nearby and threw it at the window. It shattered allowing the cool outside breeze to saturate the room.

''Round up every able-bodied person you can find and have them search the woods. Burn it to the ground if you must. I want you to find those terrorists,'' he ordered. The soldier bowed low and left the Czar seething in his throne room.

These insurgents had asked him to relinquish his power to the very people he was fighting. It wouldn't surprise him if the Koren had now aligned themselves with the Red Dawn to take his crown. He vowed to lay waste to both of them. He would destroy their cells here in his colonies and back in Europe. It was time to take more drastic actions against the group.

THE REBEL CODE

Tife remained silent and still as the truck bounded down the icy roads. She could feel the truck veer-off course and begin its journey down a rough patch of dirt road. The truck suddenly came to a stop forcing her forward in her seat. The Red Dawn soldiers let her out and removed the bag covering her head. The snowfall had abated allowing for an unobstructed view of her surroundings.

They had managed to make their way atop a narrow hill in the middle of the frozen tundra. White peaked mountains stood tall in the distance and circled the entire area. Coniferous trees adorned the base and sheer face of the mountains. In a small clearing below was a frozen lake with an icy sheet covering its surface. Despite the heavy coat, Tife shivered as the wind blew gusts of cold air across her skin.

The rest of the rebel troops disembarked from the vehicles. Yerkov got out of driver's seat and scanned the area. He took out a cigarette and lit it up, taking huge intakes before blowing out plumes of smoke from his nostrils. He gave a cursory glance of Tife before directing his attention back to his men.

They had taken a man out from the back of the second truck. He was one of the soldiers at the manor attempting to repel the terrorist attack. He had several cuts and bruises to his face and a gunshot wound to his upper right thigh. Yerkov's men held him up and took off the bag on his head as he walked towards the beaten soldier. He blew a copious amount of white smoke in his face before looking down at the wound to his leg.

''You are in pain soldier, yes?'' Yerkov asked him while grinning widely at him. The soldier only scowled in reply. ''We still need you alive and will give you the medical attention you need once we reach our hideout. Stay strong till then.'' Yerkov patronizingly patted the soldier's cheek before shouting orders to his men.

''Dispose of the vehicles in the lake and cover our tracks so we can't be followed,'' he ordered them. ''We are a long way off from base camp and need to make haste before night falls.'' Tife watched as two men took the military trucks, put them in drive before ramming them headfirst into the frozen lake nearby.

Both men jumped out of the vehicles at the very last instant. The sound of ice breaking followed by the cold embrace of the water as the trucks submerged quickly followed. The large hole in the ice would surely freeze over come nightfall.

Yerkov made his men drape the bag over the captured soldier's head once more as they began the trek through the trees, ''Don't worry, you will not have the same treatment shown to you, Emissary,'' Yerkov said addressing Tife. They made her walk ahead of them as they followed closely behind with weapons draped around their chest.

She kept up pace as they navigated through the icy trees and heavy snowfall washed across the terrain. Yerkov walked ahead of them all occasionally puffing out huge balls of smoke from his mouth and scanning the area.

They walked in silence for several kilometers and stopped occasionally only when Yerkov ordered them to. He would give the command to halt if he heard movement in the forest. It usually ended up being an animal like a moose herd but he wouldn't take any chances. He also ordered his men to constantly wipe their foot tracks as they made their way forward. He would not risk any chance they could be followed by Slovian soldiers who would eventually catch wind of their deception.

They reached further into the mountain regions of the white-covered plains. Although the snow had abated for a while now, Tife wrapped herself tightly desperately fighting the cool chill of the winter breeze sweeping across the forest. She occasionally caught Yerkov's eye who furtively looked in her direction to see how she was faring.

As a high value prisoner, it was in their best interest to keep her alive, Tife thought. They would not risk something happening to her and that thought gave her the strength to keep fighting and possibly escape when the opportunity presented itself.

The temperature dropped precipitously as darkness began to fall all around them. Yerkov ordered his men to do reconnaissance around the area before instructing them to set up a make- shift camp in the forest. They quickly went to work and began making tents from sticks in a small clearing.

Yerkov went to work setting up the fire himself. He gathered wet brush, fallen leaves and wood from trees around the area and placed them in a pile. Using his cigarette lighter, he set the pile alight waiting several seconds before the fire could catch properly.

Finally, the flame blazed to life turning the pile of forest debris into a yellow hot stack of warming fire. The captured soldier had his feet and arms bound before finally being tied to a nearby tree. A rotating armed guard took turns watching him throughout the night. Tife, Chen and Han on the other hand were allowed to remain unbound and free. They were still monitored closely by the guards who watched their every move.

The silence around the campfire was interrupted by the orchestra of animal sounds echoing across the forest. The occasional howl of wolves and the hoot of howls dominated the symphony of noises that filled the night sky as they sat around the dancing fire.

Tife wrapped herself tightly to keep warm as she was bathed in the fire's comforting glow. She looked on warily to the men with guns. They laughed and joked amongst themselves as the night wore on however they kept their weapons close to them, always wearing them across their chests.

The bags they had been carrying contained food stolen from the manor. Fresh fish and meat were taken out and placed atop the dancing flame. The smell of cooked meat and fish wafting into the air prompted Tife's stomach to grumble ferociously. She had totally forgotten her appetite since the ordeal of her abduction began.

The rebels surrounded the fire conversed merrily as they ate from the hot food. Tife on the other hand sat alone on the other side. She looked longingly at the sizzling meats and fishes on the fire but made no attempt to take one. Yerkov stood off at a distance taking in several puffs of smoke from his cigarette once again. He walked over to the fire taking several pieces of fish warming on a stick and brought it to them.

''Take it, '' he urged them, looking directly at Tife, ''You will need all the strength you have left to make it to our camp.'' Both the Chinese delegates took the fish from him and ate them eagerly. When Tife hesitated, he shoved the stick into the ground in front of her and walked away to resume his smoking.

The smell of cooked fish enflamed her nostrils as the knotting pang of hunger continued to harass her. She took the fish from its perch and took several bites into it. The long trek of the day had sapped her of all her energy. The wholesome feeling of food hitting her stomach satisfied her immensely.

She stared into the warming fire as the sounds of giddy rebel soldiers continued to fill the campsite. One by one, they retired for the night settling into their makeshift tents. At least half a dozen remained awake and continued to stand at alert for any possible danger.

The night wore on and only three guards remained awake watching the prisoners. The captured soldier had his head bowed low as he slumbered. Tife and Chen were made to sleep in the same make-shift tent while Han was given one beside them. Tife watched carefully as the eyes of the guard watching them flickered periodically. When he had fallen asleep momentarily, Tife turned her attention to Chen, addressing her in Mandarin.

''I think we should use this time to escape,'' she whispered. ''I think we can navigate our way through the forest back to the main road. We may find a patrol of soldiers along the road. They must be looking for us and would have sent squadrons in the direction we were travelling.''

Chen looked on warily at the slumbering soldiers with their weapons now laying across their knees. The shadows from the fire danced across their sleeping faces.

''I think you'll have the best chance of escaping if you did it alone'' she replied prudently. ''You could send for help once you are clear.''

Tife agreed and went over the plan once more. The rebel soldier watching them was awake now and warming himself by the fire again. Bags of sleep rested heavy under his eyelids. Tife got out of her tent and began to saunter towards the forest. The man immediately cocked his weapon and pointed it at her menacingly.

''Where do you think you are you going, woman?'' he demanded as he walked towards her, gun in arm.

''I need to use the restroom,'' said Tife calmly, pointing to the woody trees.

''You can go over there,'' said the guard, pointing his gun at a nearby bush.

''I would prefer not to attract wild animals to our location. Then there is the issue of the smell…'' she replied. The guard seemed to consider this deeply. He looked around to his sleeping colleagues in their tents. He awoke one of them and instructed him to look after the camp while he escorted Tife into the woods. They ventured deeper into the snow-covered woodland until the soldier commanded her to stop.

''Over there,'' he instructed, pointing to a crop of dense trees nearby before adding, ''Be quick about it.'' Tife motioned towards the trees before squatting down behind the thick foliage. She remained there as the rebel soldier looked through the brush ever so often. Even though the moon hovered overhead, the thick darkness of the trees made it difficult to see properly.

Tife waited a few seconds until she could make out the soldier's turned back then she made a quick dash through the trees, her feet making loud noises through the empty darkness. A warning shout from the soldier reached her ears followed by several gunshots. She ducked just in time to hear the sound of bullets striking the trees nearest to her.

She ran for several meters, making her way as quickly as she could through the darkness. The sound of the rebel soldier's boots followed closely behind. Tife stumbled on an exposed root, knocking her to the floor. Her ankle screamed in pain as she braced it with her hands.

She crawled under a bush and listened as the rebel soldier's footsteps grew closer. He turned around, frantically searching for her in the darkness. Tife pressed a hand to her mouth to keep her from making any sudden noises. The pain from her ankle grew by the second but she was determined to remain quiet. The man gave one last cursory look around before continuing down the forest path hoping to find her.

Tife remained concealed in the thick brush for several minutes. When she was convinced the rebel soldier was nowhere nearby, she inspected her throbbing ankle.

The surrounding darkness was so thick that she could not even see her raised hand in front of her. Nevertheless, she reached a hand to the portion where she felt the most pain and immediately winced in agony. The section of her ankle was inflamed and soft to the touch. She would definitely have hard time walking through the dense forest terrain.

By propping herself up with a thick branch, she managed to get up to her feet and slowly trudge through the dark forest. The pain in her leg was growing forcing her to hobble forward and to rely on the branch for support. However, she continued to make progress through the trees, determined to find her way to the main road.

Tife had no compass to direct her on which route to take however she had gleaned something important during their trek in the woods. She had noticed the moss growing to one side on all the trees they passed.

An important piece of geography she had learned of the Northern hemisphere was that moss grew exclusively on the North side of the trees to avoid direct contact with the sun's rays. If she continued in the opposite direction, she would make it to the main road which was due south of her location. If she was lucky, she may be able to encounter a search patrol on the highway. With that self-reassurance, she ventured deeper into the woods.

A large clearing came into view, shining the moon's pale glow in the circle. As Tife sauntered forward, a rustle in the bushes startled her followed by a menacing growl. She paused as five wolves emerged from the forest and stepped into the clearing. They bared their teeth and paced around impatiently in front of her.

She hopped backwards hoping to put some distance between them causing her walking stick to snap under her weight. She collapsed backwards, facing the wolves as they approached her. Drool oozed from their snarling mouths as they inched forward towards her, ready to pounce and attack.

A loud gunshot echoed through the forest forcing the wolves to flee back into the woods. Tife turned her neck around to see the smoking barrel of a gun pointing in the direction of the wolves.

The person holding it stepped out into the clearing with a cigarette balanced in his mouth. Yerkov looked at her with indifference as two other rebel soldiers appeared beside him. He motioned to them prompting them to take Tife by the arms and bring her to him. With a quick flick of his hand, he struck Tife across the cheek. She glared at him, now more defiant as ever.

‘’Try to escape again, and I will personally put a bullet through your legs, ‘’ he said, pointing the gun menacingly at her knees. They dragged her back through the trees until they reached their campsite again. All the rebel soldiers were out of their tents with guns trained on the forest. Yerkov ordered them to stand down as he stepped through. They proceeded to bound her arms and legs with a thick rope before placing her back in her tent. Chen looked on at her despondently as she turned her back to sleep again.

They were all awoken early the next day and forced to trek through the forest once more. Tife still had her hands bound as they made their way through the leafy vegetation. Yerkov had ordered his men to bind Chen and Han as well. Each was led with a long rope attached to the bounds on their hands. They walked in complete silence for several kilometers. The biting cold still lingered around sending chills through Tife's body.

The icy tundra opened up to a view of an impressive waterfall in the distance. Ice sheets floated freely at the top of the impressive geographical formation while cold water surged from above into the chasm below. The water formed a white mist which concealed the entire stretch of ravine in a hazy fog. Yerkov ordered them to wait behind a crop of trees as he stepped out to the edge.

Pursing his lips together, he made a series of high-pitched whistles which echoed across the majestic waterfall. He waited several seconds until he heard several whistles echo back through the falls. He proceeded to lead them down several narrow bluffs to the bottom of the lake below. Several men in camouflage appeared carrying assault rifles on their backs. They quickly took possession of Tife, Chen and Han and ushered them through a small opening behind the falls.

A rush of warmth greeted their bodies as they were taken down a narrow path into an expansive cavern filled with several people. The sound of triumphant shouts and screams filled the area as Yerkov trooped in with his prisoners. Men and women of various age ranges filled the space as did several children. Nearly all were mostly dressed in raggedy clothes and looked unkempt.

Makeshift scaffolding was erected in many places hosting vines which snaked up its legs. The oval cavern was carved into layers allowing for people to take up residence on higher levels within the space. Sturdy ladders allowed for them to climb to the various levels in the large space.

Several holes pierced the top of the cavern which let in a continuous circulation of air through the space. The sound of the waterfall outside could still be heard from within the rocky interior. Several fires were lit on pikes helping to illuminate the poorly lit area. On one side, pots boiled vigorously, releasing a piercing odor into the air.

Tife and Chen were taken aside and placed in an iron cell carved into the corner. Han and the soldier were placed in a similar cell several meters apart. They remained there until evening, watching the children run about the area playing what Tife could only make out as a shooting game. Half the children wore red face paint and imitated firing a gun with sticks in their hands aimed at another group wearing green face paint.

It was not long until a small celebration in the cavern broke out in the cave. The women began a chant which the men echoed in a deep tone. Many of them took to the center of the cavern and began a lively dance to the tune. The children raced across the floor, chasing themselves up ladders and disappearing into the cavities cut within the walls.

Several roasted carcasses of animals were brought out on large sticks and distributed to the hungry crowd. From Tife's cell, she spotted Yerkov looking down at the joyful crowd of people. When he noticed Tife's gazed fixed on him, he disappeared into one of the hidden compartments of the cavern.

The celebration wore deep into the night until many decided to retire into their sleeping chambers deep within the spacious chamber. The cavern emptied out and several of the lights were put out. What remained were several rebel soldiers patrolling the perimeter of the cave.

Tife balled herself up on the straw bed provided for her. She looked to Chen who had her back turned to the wall and was fast asleep now. The cell was bare save for the hole in the corner she assumed was where she would be forced to relive herself.

As Tife inspected her surroundings, a timid little girl approached her cell. Her body was awash with dirt and her dirty red hair clung tightly to her gaunt face. In her hands was a piece of meat she had taken from the celebration. She brought it up to Tife and offered it through the bars. Tife sat up and approached the bars, kneeling as she took the now cold piece of meat from her.

''Thank you so much,'' said Tife with a wide smile. The girl grinned revealing several missing teeth in her mouth. She ran away and disappeared into one of the many holes of the cavern. Tife sat back in her straw bed with the cold meat in hand. Despite the hunger prickling at her stomach, she had very little appetite.

She began to sob silently as tears streamed down her face, the weight of her predicament dawning heavily on her. She remembered her grandmother, Mama Uvewa who would become undoubtably worried about her once she did not return. Her thoughts then circled back to Abigail who still required a great deal of assistance given her disability.

She wiped the tears from her eyes knowing she would have to be strong if she was to survive this predicament. Tife had faith that Queen Yaa-Yaa would do everything in her power to rescue her once she found out about her abduction.

Tife had managed to go to sleep when the sound of gates rattling started her awake. She rushed to the front of the cell in time to see Yerkov standing behind two soldiers as they dragged the captured soldier from the cell he was sharing with Chen. He struggled briefly prompting one of the guards to strike him in the back of his neck with his weapon. They took him through an open hole at the back of the cavern and out of sight. She remained awake for several more minutes however they did not return with him.

The next morning, she awoke to the sound of a rebel soldier striking the iron bars of her cell. He had a severe expression etched across his face.

''Get up! The captain wants to see you,'' he barked. He forced her out of the cell and through the hole she had seen the captured soldier go through. It opened into a wide antechamber that cut deep into the natural formation.

The walls were smoothed and worn from centuries of rock weathering. The roof was filled with giant stalactites which trickled water from its points. On one side was a glittering side pool which glowed an unearthly blue in the dark space. A shimmering fire lit in the corner bathed the space in an orange glow warding off the darkness of the sprawling cave.

They pointed to a chair placed next to the glimmering pool. Tife's ankle was still very sore yet the rebel soldiers did nothing to help her as she struggled to walk. She managed to walk over to the seat which had several blood stains strewn across it. She sat down and was restrained with leather bounds attached to the chair.

Yerkov stood off to the side looking forlornly at Tife. He took a seat from the side, placed it in front of her and sat down. He reached for a cigarette in his pocket and lit it. The smoke billowing from his mouth made Tife cough out violently. He addressed her in his Slovinian tongue.

''You are Emissary for the African Union, correct?'' he inquired. Tife nodded her head in reply.

''Do you understand why we liberated you from their grasp?'' he asked blowing more smoke into the air. This time, Tife shook her head in response. Yerkov stood up and walked behind her chair. She listened intently as he grabbed the back of the seat, tilting it slowly backwards.

''For too long have you been a slave to despots who control you just as much as they have controlled me,'' he declared in a flowing voice, '' These autocrats rule over us with an iron fist, controlling our lives and using us as pawns to consolidate their power. Never once do they truly consider our wellbeing in all of this. Tell me, what have they told you about us?'' he inquired from her.

Tife was face to face with the head of a group which was responsible for murdering her father and hurting Abigail. For all she knew, this man may have been the mastermind behind the attack. She clasped her fists tightly as white-hot anger began to well up inside her.

''You people are terrorists,'' Tife spat back fiercely, ''you murder innocent people for selfish gain. All you seek is destruction and chaos. No good can come from your blind cause.'' Yerkov seemed to consider this before returning to face Tife again. She looked on at him with spite and fury as he took out another cigarette from his pocket. Yerkov then motioned to the two men standing guard, ''Leave us,'' he ordered. The guards quickly disappeared through the doors back into the cavern leading to the falls.

He took his seat in front of Tife again and stared at her pensively. Tife glared back at him; eyes burning with intensity.

''I used to be like you once,'' he said amiably, gazing directly into her eyes. The blue shade of the pool reflected off his eyes, ''I was once a high-ranking soldier for Czar Nicholas. I and so many others once believed in his ambition to expand the prosperity and rulership of Slovia."

"It is with that same mandate that the Czars of old set their sights on the North American territories.'' He paced across the room and crouched beside the blue pool of water. Drips of water falling from fine-point stalactites attached to the ceiling sent tiny ripples across its surface.

''We were in direct competition with the Chinese Emperor who had already established functioning colonies in the new land. It was said that we sent several warships under the guise of mutual trade between the native people in the new land. It was all a ruse to engender their trust and steal the land from under them.''

''Tales of bravery were told of the men who conquered the savages from across the Atlantic. As a young boy, I dreamed of serving my

Czar in his quest to establish order around the world. My passion was used as a tool to further the Czar's insatiable quest to subjugate as many territories as he could.''

''As soon as I was old enough, I became a soldier in the Czar's army. In service to our ruler, we committed many atrocities. We brutalized anyone who resisted our control and decimated whole peoples. I became blinded by the pride of our kingdom that I never stopped to consider the destruction we had wrought on innocent lives. That quickly changed after the attack to a neighbouring village on the borders of the empire.'' His voice became solemn as he began to narrate the details of his experience.

''The Czar ordered us to occupy the village as its high elevation provided a strategic advantage in the war against the Austria-Hungarian military. The villagers refused our orders to evacuate and were all but determined to retain their homeland.'' Yerkov's voice broke as he began to recount the events which transpired.

''When the villagers would not leave, the Czar ordered for sarin gas to be launched into the area as the villagers slept. With masks on, we were ordered to kill any stragglers who managed to escape the biological attack. As I entered a house, I was met by a family. The mother and father lay dead on the floor while their child lay in the corner with a gas mask on."

"My captain walked in behind me and ordered me to kill the little girl. I raised my weapon to the girl but could not pull the trigger. I could not bring myself to kill that innocent child.'' When Yerkov swung forward to face Tife again, tears were running down his cheeks.

''When we returned to base, my captain disciplined me for insubordination in front of the rest of the soldiers. Do you know what they do to people like me that disobey orders?'' Tife froze as Yerkov began to loosen his belt and pull down his trousers. She averted her eyes as he was now completely nude from the waist down.

''Look at what a king does to his people,'' he urged her. She turned her neck and looked in horror at what she saw. A large section of his shaft and scrotum had been sliced clean off leaving behind a gruesome scar between his legs. She could not tell if what remained of his genitals could offer any sort of reproductive functions or allow him to relieve himself for that matter.

Yerkov duly raised his trousers and adjusted his belt. He sat back on his chair opposite Tife and gazed at her non-plussed face.

''I joined this movement to put an end to the murderous system we have all become a part of. People deserve better lives. They deserve the opportunity for self-determination and to make decisions for themselves. And if it means burning this entire system to the ground and starting afresh so be it.''

''I admit the injustice done to you was unconscionable, but you cannot justify the violence your group has committed over the years.'' Tife chimed in, more defiant than ever. Yerkov straightened up, his cold demeanor had returned now.

''You have been spoiled by your life of privilege that you know nothing of why we fight for freedom. The lies your Queen spins does far more damage than any bullet we fire. You will help us of your own accord or be forced to like we did the solider we captured.'' The two soldiers who had left the room returned and Yerkov promptly ordered them to take her back to the prison cell. This time, they held her up by the hands and escorted her back to her cell.

Once they threw her back inside, they took a distraught Chen out of the cell and into the room she had just left. Tife had her back to the wall as she relieved the horrors Yerkov had showed her. She had learned of the many atrocities which the Czar had committed but never had she been exposed to it in person.

His story was compelling however she could never share the same outlook as Yerkov did. Queen Yaa-Yaa had shown nothing but kindness to her people and her rule had been marked by untold prosperity for her constituents. Tife could not envision a better system of leadership for the people of Luanda and the larger African territories.

''This blatant disregard to the treaty will not stand!'' the Chinese Emperor bellowed over the radio.

The Emissary to the AU, Jinhai Wen, held the phone away from his ear after he had informed the Emperor of the abduction of his colleague, Chen. They had received news through back channels that an attack on the state manor had led to the kidnap of their delegates much to the fury of the Chinese ruler. An official response from their Slovian counterparts had not reached them even after twenty-four hours from when the attack occurred.

As a diplomat, Jinhai was fearful of the reaction the Emperor would have to such news. Given his reluctance to accept the negotiated terms of the peace treaty in the first place, this new information would only be seen as a prelude to renewed war between the two sides.

''We have attempted to engage official channels to find out more about the incident. So far, we have been met with a block of communication from members within the local councillorship. Reports say they may have taken them to the upper Northern territories.'' Emissary Wen said.

''Send word to our military units at the border. If you receive no update on the whereabouts of our delegates within twenty-four hours, I authorize you to send several units to extract them by force.

You are to instruct them to engage and destroy any forces which attempt to deny you access.''

Hours after the peace summit, the Emperor had immediately begun his trip back to his stronghold in China in hopes of reestablishing order at his borders. The war had taken a tremendous toll on his people and he sought to use the lull of tensions to consolidate his power.

He had other concerns to contend with as well including talks of usurpers within his ranks. To maintain control of the colonies, he appointed Auxiliaries to govern the territory. They served much in the same capacity as the Councilors in Slovian colonial territories but wielded much greater influence over the region.

These Auxiliaries were said to be the most loyal members of the Emperors circle. They were chosen from a block of nobles known as the 'Gong'; families steeped in riches said to have ancestry that traced back to the Emperor himself. Two of such Auxiliaries governed the entire North American territory controlled by the Empire.

The raw material resources they supplied to the Emperor proved instrumental in their successful war campaign against Slovia. As their power spread, so did their insubordination to the Emperor. When news of rebellion began to spread, the Emperor took decisive action. He used to peace summit as an opportunity to take care of the incalcitrant proxies.

On the eve of the summit, he invited the Auxiliaries to a personal banquet at the royal palace to celebrate the ending of a long, drawn-out war campaign. Jinhai had been sent to the peace summit venue to finalize details for the arrival of the monarchs so he was largely absent for the celebration.

A hundred-year-old wine was brought out to mark the festivities. After a toast initiated by the Emperor himself, the wine was quickly ingested by the eager guests at the table. Several minutes later, the official delegation and the two Auxiliaries themselves lay foaming at the mouth and convulsing on the floor.

The Emperor had taken care of his problem but had left a leadership vacuum in the colonies. Controlling the territory still required a strong leader to govern the area in his stead. Jinhai received the Emperor at the summit and briefed him of the proceedings to happen at the event.

The Emperor in turn informed him of the treachery of his Auxiliaries and their unfortunate passing the night before. He informed Jinhai that he would now be promoted as Auxiliary to the colonies directly answerable to him.

Although several official delegations were nearby at the time, Jinhai prostrated on the ground in deep gratitude to his Emperor. He pledged his undying loyalty and life in service to the Empire. The promotion came as a surprise to several high-ranking members of the Chinese nobility. Jinhai's family did not share ties with the Gon, Hou or Bo noble classes however he was seen worthy of this new appointment.

His function as Auxiliary to what had become known as the extended Chinese estate would require him to maintain the production of mineral ores and imports from the colonies back to the Mainland. With the war spilling over to the shores of the colonies, they were in constant conflict with their enemies at the borders.

The Austria-Hungarian Empire lay to the south of their territories and controlled a sizable resource belt which the Chinese estate fought for control. The Slovians to the West fought aggressively for resources in the rich mountain regions separating their territories. Their battles were marked by the bombardment of Chinese settlements purportedly encroaching on their lands. Jinhai had a responsibility to protect the interests of the Emperor at all costs.

He travelled to the military base at the border shared by Slovia to meet with Lieutenant General Mao. Jinhai wanted a first-hand account of the military effort to invade the Slovian territories in the event that diplomatic efforts failed in locating their delegates.

He touched down on the base and was ushered into the briefing room by Lieutenant General Mao where they could discuss their plans in private. General Mao directed his attention to a map laid out on the table. Several black blocks dotted the map on the Chinese side while red blocks were used to denote Slovian troops.

''The attack happened here at the Slovian guest manor in their city stronghold of Krepost,'' Mao informed him, pointing to a region in Slovian territory close to the ocean. ''There were reports of an attack by the terrorist cell Red Dawn known to operate within their territories. So far, we have received no word from the soldiers posted to protect them. We assume they were killed in the attack.''

''How can we be sure our delegates are still alive then?'' Jinhai asked intuitively.

''The Red Dawn are not known to kill high-valued targets,'' replied General Mao, ''We believe they have kept them alive to use as leverage in any negotiation they initiate. Several of their fighters are imprisoned in Slovian jails. They will attempt to have them released.''

''Do we know where they could have taken them?''

Lieutenant General Mao pointed to the map at the region above the city of Krepost. It was the woody forest area leading into uncharted territory further North.

''We believe they are somewhere deep within the woodlands of the Northern Tundra. The extensive snow cover will make it difficult to pinpoint their location from the sky.''

''Then what are our options? The Emperor has made it clear on what action we should take.''

Mao hesitated before placing several blocks on the Northernmost part of the Chinese estate, on the boundaries of the uncharted territory.

''With a small extraction team, we could lead a search party to find the base. Once we confirmed their location, we have a standing assault team ready to extract our people.''

''And have we notified our African Union counterparts of this extraction mission?''

''I have sent word to General Sumaina on the status of the mission. He has expressed his support for the plan and is ready to support a full-scale response if the crisis escalates. His Queen however would prefer to settle the matter diplomatically. She does not want to be drawn into further conflict.''

''Then what will become of the peace treaty we signed several hours ago?'' Jinhai asked non-plussed at the seeming desire for greater military action by the generals.

Mao slammed his palms on the table in rising frustration, ''The peace treaty was dead the moment the Slovians allowed a rogue terrorist cell to abduct our citizens,'' he replied fiercely, ''We must respond with a show of strength!''

''Well, we will have a couple of hours before the deadline set by the Emperor expires. I will use that time to reach out to my contacts across the border. Let us see how we can avert bloodshed.'' Jinhai would remain on the base using the powerful communication array at the outpost to reach out to high-ranking members on the Slovian side.

He re-doubled his efforts into reaching Igor Smirnoff, the Councilor in charge of the city of Krepost. He would have better information regarding the location of any rebel base in the region he controlled.

Using an array of official and unofficial channels, he waded through several representatives who all echoed the same response. They all claimed they were not able to give any information and directed him further up their chain of command. Much to his chagrin, Jinhai could not get a hold of the councillor directly.

Jinhai was fiercely against large-scale battle and conflict. His experience as a child watching the poverty and destruction which followed each new campaign firmly entrenched his belief in the superior power of dialogue to resolve conflict. Despite his personal beliefs, he was conscripted to the war effort at a young age. He was fortunate to return him alive after his tour of service

Many of his closest friends were not so lucky. Some of them returned home maimed and broken, suffering gruesome injuries during the countless battles. They were considered the lucky ones. Many never returned at all, losing their lives on the battlefield.

Nighttime fell and all attempts to contact the Slovian leadership in the colonies proved futile. Jinhai sat in his chair dejected as he placed the telephone back on its holder. He nervously thumbed through the last strands of his greying hair with his hands. A giant bald spot sat in the middle of his head. He was sure the never-ending stress of quelling diplomatic incidents was the cause for his hair loss.

He looked over to the clock as the hour hand neared nine o'clock. Numerous shadows now danced outside his office in the bunker so he stepped outside to investigate. Mao was in the center of several troops barking orders as weapons and artillery were handed to them.

''What is going on, Lieutenant?'' Jinhai demanded.

''I have begun mobilizing troops to invade the Northern corridor,'' he replied, '' If we move now, we can deploy before sunrise.''

''But we still have a few hours before the Emperor's deadline,'' Jinhai pointed out.

Mao took Jinhai aside away from earshot of the other soldiers, ''With all due respect Auxillary, your efforts would not have borne fruit. The longer we wait, the further our people slide from our grasps.''

''We do not take any action unless we have express direction from the Emperor," Jinhai admonished.

''The Emperor has already given his consent for military extraction of the prisoners,'' Mao shot back. Jinhai stood back in shock. He had received no word from the Emperor on the plan and was surprised to hear he had already approved the mission.

Mao took him to his private office and brought out a piece of paper from his cabinet. It was lined with the royal seal from the Emperor's table and embossed with his signature. Jinhai skimmed through the secret communique for the important points, his eyes widening at the content.

In the letter sent to the outpost, the Emperor had ordered his troops to occupy the demilitarised zone and expel the Slovian presence from the region. He was determined to lay solid claim to the area using the peace summit as a ploy to catch their rivals off-guard.

Jinhai read through the letter and handed it back to Mao who stowed it back into his cabinet, ''the Emperor never wanted peace with the Slovians, did he?''

''The Emperor will not put trust in a treacherous kingdom which has done nothing but show aggression towards the Chinese people. His allegiance remains to the Chinese Empire as should yours. We will remain in service to our great leader.'' Mao led him out of his office and with one last salute, returned to the group of soldiers he was prepping for the invasion.

Jinhai was left with a feeling of deep unease as he entered the helicopter which would take him back to his residence on the east coast. The resolution by the Emperor would be a severe blow to the peace initiative he and several of his fellow diplomats had worked many years to perfect. The abduction of his colleagues was being used as an excuse to further military action in the colonies.

As the helicopter glided across the ground, he contemplated the ramifications this action would have not only in the colonies but in the mainland. The Slovians would definitely react in kind to any aggression they showed. They retaliation would push tensions in the colonies to a fever point. The bombings which devastated the border towns would continue. Agricultural produce would become scare once again leading to massive famines.

Despite all this, he could not voice his opposition to the Emperor. It would be seen as a sign of insubordination if he did. His job was to prepare the people in the colonies for the restart of an all-out war.

Knowing the full ramifications of the actions which would transpire, he set out to work as he landed in the coastal city early in the morning. He would need to co-ordinate with the army to reinforce the military installations across the colony. It would be equally important to stockpile food and grain to address shortages which were bound to occur. The survival of the people in the colonies was his responsibility and he was determined not to fail them.

STICKS AND STONES

Tife waited patiently for them to return with Chen after they finished interrogating her. She peaked through the bars desperately trying to catch a glimpse of the door which led into the empty cavern she was taken to.

After several hours had passed, the doors opened to reveal Chen being led back to the cell. They promptly placed her inside and locked the doors behind her. Chen slowly walked to the end of the cell and sat down on on the make-shift straw bed. She looked despondent and dazed; her expression filled with intense confusion.

''What did they ask you, Chen?'' Tife inquired as she inched closer to her and sat opposite her.

''They asked me for details on the military strength of the Chinese army. They also wanted to know details about a 'Project Yinzou'.''

''Project Yinzou?'' Tife echoed pensively. She had never heard the name before.

''Yinzou is a provincial administrative unit on the North-West coast of the Chinese colonies. They are known for many research projects that I am not privy to. I had visited there on a handful of occasions but was not allowed to enter the more sensitive areas in the province.''

''Then what did you tell them?'' Tife pressed.

''Anything I could. I told them where I saw military installations, the locations of bases and the layout of the region. I didn't know what else to say.''

Tife sat back and pondered deeply about the rebel's intent. Their line of questioning suggested they were trying to extract as much information as they could from them.

Unfortunately as diplomats, much of the information they had at their disposal would be of little use to their cause. Their main concern was largely focused on brokering peace between their governments and their enemies. Military movements and combat missions were outside their purview.

Yerkov and several rebel soldiers had left during the day and returned at night covered in a thick shroud of snow. They warmed themselves by a fire set up by the women in the camp. Tife watched with curiosity as several children rallied around the rebel soldiers.

Yerkov proceeded to pick up a child no older than six years old and whisk him through the air. The little boy giggled in delight as he twirled him around in circles. The other children around him quickly clamored for the same treatment. Tife watched through the bars as he spent the rest of the evening with them. They sat by the campfire as he told them lively stories from his time in the forests.

The evening wore deep into the night. Several of the children now lay fast asleep beside the glowing fire. They brought blankets to cover them and retired for the night. Yerkov was the last to leave. Tife darted out of sight as Yerkov noticed her watching him.

The light from the fire grew dim and shadows consumed the entire space now. He walked towards her cell and sat down beside it. Chen's slow, rhythmic breathing showed she was fast asleep now.

''You think of us as monsters, do you not?'' Yerkov asked as he lit up another cigarette and took in a huge intake of smoke from it, ''You believe yourself better than us because we are ready to use violence to fight for what we believe in.'' Tife remained silent giving no word in reply. Yerkov breathed out a huge sigh before turning to look at her through the bars.

''I give you permission to speak your mind freely. No harm will come to you,'' Yerkov assured her.

''Despite whatever grievances you may have with your Czar, it does not give you the moral justification to respond with violence. You believe your armed conflict is just, yet innocent people get caught in the crossfire,'' Tife replied through gritted teeth, the anger welling up inside her. Yerkov looked at her with sympathetic eyes. He grasped one of the metal bars and brought his head closer to the cell.

''You know personal loss as well, don't you?'' he asked, ''who do you still grieve for?''

''The attack at the Irin Ajo Oba was responsible for claiming the life of my father. Your misguided campaign is directly responsible for murdering and hurting the people I love. Your actions have driven the world to the brink of total destruction. Tell me how you justify all of this,'' she replied, wiping tears which now streamed down her face.

''We bear no responsibility of that attack and you equally have no evidence to prove it. Our group was framed by elements seeking to profit from the ensuing war.'' Tife turned her face away from him now, staring into the shadows of her prison cell. Yerkov stood up and dusted himself off. He crushed the cigarette on the ground beside him with the tip of his boot.

''The anger and rage you feel is good. You must now learn to channel it to the right cause. The truth is right in front of you if only you are brave enough to see it. We are not your enemies. The very institution of dictatorial autocracies and birthright rulership is. I am confident you will come to understand this one day.'' He took one last look at her before climbing up the ladders to retire for the night, leaving Tife to ponder in silence.

The attack which killed her father still haunted her to this day. She remembered how she refused to leave the house weeks after the incident occurred. Even after she gathered the courage to venture out of the house, the fear and trepidation she felt remained.

She never questioned the veracity of reports that the Red Dawn had masterminded the attack. It had the effect of galvanising the resolve of the entire empire to take swift action against all those responsible. The rallying from neighboring African kingdoms to seek justice ensured a unified war attack plan.

The intelligence gathered did determine it was the Red Dawn who carried out the attack with the support of the Solvian Czar. The result would be to destabilise the African kingdoms and lay greater claims to their territory.

Tife had gained access to the intelligence reports confirming these allegations and never once doubted their authenticity. Yerkov was calling to question this information gathered by the military. If the Red Dawn did not plan the attack, then who did?

The hours stretched on interminably. Tife could only watch the activities of her captors through the bars of her cell. The little red-haired girl who had brought her food the night before approached the cell again, this time with a cat nestled in her arms. She stroked the emerald green-eyed cat which purred silently in response. The girl knelt in front of the cage as Tife moved forward to the bars.

''Is he yours?'' Tife asked curiously. The cat had a unique coat. The length of his body was black save for his face which was separated by equal parts of black and white fur giving him a distinctive appearance.

''It's a girl,'' the girl replied with a deep frown on her face.

''I'm sorry. Does she have a name?'' the girl's face lit up now. She brought the cat closer to the bars.

''I named her Eliza, ''the little girl replied, ''people don't want her here because we don't have a lot of food to feed ourselves and they think Eliza will just be an extra mouth to feed.''

''Well, I think Eliza is a wonderful addition to this place, ''Tife said, adding a wide grin.

''Would you like to pet her?'' the little girl asked. Tife reached through the bars and stroked the cat's silky coat. The cat responded by giving a low-pitched mewl in response.

''What's your name, little one?'' Tife asked.

''My name is Katrina,'' the girl replied with a broad smile revealing her missing teeth once more.

''Well, that's a lovel-, '' before Tife could finish her sentence, a soldier yelled, ''Helicopter!'' from the front of the cave. This prompted a rush of movement in the expansive cave. Men and women scampered up the ladders and hid inside the holes cut deep into the walls.

Lit torches were smothered and turned off. Katrina herself disappeared into a hole in the wall, the cat still in her firm grasp. The cave was deathly silent now save for the sound of the waterfall which percolated into the dark chamber.

Tife listened in as the familiar sound of helicopter blades reverberated through the air. The sound became loudest as the helicopter passed overhead and then slowly faded into the distance as it travelled further off.

Several minutes passed before a solider shouted, 'Clear' from the cave entrance. A noticeable atmosphere of relief filled the space as several people came out of the holes and returned to their various activities.

Yerkov approached Tife's prison cell and gestured to the sky above.

''They seem to be searching desperately for you all,'' he said with a stern expression on his face.

''Please release us. We have done nothing to deserve this treatment,'' Chen pleaded through the bars.

''We have already initiated talks to have you exchanged for our fighters. When they have agreed on our terms, then we will proceed with the transaction.''

''What will you do with us in the meantime?'' Tife demanded tensely.

''You will remain confined to your cells until we can make the exchange. Cooperate with us and you will not be harmed. I give you my word.'' Yerkov went off in the other direction accompanied by several of his rebel soldiers. Chen slumped back in the corner with her hands to her head. She rocked nervously from side to side murmuring anxiously to herself. Tife rushed to her and clasped her hands comfortingly.

''It's going to be ok, Chen, we will get through this. We need to stay strong until then.'' Tife offered a bright smile and pulled Chen close to her. She could feel Chen's heart rising in her chest. Tife was afraid for her life as well but tried to show no indication to Chen as she comforted her.

The situation was dire and she knew it. As a strong policy point, the African Union agreed never to negotiate with any terrorist group operating within its region or abroad. The intent was to discourage terrorist groups from acquiring leverage in the form of prisoners to make demands on the empire.

This mandate only resulted in one course of action if any foreign rebel group successfully abducted the citizens of the empire. A team would quickly be deployed to locate and extract the prisoners by force. Tife knew this well and expected a team to be close on their tail tracking them. She hoped they would reach them in time before any real harm came to them.

A couple of hours had passed as Tife sat silently in her prison cell. She watched them take the captured soldier from his cell and into the interrogation room once more. It seemed they were determined to extract as much information as they could from him before the handover took place.

She lay down in her bed and thought of her loved ones back home. Abigail was restricted to a wheelchair and had no one else to help her with simple tasks. The groceries Tife had bought for her would soon run out and she would need more in the next couple of days.

Her grandmother, Mama Uvewa, would also be worried sick since she hadn't returned as scheduled. She was well into her years but somehow retained the strength to do everyday chores by herself. Her first action when she returned home would be to inform Mama Uvewa that she was safe and sound.

The soldier returned bloody and beaten as they dragged him back into his cell and thrust him inside. Tife peered through her cell to catch a glimpse of him. She could make out his bloody visage at the periphery of her line of sight.

They had become increasingly violent with him as greater attempts were made to extract information from him. She was instantly worried that the rebel soldiers too would become more violent with them as well.

Tife had never directly experienced violence in her life. Her mother would occasionally discipline her when she had done something wrong. Her father reprimanded his wife on several occasions and would always recommend less physical forms of punishment.

She recalled a fond memory of playing a game called sticks and stones in the yard with her friends from next door. Their neighbor, Mr. Hamid and his family, had come to visit them on one cloudy day in June.

Mr. Hamid was a lean man with a bright smile and a sunny disposition. He had ten children in total: nine girls and one boy. People in the neighborhood would derisively say he kept trying for a boy even at the expense of his wife's health.

Every now and then, they would come to Tife's house to visit her family or sit down for dinner. Tife and the girls would always go upstairs to her room while the boy would remain by himself in the dining room reading from a book.

On this occasion when she was just ten years old, her mother Kifunji took the boy to Tife's room where the girls were congregated. They were all giggling about a rumor they had heard in school.

''Tife, don't exclude Ali from playing in your group?'' she said. Ali scrunched his face together in annoyance, indignant that he was being forced to play with the girls.

''He doesn't want to play with us, Mama,'' Tife moaned, ''he always goes off by himself.'' Kifunji ushered him into the room and instructed him to sit in the circle the girls had made. She put her hands tenderly on his shoulders and eyed each of them wearingly.

''Be nice to your friend and your brother, girls. Don't make him feel lonely,'' she cautioned them before leaving to rejoin her husband and their friends in the living room. Ali looked around nervously at the group of girls who now fell silent as they stared awkwardly at him. Finally, Tife broke the silence.

''Why don't we play sticks and stones outside?'' she proposed. They all agreed and gathered outside on the grassy field in front of their house. They sat in a circle with five water balloons laid in front of them. Each of them outstretched their left hands in front of them while Tife explained the rules.

''You all remember how we play this game, right?'' she began, ''we all go around saying things we have never done. If you have done it before, then you curl up one finger,'' Tife raised her hand and demonstrated by pulling back her thumb,'' The first person to have all his fingers curled back loses. We yell 'Sticks and stones' and throw our water balloons at that person. Remember, you have to be honest. If any of us can confirm you are lying, we throw our water balloons at you and you are immediately kicked out of the game.''

''I'll start first. Sticks and stones may break my bones, but I have never peed standing up before.'' All the girls giggled giddily and stared at the Ali who nervously pulled his thumb back. Samba, the girl closest to Tife, continued.

''Sticks and stones may break my bones, but I've never kissed a girl before.'' All the girls looked up to Ali again. This time, he kept his remaining four fingers straight prompting them to giggle again even harder. Balela sat across from Tife and curled back one finger which prompted the others to scream in delight.

''It was on the cheek guys. I was dared to do it. There's nothing wrong with it,'' she revealed, blushing profusely.

Then came Mianda, ''Sticks and stones may break my bones, but I've never gone completely bald before.'' Ali promptly curled another finger. Even now, his scalp barely had any hair on it. His father constantly insisted he keep his hair low.

Adah came after, ''Sticks and stones may break my bones, but I've never played football before.'' Only Ali curled up another finger again.

Bibi was up next, ''Sticks and stones may break my bones, but I've never gotten into a fist fight before.'' Once again, Ali curled back another one, leaving one outstretched finger out. This time, it was his turn to ask the question.

''Stick and stones may break my bones, but I've never had a period before.'' Now all the girls stared at him with curiosity etched across their faces.

''What is that?'' his sister Kanika asked.

''You know when you girls pee blood every first week of the month,'' Ali explained. This was followed by retching sounds from all the girls sitting down.

''That's gross, Ali,'' Bibi intoned, sticking out her tongue in disgust. Ali shrugged in reply.

Tife gave Fajah a nod before it was her turn to speak up, ''Stick and stones may break my bones, but I've never broken a bone before.'' Fajah knew well enough that her brother had a nasty fall on his bicycle after his seventh birthday requiring him to wear a cast. It took him several weeks to recover from the incident. It was their goal to kick Ali out of the game and make him lose interest in playing with them.

Ali pulled back the last of his fingers and braced himself as the girls stood up, grabbed their water balloons, and pelted him with it. He stood up and ran to the wall as they continued to drench him in water. Tife ran over and pressed one of the water balloons directly on his head. Ali responded by pushing her back, knocking her to the floor.

Tife stood up enraged and with a running start, pushed his body back against the wall. Ali struck it with a loud thump prompting him to cry out in pain. Tife stood over him, her face contorted in rage as he howled in agony.

''What is going on here?'' her mother Kifunji demanded as she rushed outside of the house. She caught Ali splayed on the ground with Tife looking down over him. Ali pointed accusingly at Tife as he shouted, ''She pushed me!''

''He pushed me first,'' Tife shouted in defense, ''I only pushed him back.''Kifunji grabbed Tife and brought her inside to the kitchen. She took out a ruler from a nearby drawer and instructed her to straighten out her arms. Tife knew what was coming and balled her fists in anticipation.

''Stretch out your fingers, Tife!!'' she ordered. Tife reluctantly complied, bracing her body for the pain which was about to follow. With a swift motion, Kifunji brought down the ruler on Tife's outstretched fingers.

The pain was sharp and intense. Tife cried out in reply as tears began to run down her face. Another swoop of the ruler caused her to scream louder as the pain registered even deeper now. Eli could hear the commotion from the other room and marched into the kitchen. Tife ran and grabbed her father by the waist as he appeared before them.

''Why are you beating her, Kiffy?'' he probed, a look of concern plastered on his face.

''She hurt Mr. Hamid's son when I asked them to play together,'' Kifunji reported. Eli looked down at Tife who still held him by the waist.

''Is this true, Tife?'' he asked.

''Yes, but he pushed me to the ground first, Papa,'' she explained.

''I'll take care of this, Kiffy. Come with me Tife,'' he instructed her. Eli took her upstairs to her room, closed the door behind him and sat down across from her on the bed.

''I've told you in the past that you need to learn how to control your anger, Tife,'' Eli began, ''acting violently in response to violence does not solve anything.''

''It wasn't my fault Papa,'' she replied in protest with tears still climbing down her cheeks, ''the girls can tell you Ali was the one who pushed me first. I only returned the favor.''

''And tell me what that solved, my angel. How are your actions any better than his?'' Tife stared at her feet in silence. Eli lifted her head by her chin and wiped down her cheeks with a gentle rub of his palm.

''You need to understand my love that an eye for an eye will only make the whole world blind. Acts of aggression will only breed more aggression if we do not break the cycle. What you did to Ali did not solve anything. You would have stood more to gain if you first reported to us. One day, you will be faced with similar decisions. It is up to you to make the right choice. Do you understand?''

''Yes, Papa,'' Tife replied, looking up to meet his gaze. He returned hers with a wide smile plastered across his face.

''Now, you know your mother will not be happy if I just let you go without proper punishment. You will be grounded at home for a month. You will go to school and come back as soon as you finish. No visits from your friends will be allowed either. You will also be responsible for raking the leaves outside and doing the laundry during that time.'' Tife moaned in reply as he listed out her punishment. Eli held up his finger to her face.

''No complaints, young lady. I also want you to go back in there and apologize to Ali for hurting him. And I do not want to hear a word in protest,'' he warned. He took her back to the living room where Ali sat alongside his parents. A band aid had been fixed to the side of his head which had struck the wall.

''My daughter has something to say to your son,'' Eli announced. He held Tife by the shoulders and pressed gently on them.

''I'm sorry for pushing you and hurting you, Ali. It won't happen again,'' Tife said, looking away in embarrassment.

''And I am sorry for pushing you too, Tife. I got mad that I lost, and I took it out on you,'' Ali replied.

''See, was that so hard, now?'' Eli asked with a wide smile, ''Now you both go back outside and remember to play nice.''

Tife remembered that memory vividly as she sat in her cage. Events in her life such as that one had framed her world view from a young age. Her father had always preached peace to her and the need to deescalate tensions whenever possible. Advice like that had become motivating drivers in her quest to be front and center in politics.

The very inspiration to become an Emissary to the crown was hinged on her strong belief in the power of diplomacy in settling disputes. This ideology evolved quickly when she became more involved in the political discourse between their warring empires.

The war raging across the different territories was sponsored by parties who only saw the benefit of aggression in responding to disputes. Her views on peaceful discourse however evolved every so slightly the more time she spent with the military elite who always proposed a violent response as solutions to the empire's most pressing challenges.

Although her views were more tempered and measured, she found a way to balance the need for peaceful discourse with the need for a strong show of force to deter further aggression. Deep down however, she admitted that she was still that little girl who was ready to respond with force to any slight directed at her. In memory of her late father, she suppressed those violent tendencies as best she could.

Yerkov returned a few of hours later accompanied with a regiment of his rebel troops. He pointed to the bloodied soldier in his cell. His men proceeded to grab him roughly by the shoulders, place a blindfold over him and lead him towards the exit of the cave.

''Bring them too, '' Yerkov ordered, pointing to Tife and Chen's cell, ''I want them to witness this.'' Two rebel soldiers approached their cell and flung it wide open. The soldiers ordered them up and marched them out of the cave before making them drape on heavy coats to stave off the winter cold.

Tife had not been outside since they were abducted days ago. Her prolonged time in the dingy cell made her tragically lose all sense of time. The frigid air stung deeply as they stepped outside. The night sky was dimly lit as a snowy haze blanketed the area.

They took them to two dog sleighs waiting just outside the waterfall cave. Two teams consisting of ten dogs each were attached with leather straps to the wide sleighs. Tife and Chen were made to board one alongside two other soldiers while Yerkov took the reins of the second sleigh joined by his rebel colleagues and the blindfolded soldier.

With a loud 'Haaaa' sound, the dogs began down the white trail. An icy mist rose from beneath their feet as they bounded through the frigid wasteland. The journey took them down the sloped path giving them an impressive view of the mountain ranges standing majestically in the distance.

They travelled several miles until they reached a virgin clearing in the distance. From here, Tife could catch a glimpse of the main road which cut a clear path through the dense, snowy forest. They stopped within a few meters of the clearing and disembarked from the sleighs. The dogs whimpered silently as they waited patiently in the cold.

Yerkov took the bloodied shoulder roughly by the neck and dragged him off the dog sleigh. He ripped off the blindfold from him and shoved him forcibly into the clearing. The distraught soldier looked frantically around his surroundings as they let him loose. The bounds on his hands remained fixed though.

''Tell your bosses what our demands are, soldier, '' he shouted into the wind as a cold gust undercut the air. ''Tell them we are ready to trade their people for ours which they keep locked up in their cages. They have three days to decide. We will meet back at this exact location if they decide to honor our terms.''

Yerkov took out a flare gun from his pocket. He raised his right hand into the air and fired the small gun. A blinding, red trail of glimmering light lifted into the air and exploded in an impressive red glow which filled the sky above. Yerkov then ordered his men back unto the sleigh and departed hurriedly from the spot, leaving the injured soldier in the cold.

They arrived back at the hideout hours later. The dogs were removed from their harness and taken away through another entrance into the cave. Yerkov, accompanied by his men with Tife and Chen in tow, walked into the oval cavern to see several inhabitants of the cave arranged on the different levels overlooking the expansive space.

Down below was a man dressed in military fatigue with several rebel soldiers surrounding him. He had deep, long, red hair and a scruffy unkept beard. Attached to holsters of his outfit were knives which adorned the side of his jacket and trouser. Silence permeated the space as they walked inside.

''What is the meaning of this, Dmitri?'' Yerkov demanded, pulling off his snow goggles as he marched into the cavern.

''You released the soldier without our collective consent, Captain,'' Dmitri shot back fiercely. ''He could have still provided us with intel against the fascist regime. And even more alarming is that you potentially expose our location by your actions!'' The armed soldiers flanking Dmitri nodded in agreement. Concerned murmuring filtered through the cavern as the people whispered amongst themselves.

''The soldier had nothing left to reveal to us, Dmitri. I personally made sure of that,'' Yerkov responded stiffly. Dmitri sauntered across the cave floor eyeing Yerkov with intensity.

''You have become increasingly reckless over these past few months, Captain,'' Dmitri declared, raising the level of his voice now so that everyone in the cavern could hear him.

''First, you storm the Krepost stronghold to abduct these foreigners,'' He pointed at Tife and Chen who were standing in the back, ''and now you release an enemy soldier without consulting your loyal troops. I am beginning to wonder where your allegiance truly lies.''

‘’Do you question my resolve to the cause?’’ Yerkov replied through gritted teeth. He placed a weary hand on his side arm prompting Dmitri to raise his hand in submission. A dangerous grin spread across his face.

‘’I only question the decisions you have been making. You endanger our lives as well if you make the wrong ones. My line of questioning is not unusual. After all, you used to work for the Empire as a soldier, did you not? You once represented the very thing we all fight against now. How should we in good faith put all our trust in you?’’

The murmuring grew even more intense now with several people in the cave speaking up in agreement to Dmitri’s words. Yerkov looked around the room before walking to the center of the cave. He took out his gun and placed it on the floor. He also reached into his breast pockets and took out several knives hidden in them. He raised his hands into the air as he addressed the crowd once more.

‘’I have lived many lives in my quest for meaning in this world. In the past, I did live as a soldier for the Empire. My actions helped to prop up the monarchy which has now become a bane on all of our lives. But when I was asked to sell my soul to the Czar, to act in a way which is fundamentally inhumane and unjust, I made the right choice. I paid a hefty price for that action, but I am glad I bled instead of committing more evil. ‘’

‘’I more than anyone else know of the wickedness of the Slovian Empire. It is for that reason that in the life I have chosen now, I seek redemption for my past transgressions by liberating the people from their tyranny. But any victory we gain will mean nothing if we do not do everything in our power to come to the aid of our captured brethren."

"That is why I released the soldier and intend on releasing these prisoners in exchange for our people. If that is wrong, then lock me up and make sure I never see the light of day. If I am right, then aid me in my attempt to reunite our kin with us. We are stronger only when we are together and united! ''

The cavern fell silent as he finished his speech. Dmitri stared at Yerkov with hollow eyes as he returned his gaze. After several seconds, Yerkov walked past Dmitri and through the doors leading deeper into the cavern. The soldiers returned Tife and Chen to their cells as the crowd of people in the central cavern slowly began to disperse.

Hours pass and Tife lay on the floor of her cell. The night activities had resumed once more with the children playing in the cavern. The heavy smell of food wafted through the air as women stirred long spoons in smoking cauldrons on one side.

Minutes later, the cave inhabitants lined up one after another with the children going first to get a portion of food in makeshift bowls made from curved wood. They poured the steaming gruel into the bowls and handed a sliver of bread to the children as they stepped up one by one. The bread quickly ran out just as a girl stepped up to collect her portion. Tife watched as she sobbed silently and walked away dejectedly into the corner.

After everyone had been served, the woman distributing the food called over two rebel guards and pointed in Tife's direction at the far corner. She poured three more bowls and asked them to bring them over to the cells. The rebel soldiers begrudgingly took them and walked over to her. The soldier bringing her plate of food stopped abruptly in front of her cell and dropped the bowls onto the floor. The brown porridge spilled all over the ground and unto his shoes.

''Eat up, '' he intoned before walking away with a mocking grin across his face. Tife stared forlornly at the spilled food on the floor. Their captors had not been scrupulous in feeding them regularly. At this point, she was grateful when they did. She was deathly hungry after their excursion outside and longed for the feeling of warm food filling her belly.

Chen rushed over and grabbed one of the bowls from the floor. She proceeded to scrape its contents off the ground and into the bowl. Chen gave Tife a bashful look before returning back to the far corner of her bed to voraciously eat the food. Tife sat back on her bed, unwilling to eat the spilled food. Her stomach growled intermittently but she ignored it, opting to attempt sleep instead.

She had managed to doze off when another soldier walked by. He ordered Tife out of the cell and bound her hands again.

''Where are you taking me?'' she asked.

''Captain wants to speak to you,'' the rebel soldier informed her. He took her further into the cave until they reached a narrow space with a singular tunnel leading into it. Inside was a miniature waterfall pouring into an overflow pool just below the raised access point.

The cave was lit up with an ethereal glow coming from the stalactite formations hanging above the pool of water, bathing the space in an unearthly, red glow. Tife spotted Yerkov sitting at the far corner with a lighted cigarette at the end of his mouth. He pointed towards a spot overlooking the pool and ordered her to sit there. The small space reverberated his voice giving it a melodious quality.

''You watched the drama which unfolded a couple of hours ago, did you not?'' he asked bluntly. Tife responded with a blank stare at him.

''I can feel my soldiers losing trust in me as each day passes,'' he admitted, taking a long intake of smoke from his cigarette, ''it is hard to maintain ranks when you have hardliners like Dmitri seeking to usurp control.'' He shook his head forlornly and heaved in a deep sigh.

''What do you want from me?'' Tife demanded. Her body was still exhausted from not eating for several hours. He turned to look at her suddenly, peering deeply into her eyes.

''You are an Emissary to Queen Yaa-Yaa of the African Union, correct?'' He asked. ''Tell me, faced with a possible mutiny of your own men, what would you do?''

''You abduct me and keep me as your prisoner. Now you ask for my counsel?'' Tife asked incredulously.

''It is specifically because you do not represent a faction within our ranks that I can respect your advice,'' he replied, ''an outside opinion may be useful to me.'' Tife remained silent and returned his gaze with a fierce one of her own. Yerkov stood up and marched towards where she sat. He leaned against the wall closest to her and looked down at her.

''Despite appearances, I have shown you nothing but kindness since we took you from the State Manor. Others like Dmitri see no reason to keep you alive. They doubt the word of the fascist government in releasing our captured brethren in their possession. The Red Dawn is in many ways their creation. It was used as a tool by the Czar to retaliate against his enemies. I learned of this when I became a leader of the faction in the colonies.''

Tife looked up at him now with renewed interest. Reports of the Red Dawn working with the Slovian empire were common knowledge but never had she heard a direct admission of guilt from within the Red Dawn ranks. News of this would only sow greater discontent for the dictatorial regime in the eyes of the international community.

''You remind me of her, you know?'' Yerkov added suddenly, his voice taking a mournful quality now, ''your spirit that is. I see her in you.'' Tife looked up at him as he stared sorrowfully at the pool swirling with water falling from above.

''You have lost someone close to you, haven't you?'' Tife asked intuitively. Yerkov looked back at her passively before returning his gaze to the pool.

''My partner, Galina. I rescued her from being taken to the gulags for apparent crimes against the Empire. It was to be her punishment for hiding two children accused of stealing food. She fought valiantly for the rebel cause but was captured on a food run many months ago. The prisoner exchange may be my last chance to save her.'' Yerkov returned his gaze to Tife. The look of indifference which had been a trademark of his face was now replaced with a forlorn one. Tife saw a man desperate to reunite with the woman he loved.

''I will not pretend that you understand these things. You clearly have lived a life of privilege. You know nothing of struggle and suffering that we bear under the hands of ruthless dictators. I assure you that we will return you to your life of privilege soon. We will trade your life for our comrades and you can put this ordeal behind you.''

Yerkov reached into his pocket and pulled out something wrapped in newspaper. He threw it at Tife who promptly caught it. She unwrapped it to reveal a tiny loaf of bread concealed within. Her stomach churned hungrily at the sight of it. She bit down swiftly into it not minding it being cold and damp.

The spongy dough hitting her stomach filling her with delight. She took several more bites from the bread before rushing to the side of the pool of water. Cupping her hands together, she managed to take in huge mouthfuls to satiate her thirst. She looked up to see Yerkov eyeing her with interest once more.

''You asked me what I would do if I suspected an impending mutiny on my hands, '' Tife spoke up while wiping her mouth with the back of her hand. ''If I were in your position, I would take away the support base which your competitor enjoys. A large gesture of goodwill extended to everyone would re-balance the scales in your favor.'' Yerkov replied with a silent nod of acknowledgement before calling on the soldier outside the door.

''Return her to her cell. I have nothing else to discuss with her,'' he ordered the soldier. Tife was led out and returned to her prison cell. Chen stirred awake momentarily but quickly fell back to sleep as the seconds passed by. Tife was left to brood alone washed in the faint orange glow of the flickering torches.

With the knowledge of splitting factions within the terrorist ranks, she understood the greater peril she and the rest of her abductees were placed in. Given how heavily they were monitored, another attempt to escape would be unwise.

The very next day, Tife watched as Yerkov led a large group of men outside the cave. The night which followed saw them return with a large cache of meat, grain, fresh vegetables, and fruits wrapped in large linen cloths. The celebrations which came at night saw the inhabitants fill the central cavern for the ensuing feast. The women cooked the meat in open flames by the corner. The grain was cleaned and pressed into starchy balls which they lined on stacked leaves.

The entire cavern was filled with energy as the rebel soldiers, children and women alike sat down to enjoy the bountiful feast they had amassed. Tife noticed some of the men bringing food to heavily pregnant women seated in the corner. The sound of happy children's voices spread through the air as they chased one another in the brightly lit chamber. Dmitri on the other hand sat in the corner smoking and gambling alongside several men in his company.

A few hours passed before Yerkov arrived. Tife could barely make him out as he stood on a raised platform at the highest point in the cavern. The merry voices dominating the cave slowly came to a halt as he mounted the stage.

''Comrades,'' he began, '' I trust you are all enjoying the spoils of our current venture from pillaging the fascist's food reserves. We obtained this haul from the private storehouses dedicated solely to the political elite in Krepost and the neighboring colonies. While the people starved and toiled in hardship, they became fat from the forced labor of the people. We have only taken back what is ours!'' Yerkov's words were met by cries of praise which rent through the air. After a few moments, he raised his hand to quiet them down again. He resumed addressing them once again.

''I know we have fallen on difficult times recently. Food especially has come in short supply recently. Our numbers have dwindled with each passing day. Many of our brethren have succumbed to disease or death by the hands of the fascist regime. But in these challenging times, let us remember what we are fighting for.'' He pointed in the direction of the pregnant women in the corner.

''We fight for the future of our children. We fight so that they may grow up to live in a world where they are free to choose and make their own decisions; to make their own mistakes without fear of being sentenced to death for petty crimes.''

''We fight for our liberties which were never given to us. It is time that we break the chains of oppression which have been foisted upon us by an Empire only seeking to advance the prosperity of a small group of people. To accomplish all of this, we need the full might of all our people. Tomorrow, we will be reunited with our kin who have been away from us for too long. I trust even the likes of Dimitri would appreciate this. Tomorrow will be remembered as a day of victory!''

Immediately he finished his speech, he made a point to turn in the direction of Dmitri who scoffed and walked away with his cadre of men in tow. The entire cavern erupted in a sea of applause and cheers of adulation. Yerkov stepped down and returned to the floor of the cave to rejoin his people in the festivities. Tife watched him intently from her cell as he received congratulatory handshakes and pats on the back.

Tife more than anyone understood the complexities of the power move Yerkov had just played. She had been even more surprised that the rebel leader had taken her advice on the subject. The large gesture may be effective in staving off a coup d'état in the short term but without solidifying action to bolster confidence in his leadership, the effects would quickly dissipate with time.

She knew a successful prisoner exchange would only consolidate Yerkov's power and control over the group. For her sake and the sake of Chen and Han, she could only hope they would be released back safely to their military forces.

ACCEPTABLE LOSSES

''Bring that one too!'' Igor demanded, pointing to an unkempt woman sitting in the cage. He cradled what was left of his right hand and propped it up to prevent greater loss of blood. He had about fifty of the rebel filth locked up in these cages.

Three days ago, they had found the captured soldier from the State Manor raid on the side of the road during a routine patrol in the Northern enclaves. According to him, the terrorists had demanded all their fighters be released in exchange for the diplomatic prisoners in their custody.

The prisoner exchange would happen today in the same location they had found the soldier. Despite the grievous injuries to his arm, Igor was determined to see the prisoner exchange through personally. The amputation of his right arm would pale in comparison to the tortures the Czar would have in store for him if he failed in his mission.

A soldier dragged the woman out by her hair prompting her to kick and scream in reply. The soldier responded by kicking her square in the stomach forcing her to double down on the floor in pain. She was placed in handcuffs and led outside to the transport truck.

Nineteen other prisoners were led out to the trucks and secured tightly in their seats; their mouths gagged as well. Two of said prisoners had to be placed in stretchers and laid in the trucks alongside the prisoners.

Indeed, Igor had selected only the most sickly of the prisoners in his care for the exchange. He would not stand the risk of propping up the terrorist cell by increasing their available manpower. He was determined to do everything in his power to rout the rebels and destroy them once and for all.

Igor got into the passenger seat of the vehicle as it started up. They proceeded from the city of Krepost out into the open roads leading to the Northern enclaves. The Slovian empire had laid claims to a substantial portion of the lands but experienced significant resistance from the Chinese Empire seeking to subjugate the territory.

Through the newly signed peace accords, a sharing formula to allocate the lands accordingly had been reached offering new territories to the Slovian kingdom. Their routine patrols of the area were made to monitor any activity or aggression from their Chinese counterparts who had a habit of encroaching on their lands. Now with the peace accords in place, any action they took on the land could easily be misconstrued as a breach of the agreement and an act of war.

Largely due to its inhospitable location, the northern enclaves had become ripe with activity from the terrorist cell. The rugged terrain and considerable vegetation cover offered excellent protection to carry out their nefarious activities. Pinpointing their base of operation had even been difficult from the sky. The prisoner exchange offered the chance to narrow down their search zone so that they could destroy the heart of their operations once and for all.

As they reached further North, Igor fidgeted uncomfortably as the truck bounded down the snow-covered roads. It would take them several hours to reach their destination. The considerable poor visibility prevented the use of helicopters to travel quickly to the exchange point.

Accompanying the two transport vehicles holding the prisoners were three other vehicles containing eighteen soldiers in total. They were present to guarantee a successful exchange and to provide support to any resistance they encountered in the process. Igor held no trust in the rebels and was prepared to utilize force if required to make the exchange.

After many long hours of travelling, they arrived at the drop-off point. The thick vegetation in the area was interrupted with a frozen lake which cut a large area of land in the icy tundra. The vehicles they had come in would be parked beside the road while the prisoners would be let out once they had visual confirmation of the abducted diplomats.

Igor swallowed several more pain killers as he scanned the area from inside the truck. The wind picked up substantially leaving the area in a blurry, white haze. As he struggled to look through the dense fog, a soldier shouted that he had made visual confirmation, pointing to an elevated hill overlooking the icy lake. Igor demanded for a pair of binoculars to inspect the high ground the soldier had pointed to.

Looking through the lenses, he could make out a mounted pole with a flag flying in the wind. The flag had a white background with two red crosses cutting through it diagonally. Igor immediately recognized it as the rebel coat of arms. He had no doubt that they were stationed somewhere in the outcrop of trees waiting for the exchange to take place.

Igor ordered all his men out of the transport vehicles and made them spread out across the terrain. He then instructed the prisoners out of the vehicle and made them stand in the cold. He wanted to make sure the rebels had a clear view of the prisoners.

He needed the diplomats returned in once piece and would do what was needed to guarantee that. However, losing his arm had driven up his malcontent towards the terrorist group considerably. He was determined to strike a twin blow against them on this day thereby bringing their misguided cause to an end. He hoped his success would please the Czar and restore him back to his graces once again.

Tife, Chen and Han had their hands tied behind their backs as they waited patiently for the exchange to commence. They were flanked by several rebel soldiers as they made their way down through the trees until they were at the edge of the frozen lake. The men watching them peaked anxiously through the trees waiting for visual confirmation before they proceeded. Yerkov on the other hand remained perched on the hill beside a mounted flag flying in the wind.

Through the static of the radio in possession of one of the soldiers, Yerkov's voice buzzed in. He had confirmed the release of their prisoners to be exchanged for the diplomats. Tife was shoved roughly forward and made to march across the icy surface with her hands tied behind her. Ambling closely beside her were Chen and Han. Chen looked distraught and worried as she proceeded down the glacial floor. Han continued to look behind him anxiously as they marched further.

Tife turned back towards the hill they had come down from and was still able to see the outline of the rebel flag from down here. The haze of the light snow continued to cover the area in a white blanket. Through the mist however she could still make out the troop of rebel prisoners who marched forward in their direction.

There were two groups, each holding a man on a stretcher. Both were heavily wrapped in band aids and thick clothing. The pain and suffering they endured in detention was evident on each of their faces. Each had wild hair, unkempt beards, raggedy clothes, and faces covered in dried-up blood.

Time seemed to pause as Tife, Chen and Han walked past the group. The rebel prisoners stared back at them with glassy and empty eyes. Years of torment were evident in their gaunt and pale physiques.

The sight left a deep lump in Tife's throat. Although they were members of the terrorist group which took her father away from her, she could not imagine the horrors they were made to endure. Maybe the brief time she had spent in the enemy camp had softened her stance towards them. Either way, she was glad to finally be out of their control.

They trudged past them looking ahead to the bevy of Slovian soldiers who watched them warily with guns raised to eye level. As they proceeded further, three soldiers stepped forward with guns in hand. They forced Tife, Chen and Han to the ground and searched their bodies thoroughly before lifting them up and hurrying them to the waiting trucks.

''Clear,'' the soldier announced through his radio. At that very moment, a loud explosion ripped through the air. Tife instinctively ducked for cover as a rush of snow washed over her. A second loud explosion ripped through the air sending showers of ice in their direction.

She turned back to see a large hole in the ice. The rebel prisoners had completely disappeared from sight, their bodies surely sunken in the icy waters of the frozen lake. The soldiers hurriedly rushed her into the truck as they made to escape the site. Tife ducked once more as a hail of bullets struck the side of the transport truck.

The tires shrieked on the road as the trucks made their way down the road under a barrage of bullets. In the chaos, Tife had lost sight of Chen and Han who were not present in the truck with her. The air was awash with sounds of gunfire and the cocking of guns. She braced herself in the truck, covering her ears to the horrific sounds of death streaming uninterrupted from outside.

Another loud explosion rent through the air sending the truck she was being transported in to its side. Tife was held down by the seatbelt which prevented her head from striking the truck's ceiling. It skidded down the road until it abruptly came to a complete stop, hitting a tree in the process.

Yerkov looked through his binoculars as he watched the prisoners walk past each other on the frozen lake. He was wary of the Slovian troops standing on the opposite end with guns raised at their people. He counted twenty prisoners arranged in groups of ten, a far cry from the hundreds more they held in their secret detention centers scattered across the area.

The decision to proceed with the prisoner exchange was made. He would rather have twenty of his brethren back than none at all. His soldiers would be kept on high alert in the event foul play was suspected.

Yerkov had been blessed with photographic memory, a useful quality when managing large groups of men and women. For that reason, he knew the faces of every freedom fighter within his command. Several attempts had been made in the past to infiltrate the group by sending in spies to join their ranks. A prisoner exchange of this kind would be an excellent opportunity to attempt this strategy once more, a thought ever present on his mind.

Yerkov scanned the sea of faces for one in particular. A silent wave of relief washed over him as he spotted Galina walking at the leading edge of the first group. She walked ahead of the people carrying a man on a stretcher. Yerkov recognized the faces of the bed-ridden men. They had served under his direct command before their unfortunate capture. No doubt they had been violently tortured to give up the location of their base.

Their prime directive in the event of capture was never to disclose information about the group even in the face of death. Many of their captured brethren would have their loyalties put to the test time and time again. So far, all had been ready to sacrifice their lives for their cause, never revealing the location of their hideouts.

Galina looked up to the waving rebel flag perched on the hill. Through the binoculars, Yerkov could make out her weary, dirt-covered face. Her curly hair was flecked with dirt and sores covered the exposed parts of her body. He traced a weak smile from her as they inched closer to their side of the exchange point.

His soldiers had moved closer to retrieve them when the first explosion ripped from behind. The group behind Galina had disappeared in a billow of powdered ice and snow. The ice gave way under them and their people plummeted down to their icy deaths below.

Before he could react to the first explosion, a second one struck, this time in the group Galina had been travelling in. He watched her disappear under the ice as the explosion took them all from sight.

Yerkov let out an unearthly scream as he watched his partner die in front of him. He took out a flare gun and shot it into the air; the signal to attack the Slovian convoy. While some of his men attempted to rescue any survivors from the explosion, others raced through the trees shooting at the military trucks as they made to flee the scene. Yerkov shoved one of his men aside and took a grenade launcher hidden under a tarpaulin. From his vantage point, he had a clear view of the enemy trucks.

With tactical precision, he launched a shell at the leading truck holding the coordinator in charge of the prisoner exchange. The missile unfortunately missed, striking the roof of the second truck instead and causing it to explode in a shower of metal pieces. The lead truck managed to escape and zipped out of sight.

The three other vehicles following closely behind struck the disabled truck, causing them to careen off the road and into the ditch by the side of the road. Yerkov rushed down the side of the hill to the icy lake hosting the scattered remains of his brethren. Patches of ice floated alongside their corpses.

He searched through the bodies until he saw her. Galina's body was floating beside a large chuck of ice; her face severely burned from the explosion. He jumped into the frigid water and dragged her body to shore. Her deep blue eyes once brimming with life were now glazed over. Her face was pale and lifeless. Yerkov doubled over with her body in his arms, his heart heavy with grief. He had lost the love of his life.

His sadness turned to rage as he dragged her body and laid it ashore. In the bitter cold of the icy tundra, he raced through the trees to the location of the now disabled trucks laying by the side of the road.

His men had their guns trained and pointed around the stricken vehicle. He ripped open the truck's back door to find several dead soldiers within the vehicle. The force from the grenade launcher had ripped open the roof, killing the men inside instantly.

The vehicles behind it lay immobile on their side lying next to a tree. The trucks' back doors suddenly blew open as the remaining Slovian soldiers poured out, firing randomly in several directions in a bid to kill the rebels. Yerkov quickly ducked behind a large boulder and returned fire. One by one, the Slovian soldiers fell dead to the floor as the sound of guns filled the air.

Once he was sure they had all been slain, Yerkov ordered for his men to seize fire and to inspect the truck for any survivors. A quick search of the vehicles revealed all the men to have been slain in the ensuing chaos.

All that remained was the last truck which stood propped on a thick patch of trees. Yerkov advised for caution as they approached the vehicle. He dispatched the driver with a single shot as he made to flee from the vehicle. Another man who jumped from the passenger seat was shot dead in an instant by another of Yerkov's men.

They cautiously approached the side of the vehicle till they reached the truck's back door. Yerkov pulled out a small explosive device and placed it on the truck's opening panel. They cleared away just in time to hear the explosion rip open the truck's door, exposing its inhabitants inside to the bitter winds.

A glance of the interior revealed three active soldiers within; their guns raised in anticipation to the storming of the rebel troops. Their former prisoner Tife lay huddled in the back behind one of the soldiers.

In a coordinated approach, Yerkov and his rebel fighters swung in front of the truck's exploded doors and took out the first two soldiers before they could give off a shot. The last Slovian soldier proceeded to grab Tife and place her between himself and the incoming rebel troops. His eyes glinted with murderous intent as he trained a gun at her head.

''Get back or I will shoot her,'' he demanded, pressing the barrel of his gun deeper into Tife's temple. The rebel soldiers looked to Yerkov for instruction as the standoff proceeded. He ordered them to step aside as the soldier stepped out of the vehicle holding Tife in his firm grasp.

The Red Dawn rebels trained their weapons at him as he trudged through the snow dragging his hostage in tow. They searched for an opening where he could be neutralized and have his hostage spared.

The opening was found when Tife drove her head into the Slovian soldier's temple and ducked for cover. This offered enough time for Yerkov to raise his gun and shoot the soldier square in the head; his body falling stiffly into the snow. He approached Tife who still lay on the floor. He lifted her up to her feet and took her back to the waiting dog-driven sleighs sitting atop the hill.

They rode in silence as they made it back to their base in the waterfall. Yerkov ruminated in silence at the deceit shown by the Slovian troops. They had attempted to find survivors who had fallen into the ice after the explosions hit but only recovered dead bodies from the lake. The bodies of the Chen and Han had also been found laying beside the road. In the ensuing chaos triggered by the Slovian duplicity, they had been caught in the crossfire between the two groups.

Not only had he lost a significant portion of his leverage against the empire, but he had possibly exposed the location of their hideout to Slovian forces. Despite his internal grieving for his lost love, he had to consider the possibility that they were compromised and needed to relocate from their current location.

They arrived several hours later at their base in the waterfall. Several troops and medics rushed out to greet them as they entered. Preparations had been made to welcome the prisoners from the Slovian jails who would no doubt be requiring medical attention when they arrived. The sullen faces on the returning soldiers made it clear that wouldn't be required.

Inside, many of the cave's inhabitants had arranged themselves on the various levels in the main atrium hoping to catch a glimpse of their returning comrades. The dejected look of their soldiers made it clear they would not be reuniting with their friends and family today. They slowly dissipated back into the many caverns of the expansive hideout. Yerkov directed his attention to one of his men.

''We need to have our lookout parties on high alert. We may have Slovian troops in the area and must prepare for …'' Yerkov's voice trailed off as he had the butt of a gun strike the back of his neck. Several rebel soldiers rushed from behind and menaced Yerkov's party with guns raised to their heads.

They ordered them to relinquish their weapons, then forced them to the ground and bound their hands and legs. They forced Yerkov up just in time to see Dmitri stroll into the cavern with a severe look on his face.

''What is the meaning of this, Dmitri?'' Yerkov demanded through gritted teeth. The cave inhabitants slowly reconvened in the cavern to witness the tense situation take shape.

''Your weak leadership has put us in jeopardy for the last time, Captain. Despite my reservations, you proceeded to embark on a prisoner exchange which has cost the lives of over a dozen of our soldiers.'' Dmitri turned his attention to the group of onlookers above, raising his voice so that they could hear him clearly. Heavy murmuring ripped through the crowd as they observed from above.

''Maybe that was his plan after all; to destroy us. We have been betrayed! Our captain has conspired with our enemies to eliminate us. It's time for fresh blood to take the helm of affairs.'' He turned his attention back to Yerkov, grabbing him roughly by the chin and lifting his face up to his.

''You will never see the outside of a prison cell again, traitor,'' he menaced before ordering the soldiers to throw him in a nearby cell. Tife too found herself locked up in an adjoining cell to his. Four rebel soldiers stood guard in an attempt to discourage any sympathisers to Yerkov from attempting to release him.

The sudden turn of events had jolted Tife. Not only had she now lost Chen and Han, but she had also become a prisoner once more. Her situation had become even direr given the mutinous coup which had just occurred. From what she had gathered so far, Dmitri possessed even greater murderous intent than Yerkov ever did. He appeared far less reasonable and compassionate than his predecessor.

Tife's presence also made her the perfect sacrificial lamb and scapegoat for Dmitri to capitalise on. The simple gesture of terminating her life in front of the cave's inhabitants would solidify his grasp over the group permanently and put an end to any dissenting voices within their ranks. With no one else available to come to her aid, her life was no doubt in danger. She did not have long before she would be sacrificed to Dimitri's cause.

The fading light streaming from the holes in the cavern suggested evening had fallen once more. Unlike her time as prisoner under Yerkov's rule, there had been no attempts made to feed them. Tife looked on hopelessly as food was distributed to the cave dwellers.

Katrina, the gaunt, red haired girl came up as usual to receive her portion of food for the night. She stared at Tife forlornly as she held the gruel in her hands. The intimidating soldiers still stood guard over her preventing anyone from coming close to her cell. Tife offered her a weak smile as she plopped down in a corner to eat.

Nightfall brought with it the heavy, rushing sound of the waterfall into the large cavern. The soldiers watching them had fallen to just two and both lay fast asleep on the ground beside their cells. Without the glow of the lit torches, the temperature dropped precipitously in the large cavern.

Tife balled herself together, hoping to gather as much warmth as she could. Her body was weak now and aching from the deplorable conditions she was made to bare. At this rate, she would succumb to the hunger or the cold long before Dmitri could use her as a tool to prop himself up.

''You must be disappointed,'' said Yerkov weakly, his heavily intoned voice filtering through to Tife's cage. ''Yesterday, you thought you would be reunited with your loved ones. What a difference a couple of hours can make.'' Tife remained silent in her cell. The heavy sound of falling water still present in the air.

He continued, 'For all his brashness, I agree with Dmitri on one point. My desire to have our people returned to us blinded me to the dangers of initiating an exchange with that fascist government. I should have known better. Now I carry the burden of over a dozen lives needlessly lost to our cause.'' Tife remained tightly curled up to stave off the cold but listened intently to what Yerkov had to say.

''You may yet be reunited with your loved ones. I expect the Slovian army may be able to track our base now that they can narrow their search. We may not have a lot of time before they find us.'' This news piqued Tife's interest. She shuffled towards the front of her cell to hear Yerkov better.

''How long do you think we have before they locate our position?'' Tife inquired.

''Days at most. The army uses trained dogs to sniff out the scent of enemy factions. We always try to conceal our trail in the snow but that will not stop them from narrowing down our location. You may believe it be in your best interest for them to find us, but you cannot trust the Slovian government. They murdered my people then escaped when we returned their aggression. You saw how the soldiers were willing to sacrifice your life to save theirs. They would sooner have you executed than have you returned to your people.''

Tife considered this deeply. Her continued abduction already put the newly signed peace accords in jeopardy. However given recent events, she had little faith in the Slovian army's ability or desire to save her from her predicament. Her best chance lay in her Queen ordering a rescue party to extract her from the rebels. She would have to remain alive until then.

''Have you tried to convince Dmitri of this?''

''He will not listen to me now. My words will only fall on deaf ears. Even my own men have turned their backs on me. He has managed to convince many of them that I am a traitor.'' Tife sunk back to the ground and balled herself up once more.

Like being at the head of a raging bull, Tife felt gored from both sides. On one hand, she could not trust the Slovian army to bring her to safety. On the other hand, Dmitri seemed irrational and would not listen to logic or reason. She pondered on the best solution as the night took her and she fell fast asleep.

She awoke the next morning to hear a flurry of activity in the main atrium. Dmitri walked out with a wave of soldiers behind him. They dragged Yerkov out from his cell who protested violently as he was being led out.

A series of blows to the back of his legs and his back forced him to go limp as they carried him to two hanging ropes attached to the upper platforms. His legs dangled in the air as they lifted his body up from the ground. Yerkov screamed in protest prompting the cave's inhabitants to gather once more in the atrium.

A rebel soldier handed Dimitri a tightly wound whip which he grasped tightly in his right hand. He looked up to the people gathered in the cavern, ready to address them.

''This traitor has brought great misfortune upon us. We lost many of our brethren in that poorly executed prisoner exchange. He knew of the risks involved and proceeded to put our lives in danger. He deserves the most severe of punishments.'' Dmitri walked around till he was behind Yerkov. He cracked the whip backwards before violently striking Yerkov's back. Yerkov gritted his teeth in pain as the whip tore through his shirt, leaving a jagged, bright red line across his back.

''Dmitri...you must listen to me...'' Yerkov piped up through breathless gasps, ''we must evacuate from this location before Slovian troops find us. They will send reinforcements to scour the area now that they have narrowed down our position. ''

''Do you hear him, my comrades? Even now the traitor wishes to rub salt in our wounds by asking us to leave our base to die in the wild,'' Dmitri shot back. He responded with another crack of his whip and a strike to Yerkov's back.

Several more strikes followed leaving bloody trails across the cavern floor. The inhabitants watched along in silence as Yerkov's screams of pain echoed through the chamber. Tife watched in terror as they whipped Yerkov to an inch of his life. Finally, she had enough.

''STOP! YOU'RE KILLING HIM!'' She cried from her prison cell. Time seemed to pause as all the cave's inhabitants turned their attention to her. Dmitri halted his beating to eye her curiously.

''You see, my brethren. The traitor now has found allies in the very people who have direct responsibility for the death of our people. If it were not for the attempt to return them back to their government, our people would not have met their untimely ends. Her presence here jeopardizes all of our safety.''

''If what he is saying is true, then you don't have much time to flee this location, '' Tife added, ''the longer you stay here, the more likely you will die once they bring their armies here.''

''It is fitting that you ally yourself with the likes of her, Captain, ''Dmitri said derisively at Yerkov. ''Even from her prison cell she threatens us. For crimes against our people, we sentence you to death. You and your traitorous ally will hang tomorrow in the same way as our men who were executed in the Red Square. ''

He ordered them to take Yerkov down from his restraints and thrown back in his prison cell. The entire floor under him had turned a bright pattern of crimson red. Several women came forward later to wipe the bloodstains from the floor.

Tife listened closely to the sounds of shallow breathing coming from Yerkov's cell. She waited until the soldiers guarding her had fallen asleep before she attempted to reach him in his cell. A groggy voice answered back through the bars.

''You have signed your own death warrant little girl, you know that?'' Yerkov asked as he straightened himself up and propped himself on the wall, ''Now we will both hang tomorrow.''

''You know these caverns better than I do. There must be a back passageway where we could escape.'' Yerkov let out a weak chuckle which quickly devolved into a bloody cough.

''You still believe you can cheat death despite your dire circumstances. I admire your resolve to live, little girl,'' he said scornfully. Tife slunk back in her cell as the guard watching them stirred in his sleep. She waited for him to roll over before pressing her face close to the rusting prison bars.

''Now more than ever, your people need you to lead them. Think of the innocent women and children who will be slaughtered if you do not do everything in your power to help them escape.'' Tife's mind wandered to the little red-haired girl who offered her food in her cell. From what she could gather, many more children like her littered the cavern. Any attack on the base would surely lead to their deaths.

''Why would you care for the people who abducted you and locked you up; took you away from your friend and family?'' Tife paused as she thought deeply about this. She had borne witness to the death of Zala, Chen and Han during her capture. She had so far been forced to live in decrepit conditions since her imprisonment, made to endure psychological and emotional torment and had been starved half to death.

But despite all of these things, her time with the rebels had exposed the daily struggle these people faced. The horrible conditions foisted upon them by their empire must have been unbearable for them to resort to such barbary instead. Her own mother had made sure to teach the important lesson of compassion and the need to consider the needs of others before herself. This situation though perilous did not dampen her empathy towards other people.

''All my life, I have been a witness to pain and suffering. From my mother's slow passing to cancer to my father's violent end in the attack at the coronation. Pain only begets more pain it seems. We must do our part to break the cycle.'' Yerkov listened to her in silence. He piped up after she finished speaking, his weak voice streaming into her cell.

''Wise words for a little girl,'' he said finally, ''I have to say I admire your spirit and courage. There is a secret exit which leads to the mountain's exterior. I may be able to guide us out of the base if we can escape our cells.''

Tife looked around her small cage. Centuries of weathering had smoothened the limestone rock lining the walls. There were no visible signs of failure she could take advantage of. She also remained weak from not eating for the past couple of hours.

Another concern was Dmitri. If he caught wind that they were attempting to escape, he would have them executed on the spot. If they had any chance of escape, they would have to time it when he was away.

''I may have an idea,'' Tife said finally. ''For it to be successful, we must work together. We must also prioritize getting the children and pregnant women out first. Only then will I agree to help.'' Yerkov let out a raspy cough which devolved into a silent chuckle.

''I accept your terms. What is your plan?'' Tife proceeded to explain how she thought they might be able to escape. They agreed Dmitri would have to be out of the hideout for it to work.

Rounding up all the women and children in time may prove challenging but they were the most vulnerable group and Tife insisted they be protected. There was also the issue of arming themselves if they came up against any resistance. When she had finished, Yerkov remained silent for several moments.

''Well?'' Tife prodded. ''Can this work?''

''In the interest of my people, it must.'' he said finally. ''Too many people I loved have died already. I will do whatever it takes to protect the rest of them.''

''Then we are agreed then. By the way, what do I call you?'' Tife inquired. She had heard the soldiers and even Dmitri calling him 'Captain' but never had they used his real name.

''My real name is Michail but I abandoned it long ago when I joined this cause,'' he replied. Tife sank back in her bed on the floor. Without any assurances that the Slovian army would be able to rescue her safely, she realized it was up to her to escape the perilous situation she had been placed in. She would employ all of her diplomatic skills to return back home. She could only hope that a joint regiment of Chinese and African Union soldiers were nearby.

If she was to return home safely, she would have no other choice then to trust the man who was responsible for abducting her in the first place, a prospect which provided her with a great deal of unease.

The day of their execution had arrived. Tife was less concerned about her potential fate and more concerned for Dmitri's movement throughout the day. Their cells were guarded by two armed men with most of the cave's inhabitants away from the central cavern. She became anxious as time passed with no sign of Dmitri.

During her stay as captive, she noticed they ventured out of the hideout at least once a day to find food for the people. Michail confirmed it was also an opportunity to scout the area for any foreign troop movement in the area. Their plan was hinged on his departure from the hideout for a short period of time. They could not enact their plan otherwise.

As Tife was just about to lose hope of escaping, Dmitri stepped out of the exit on the far right of the cave flanked with several of his men. He walked up to Michail's cell and ordered his men to bring him out of it. Two rebel soldiers stepped inside and after several seconds of struggle, they dragged him outside by his hands and dropped him in front of Dmitri. Michail's face had several more open gashes from the blows he had just incurred from Dmitri's men.

''You look pathetic now,'' Dmitri began as he looked down at Michail with a severe expression on his face. Michail looked up at him; a toothy smile laced with blood now lit up his face.

This seemed to enrage Dmitri even more. He balled his fist and struck him across the cheek, sending blood splattering across the ground. He followed it up with a hard kick to the gut with his boot forcing Michail to the ground.

''You were always a weak leader, Michail. When we return, you will die for your treachery,'' he turned to Tife's cell as she watched the drama unfold and added, ''You as well, little girl. Make peace with your gods. You will be meeting them soon.'' He motioned to his men to return Michail back into his cell before they slammed it shut again.

Dmitri walked out of the cave with his men in tow. Tife looked on in resignation, unable to offer any assistance to Michail. Their opportunity had arrived though. With Dmitri gone, they could enact their plan to escape.

Although she had no watch, Tife had estimated the scout party would leave the hideout for four hours on average. Tife and Michail had agreed to wait at least an hour before initiating their plan. When the time had arrived, she lightly tapped the bars of her cell twice. This was the signal Michail was waiting for. At that precise moment, he began to howl and scream in pain from his cell; the noise echoing throughout the cavern.

''Hey, someone help! Something's wrong with him!!'' Tife cried from her cell to the two soldiers guarding them. They rushed over and peered inside as Michail writhed in pain on the ground.

''Don't just stand there, help him,'' she implored. The two guards looked at each other, unsure of what to do.

''If he dies before Dmitri can have the honor of executing him in front of everyone, then you two will surely have to explain yourself to him,'' she added. This seemed to get their attention and they proceeded to open the cell doors and attend to him. Michail continued his faked howl in pain as they entered.

Tife could not see what was happening but could hear grunts and loud blows as Michail proceed to disarm the two soldiers quickly. Moments later, Michail emerged from his cell. He had the guards locked up in his cell and proceeded to Tife's cell with a ring of iron keys in hand.

''We do not have much time,'' Michail warned as he unlocked her cell, ''we must round up the women and children and depart as soon as possible. I will get the dog sleighs prepped and ready. We keep all the pregnant women and children in a large room through that space,'' he pointed to a hole directly facing her cell. ''I need you to go there and lead them to the back of the cave. I'll wait for you there.''

''Why would they listen to me?'' Tife asked. In response, Michail pulled out a necklace with a single star pendant strung onto it. The pendant itself was made of pure gold and had the inscription 'KЗ' on it. Tife recognized the symbol to be the initials for the Red Dawn translated into Slovinian.''

''This symbol still means something. The gold is rumored to be made from mined ores within your borders. It is one of seven which exist and was how our founders recognized themselves. They called themselves the ''Rebel Alliance'' back then. This movement for freedom stretches across different continents, yours included. If you show this to them, they will follow you.''

She took the necklace from him and admired it. The exterior was flecked with small marks across its surface. Nevertheless, the pendant still had a brilliant quality about it. She silently wondered how many people had owned it before Michail.

''Hold on to this as well in case you run into trouble,'' He handed her a gun that he had taken from the unconscious solder. She had never fired one before and reluctantly accepted it from him.

''Hurry now before the guards regain consciousness and alert the others,'' Michail said before rushing across the floor and disappearing through a recess in the wall. Tife made her way across the floor and through the hole opposite from her cell until she reached a chamber with several make-shift beds lining the floor. Several of the pregnant women lay in clusters speaking to themselves while others lay on the ground sleeping. Some children sat in circles playing games with themselves.

''Do not be alarmed,'' Tife said as she walked in. Several of the women gasped in terror as she appeared before them. She quickly took out the pendent and showed it to them.

''The Captain sent me to take you all to the back. He fears an attack on the base is imminent and wants to evacuate before that happens. I am sorry for all you have been through but now is the time to save yourselves and the lives of your unborn children. You must trust me,'' she pleaded. The women huddled together, murmuring amongst themselves but not moving.

Tife looked on at them in desperation. She did not know how much time they had left before their escape was discovered. It was imperative that they moved quickly. From the corner of the room, Katrina the red-haired girl, walked over to Tife with her cat nestled in her arms. She took hold of Tife's hand and smiled brightly at her.

''I trust you,'' said Katrina with wide, innocent eyes. Another girl stood up and walked to join Tife and Katrina. Several more children rallied around her until finally, the women too walked over to her side.

''I think I can get us to the back without being detected, '' Katrina offered. They gathered as much as they could and with Katrina leading the group, they made their way down through several recesses in the wall only able to admit one person at a time.

The recess opened up into an impressive space filled with interesting shapes adorning its roof and walls. The light illuminating the space came from suspended glowing rocks which sparkled with a bright greenish aura. Several of the stalactites which hung from the ceiling glowed with the same ferocity as the crystals attached to the walls.

At that moment, a loud shout echoed through the chamber. Several more followed and was accompanied by scuffling noises through the cavern's recesses. Tife surmised the soldiers had realized the women were missing and would be searching for them throughout the cave.

''This way,'' Katrina urged as they raced deeper into the cave's interior. They hurried through another opening as loud footsteps began to echo behind them. Several armed rebel soldiers appeared with guns drawn in their hands. They ordered the women and children to the ground as they approached them slowly.

''Put your weapon on the floor, now!'' the rebel soldier said, pointing to Tife's holstered gun. She took out the gun Michail had given her and placed it on the ground. The rebel soldier proceeded to order Tife to the ground, bound her arms with a tight rope and dragged her back to her feet.

A loud grunt followed by scuffling noises ensued behind her. Tife turned around to see Michail storm inside. He had a weapon pressed to the temple of one of the rebel soldiers. The other rebel soldiers trained their weapons on him setting up a standoff.

''Release him, Captain,'' one soldier ordered with several others echoing it in refrain. Michail had a wild look on his face as he watched the soldiers with unease. Soon, more men would come pouring in from behind and would easily overpower them. The women and children cried and whimpered as they lay helplessly on the ground. Their escape would be cut short and would surely be followed by Tife's swift execution.

A blaring sound echoed throughout the entire base. The women and children covered their ears at the deafening noise. The soldiers looked around perplexed at the meaning of the loud sound.

''Do you hear that, comrades? That sound means the scout party has detected signs of enemy movement within the area, '' Michail informed them, ''the Slovian army has found our location. If we do not evacuate now, they will kill us all.''

As if to buttress his point, several loud explosions shook the walls of the cave sending several crystals falling from the roof. Screams of terror reverberated through the cavern walls as more explosions rocked the hideout. The rebel soldiers ducked for cover, racing out through one of the recesses in the walls. Michail released the one he had at gunpoint who promptly joined his colleagues escaping to the front of the cave.

''Quickly, everyone!'' Michail urged the large group as they sprinted down through the cave tunnels; the sound of explosions rocking the walls of the hideout. He cut Tife loose and together, they led the group of frightened women and children. Large pieces of rocks began to fall into their path as they ventured through the narrow nooks. Tife ducked down as a large pillar crashed in front of her.

''The exit is not far from here,'' Michail informed them as the group arrived at an icy grotto branching into multiple passageways deep within the mountain complex. Large columns of ice wound their way from the top to the bottom of the space leaving an intricate array of ice pillars lining the space. The weather dropped precipitously as they entered the chamber. A dim, bluish glow lit up each of the tunnels in an eerie haze.

''Through here,'' Michail ordered pointing to the far-left passageway in the corner. At that moment, a gunshot rang from behind prompting screams from the group of women and children. Dimitri emerged into the icy grotto with a horde of his men flanking him. He fired several more times into the air as he raced towards them. Michail doubled back and returned several shots forcing Dimitri and his men to take cover behind the icy columns.

''Go!'' Michail yelled as he produced several more rounds at the incoming rebel soldiers. Tife urged the group into the passageway all the while as gunfire and explosions raged above them.

She looked back to notice Michail now clutching his jacket tightly. Even in the dim light, she could see the thin streak of blood begin to pour down from his belly.

She looked to him in horror as he undid his jacket revealing of mess of wires connected to small boxes lining the inside. Through his pained expression, his intent was clear and Tife rushed the last of the group out the tunnel to the exterior.

She looked back at Michail for the last time who returned her gaze with one of peaceful resignation. She swiftly followed them to the waiting group of dog sleighs tied outside. Shortly after, a loud explosion tore from inside the cave collapsing the exit they had escaped from.

They had emerged into a heavily wooded area with trees concealing their position from above. The sound of helicopter blades rattled above as they loaded unto the sleighs. Tife took the reins of one while others rushed to control the rest . With a loud whip from the reins, the dogs started through the forest, leaving behind the chaos and explosions in their wake.

THE PROPHECY

Accompanied by her servant, Queen Yaa-Yaa travelled to the secluded shrine deep within the woody forest on the outskirts of town. The open window allowed the heavy, moist air to seep into the car. Even the constant fanning by her servant did little to allay the humidity which filled the interior.

The heat was made worse by the regalia which the Queen chose to wear. She wore a white, lace top bejeweled with sapphire and gold threads intricately woven into the fabric which she paired with a similarly gold wrapper around her waist. To adorn her head, she wore a beautiful hair tie which radiated in the intermittent sun's brilliance.

Tall palm trees lined the road leading to the Agura's temple breaking the sun's gaze as they passed through. She had travelled there many times in the last couple of years. Her visits had become more frequent these days. It was her hope that the Agura would offer her the answer she so desperately seeked.

The car rolled to a stop as they approached the large, stone-patch wall which lined the shrine's palatial compound. A small river cut through the back of the acreage. There was no gate into the estate as it was not needed. No man or woman dared enter uninvited into the Agura's den without her express permission and invitation.

Even the Queen was not immune to these rules. Only she would be allowed inside for the ritual. Her servant would wait on her outside by the car. He took out a metal urn filled with gold nuggets and knelt before the Queen with it, raising it up to hand it to her. This would be the offering for today's ritual and would be presented to the Agura before the ceremony began.

She walked through the opening into the compound with the metal urn in hand. Inside were several buildings, many of which were built with red-brick mortar and thatched roofs. Several unsettling images marked the building exteriors depicting frightening creatures. Beasts and creatures with large horns, twisted backs and long bony fingers featured on many facades.

As she walked further along the granite floorwork, images of prominent gods now became more dominant. Sango, the god of thunder had his profile drawn showing the god summoning fiery thunder from the sky. In his hands were his two ax weapons which he used to deal punishment on anyone who was deserving of his wrath.

She recognized Ozain, the god of the forest depicted on one of the walls mosaics. Large roots were depicted to grow out from his charcoal-colored body. Gold beads adorned his neck and provided sharp contrast to his ebony body.

Several other statues also filled the grounds showing various iconic minor gods in majestic fashion. Her favorite depiction was the statue of Orunla, the god of wisdom. This statue featured atop the Agura's temple mounted on a long, raised platform. The carving showed Orunla looking heavenwards with his hands fixed around an elliptical blob representing the universe.

Orunla was said to be present at the moment of creation and was responsible for the creation of souls. He therefore knew the destinies of each and every living thing on earth and was called upon when divination was undertaken.

The Agura's temple itself was by far the largest building in the compound and sat atop the highest elevation in the area. Looking at it from above, you would see a small, circular atrium with a long passageway leading to a much larger dome at the end. Dark smoke billowed from a nearby chimney stack which emptied into the air.

The temple itself was carved from the limestone outcrop giving it an ethereal look in the tropical sun. Queen Yaa-Yaa ventured up the numerous marble steps until she came upon the entrance to the shrine.

Two men flecked with white spots greeted her at the door. They both had red cloth draped over their shoulders and carried a bronze staff in their right arms. Both stood in silence staring off into the distance. Queen Yaa-Yaa had never heard them speak before and believed them to be mute.

Their function was simple, to enforce the rules of the temple Agura. Queen Yaa-Yaa placed the metal urn on the ground and began to unfasten her sandals. Then she removed her hair tie revealing her long, braided hair. She handed both of these to the temple guards and walked inside with the urn in hand.

The interior was lit with torches which stretched down the length of the long passageway. The floor was carpeted red, with colorful drawings filling the walls and archway in a beautiful tapestry of artwork. The obnoxious heat in the shrine's interior made sweat drip down the length of Queen Yaa-Yaa's back. She pushed forward until she arrived at the central dome of the massive building.

The red carpet which lined the archway passageway ended with a bare, stone patch groundwork which covered the area. A raised table was mounted squarely in the center of the room. Lit torches still hung around the circular periphery but now under each one stood haunting figures shrouded in the flickering shadows cast by the flames.

The masquerades under the torches were draped in straw tendrils which ran the entire length of their bodies. Each wore a black mask with various expressions casted onto their face. Some faces were contorted in pain, others showed happiness while others still showed rage and anger.

Directly opposite from where she stood was the silhouette of a woman in front of a fireplace. Her entire body was nude and covered in white paint from head to toe. Her long, twisted braids ended in glittering beads which framed her elegant back.

The Agura was a tall woman with a slim, sultry build which contrasted sharply with the violent fire raging in front of her. Her hand was hard at work sawing something mounted in front of her. She paused momentarily to reach inside what she was working on and threw what she found into the fire.

Blood dripped down from mounted table into a bowl placed underneath. At that moment, the woman turned her head around to acknowledge the Queen's presence. She washed her hands in a nearby basin and dried them off before turning to meet the Queen's gaze.

The signs of youth were clear from the delightful shape of the Agura's body, something the Queen herself was envious of in her old age. The white paint pronounced the sharp outline of her perky bosom. Her hips dipped into a beautiful arch ending in toned legs as elegant as a giraffe's. Her graceful neck was adorned with intricate beads made of gold and silver.

Individuals like herself were trained from a young age to bear the prestigious title. During their service to the temple gods, they would remain virgins until the end of their tenure, which usually ran well into their late forty's. In her desperation, the Queen had visited several of these over the course of many years but had settled on this temple priestess in recent months. Something about this one gave her hope that her long lost search for an heir would finally come to an end.

The Agura herself bore no name to speak of and was addressed solely by her title. She approached the Queen and took the metal urn from her grasp, resting it above a metal stand in the center of the fireplace. She then returned her attention to the Queen. Her eyes threw back the reflection from the torches mounted on the walls.

''Please hand your wrapper and lace top to them and lay down on the table,'' the Agura said, motioning to the two masquerades which approached her now. This had become a standard request each time she visited the temple and she quickly began to remove her clothes. She handed the wrapper and top to the waiting masquerades who placed them in baskets at the far corner.

Wearing nothing more than her shear underwear, she lay down on the table with her gaze fixated on the white, limestone roofing. The Agura returned with the bowl filled with blood and placed it by the Queen's head.

''I need you to relax, my Queen,'' she said with a wide smile. Queen Yaa-Yaa took a deep breath as the Agura dipped a pointed stick into the bowl and began drawing several symbols across the Queen's forehead, hands, and feet. The Agura left and returned with the metal urn filled with gold coins. Queen Yaa-Yaa looked over anxiously at the boiling pot of gold which radiated heat from its hot surface.

''This will hurt slightly, my Queen. Please try not to scream.'' The Agura took a metal probe and dipped it into the hot liquid. The Queen braced herself as the hot fluid touched her belly, searing her flesh. She gritted her teeth and grabbed the table tightly as the Agura drew complicated symbols on her belly.

She quickly finished and returned the metal urn to the fireplace. The excruciating procedure had left tears running down the Queen's face. She breathed in rapidly as the agonizing pain began to recede now with each passing second.

The masquerades now inched closer to the bed as thick grey vapor began to fill the room. A high-pitched scream ripped from the Agura's mouth followed by several incoherent words. The masquerades spontaneously began to dance in unison around the Queen who began to feel more light-headed as the ceremony progressed. The more breaths she took in, the more her mind gave way to strange images.

She looked around the room to see a haze of blurry images moving around her. The heat from the flames made her sweat profusely. The moving figures around her seemed to grow more avid as time passed. Her heartbeat swelled in her chest at the loud sounds and screams being made around her, rising to a crescendo before falling shortly after. The haze of figures slowly receded off into the distance as a cold hand grabbed her face and split her mouth open.

''Drink this, my Queen. It will clear your head,'' a voice whispered into her ear. The Queen gurgled several mouthfuls of the bitter concoction before coughing violently to the side. Her head still swirled dangerously as she sat up from the table.

The voice now urged her to take in deep breaths while gently patting the length of her back. Her mind began to slowly clear and the room began to take focus once more. She looked around to the masquerades who were now crouched down under the torches. Each looked down solemnly to the ground, unmoving and lifeless.

After several minutes, the Agura ushered the Queen to sit on a straw mat beside the fireplace while she took a kneeling position opposite her. She emptied several small bird bones in front of her and began vigorously rooting through them.

Finally, she found the piece she was looking for: the exposed frontal keel bone of the bird which she promptly swallowed. The she took the bowl of remaining blood and swirled her index finger inside of it. Seemingly satisfied, she returned a wide smile to the Queen and turned her full attention to her.

''Orunla has offered you a favorable response this time, my Queen,'' came the Agura's soft, soothing voice. ''You will be pleased with the answer he has for you today.'' She picked up another bone from the pile in front of her and examined it carefully. It looked like the femur bone of the bird.

''Orunla knows how hard you have been trying to conceive a female heir to succeed you.'' The Agura's body twitched curiously as she continued to analyze the bone carefully, as if the answers were etched across its surface. ''He says your search is coming to an end.'' She threw the small bone into the fireplace causing wild embers of fire to shoot out of the grotto.

She picked up another bone and felt around its rigid surface. It was the bony vertebra of the bird. Her face began to become more animated as a smirk peaked the side of her mouth, 'Power, love and strength,'' she continued, ''you will lose all three as a sacrifice towards your desire for an heir.''

''I do not understand,'' said Queen Yaa-Yaa, perplexed.

''You will when the time arrives,'' the Agura assured her. She threw the femur bone into the fire sparking even larger embers from the fire.

Lastly, she picked up the bony skull of the bird and turned it over inquisitively. A wicked smile spread across her face causing her to burst out in a raucous fit of laughter. She shouted several more incantations from her mouth as she clutched the skull in her mouth.

''What is it?'' Queen Yaa-Yaa pressed as she stared at her with wide eyes, ''what did you see?''

''I see death which will bring forth life, my Queen,'' she replied cryptically, ''You will surely conceive your heir. I have no doubt about that.'' The Queen smiled brightly at her response. Reassurance like that would put her mind to ease. Agura's were known for the accuracy in their prophecies. Their continued service in the temple relied on this fact.

Once an Agura's prophecy proved false however, it signaled her inability to commune with Orunla to access her divinations leading to dire consequences, usually resulting in her death. As she pondered the prophecy's meaning, the Agura threw the skull into the fire, prompting purple flames to shoot out from inside. Queen Yaa-Yaa gazed into the fiery curtain of flames as they danced avidly in the room. One question remained and lingered in her mind.

''Who is the man who will help me conceive my heir?'' she asked. The Agura looked through the mess of bones again, examining each new piece she brought out and throwing it aside. She cast a desolate look back at the Queen, spreading her hands on the ground in resignation.

''I unfortunately do not have the answer to that question,'' she replied, ''the Orunla will only tell me that the man to father your heir will come from the east. The Orunla demands your patience.''

But patience was a virtue she had already expressed in her many years of waiting, the Queen thought. Her days of having the ability to bear children would soon come to an end and it was her moral obligation to ensure she had an heir before then. She stood up abruptly and took her clothes from the basket in the corner.

''I only offer you what I have been told, my Queen,'' the Agura added but the Queen was not listening. She would scour her kingdom if required to find a suitable male to suit her purposes.

''One last warning, my Queen,'' the Agura called out as Queen Yaa-Yaa made her way to the door, ''your enemies are numerous and all around you. Be wary of those who you surround yourself with.'' The Queen turned her gaze one last time to the Agura before storming out of the temple.

Conceiving a female heir was only one of many challenges she faced as Queen. Tensions in the Eurasian continent had sent waves of migrants unto her shores. Many had come to settle in Luanda over the years with the Queen being magnanimous in her decision to grant them refugee status in her borders.

She had done all she could to prevent being drawn into the conflict and that included not sending troops into war. Her principal concerns were to her kingdom however she would not turn her back on desperate people seeking to flee the unending violence.

Her decision to host the refugees was not without price however and caused significant tension within her borders. The resilience which these migrants displayed quickly translated to a range of successful business endeavors offering them considerable built wealth and power. As a result, many began to face increasing discrimination and jealously within their communities. Attacks on their businesses became increasingly common with the Queen's royal guard having to step in to maintain the peace.

To add to her problems, the Chinese Emperor began to exert mounting pressure on her to send troops to aid his war against the Slovians. Her new post as Sovereign of the African territories had placed her in command of the largest army reserve on the planet. Lending her support to any side in the conflict would certainly lean the war effort in their favor.

Queen Yaa-Yaa had no appetite for war neither could she risk leaving her kingdom exposed to attack. Land disputes with dwindling British and French monarchies in the North had occupied them for several decades leading to a stalemate in recent years. Any depletion of their troop numbers would mean significant gains for their enemies seeking those territories as their own.

Her challenge of not being able to conceive a child had only exacerbated the problems she faced. Rumors of her infertility trickled through the population like wildfire. So concerned of outright revolt that she began to send her agents to local bars and restaurants to find out what the people were saying.

Feedback from her spies only confirmed her suspicions. Talks of upturning the monarchy and the military seizing control were abound across the land. 'This is definitely a sign that the monarchy has outlived its use,' many said as they spoke of the abolishment of the monarchy.

Even more concerning was talk within the rank and file of the military which began to echo those sentiments. The words of the Agura concerning enemies around her ranks were indeed true. She needed to be more careful if she would maintain law and order.

With usurpers all around her, Queen Yaa-Yaa looked on with greater scrutiny to those who she surrounded herself with. She used her considerable powers as Sovereign to expel many high- ranking members of the military and replaced them with those who were more pliable and loyal to her.

Her network of agents were also able to track the movements of the Red Dawn operating within her domain. Many of their members were said to have infiltrated various levels of their kingdom lending her even greater pause to who she surrounded herself with. Like a cancer, their calls for the abolishment of monarchies worldwide had reached their shores.

As Queen of Luanda, she was under no obligation to have a husband and her predecessors only entertained the idea in unique circumstances. In light of her difficulty in bearing a child however, her advisors strongly advocated marrying a king to solidify her claims to power.

For centuries, her family had successfully retained power within the enclaves of her gender and was determined to not have her power seeded into the hands of a dirty king. Nevertheless, she indulged requests by rulers within neighboring territories asking for her hand in marriage but never committing to one.

Her fiercest suitor vying for her hand came from King Dinga of the Zulu empire. Despite having several wives of his own already, he fought hard to win the affection of Queen Yaa-Yaa, sending her gifts of rare perfumes and beautiful necklaces to her palatial estate. He would constantly make personal visits to her residence, making a grand spectacle in the streets for all the people to see.

On a particular visit to her castle, King Dinga had several elephants decorated in brightly colored outfits accompanied by a lively band of street musicians. He himself mounted a majestic black steed as they entertained the throngs of people who filled the street to catch a glimpse of the parade.

The jubilant gathering of performers stopped in front of the Queen's residence, shaking the walls of the castle with their spirited music. Queen Yaa-Yaa stepped out to see the intriguing show unfold. Her appearance was welcomed by screams and lively chants by the crowd. King Dinga leapt from his horse and knelt before the Queen as they approached the imposing gates leading into her royal estate.

''My fellow Africans, I stand before you today humbled to visit your prosperous kingdom. I am even more humbled to grace the presence of our Sovereign and your beautiful Queen who has brought untold prosperity and harmony in our lives. May her reign be long and prosperous.''

''MAY HER REIGN BE LONG AND PROSPEROUS,'' intoned the crowd.

King Dinga continued, ''I stand here today hoping that our Sovereign would grant me her audience on this fine, sunny day.'' He bent low as he waited on a reply from her. The crowd stood waiting patiently for the Queen to respond. An amused smile peaked around her lips as she stared at the kneeling king. She straightened up, projecting her voice to address the crowd.

''I welcome your presence to my castle and accept your request,'' she responded which was quickly followed by jubilant screams and chants from the crowd. King Dinga rose and walked alongside Queen Yaa-Yaa as they proceeded into the castle.

They quickly made their way through the spacious hallways and decorated staircases until they arrived on the third floor of the building. Here stood the impressive grand living room where she entertained her most famous of guests. A ten-layer diamond encrusted chandelier hung overhead. Large, archway windows overlooked the clear blue fountains scattered across the castle grounds.

Waiting on them were the Queen's servants, men and women alike dressed only in white cloth wrapped around their waist. The women wore intricate red beads around their neck which partially exposed their buxom breasts. Each held a plate filled with an assortment of fine dishes from calamari to exotic fruits which they periodically brought to the seated regents.

King Dinga settled down comfortably in his chair and held up his long wooden pipe, periodically bringing it to his mouth and exhaling dark plumes of vapor which lingered in the air.

''You did not have to make a grand entrance to my residence today, Dinga. After all, I invited you here to discuss your coronation.'' Queen Yaa-Yaa addressed him as she settled down in one of the luxurious seats.

''The commoners seem to enjoy the spectacle, Yaa-Yaa,'' King

Dinga responded, ''it is our duty to not only govern but to entertain them now and then.'' He signaled to one of the servants who brought a calabash filled with sweet palm wine inside. The servant dutifully filled the king's glass to the brim. Several seconds later the glass was empty, and the servant filled his glass once more.

''I see your penchant for drink has remained as healthy as it has always been, Dinga.''

''I like to enjoy the finer things in life Yaa-Yaa. There is no crime in doing so.'' He raised a glass to her before emptying another glass full down his throat.

Queen Yaa-Yaa returned a wry look of exasperation to King Dinga. She did not want to admit it, but King Dinga was a handsome man. At fifty-nine years old, he had retained his boyish good looks as well as his wild personality from his youth. He sported a short, finely trimmed white beard which matched his white hair concealed under his regal crown.

She cleared her throat before continuing, ''I would like us to return to the matter at hand. Your coronation ceremony is coming up in less than a year. It is important that we prepare the modalities for the transferal of power.'' The king simply waved his hand at her in disinterest.

''Yaa-Yaa, our kingdoms have rotated power for centuries without a hitch. There is little to discuss in the matter. I would rather much discuss what a union between us could mean for the future of our domains.'' The queen grew warm with embarrassment as the king openly displayed his affection to her. The servants looked uneasily at each other as they stood and watched silently.

''Leave us,'' the Queen ordered. Each of the servants promptly shuffled out, closing the door behind them as they left.

''Dinga, I have a responsibility to prepare you for the role you will be adopting soon. During the last cycle, it was your father who held the position. Now the title falls on you. You would do well to show some seriousness in the matter.''

''I know well enough that other concerns dominate your mind, Yaa-Yaa. I have heard of your struggles to bear an heir which has placed your claim to the throne in jeopardy. Once your tenure as Sovereign expires, challenges to your authority will grow anew. Perhaps it is time that you chart a new path for your kingdom and for your people.''

The king sat up from his chair, momentarily fixing the wrinkles in his flowing kaftan before proceeding to the table across from his where the calabash filled with palm wine stood. He poured two drinks full and walked over to the Queen with both in hand. The Queen smiled weakly as he offered the glass to her.

''Do not let your stubbornness get in the way of progress, Yaa-Yaa, '' he said as he raised his glass for a toast. ''A marriage between us would ensure the survival of both of our kingdoms and give us considerable power over our neighbors.'' Both regents drank from the sweet drink which filled their glasses.

Despite his jocular disposition, Queen Yaa-Yaa could appreciate the king's counsel. The truth in front of her was hard to accept but clear as day. It was her duty to keep her royal legacy alive and a marriage to Dinga would solidify her grip on power.

Their marriage would also display strength in a time where leadership within the military ranks were actively contemplating a hostile takeover. Despite her reservations, she agreed to a union with Dinga and would formally make their intentions public after his coronation.

With a tacit agreement in place, both regents would be seen in public more often. Rumors swirled of a growing romance between them but without an official announcement from the town crier, they remained as such.

Meanwhile matters of state still occupied the Queen in her daily engagements. News from their territories in the north reported fiercer clashes between the combined British and French armies now known as the Western Coalition and the armies of the African Union.

The AU had managed to capture large areas of land on the Western tip of Europe in reprisal for prior invasions on African soil. Since then, they had retained claims to these lands for centuries despite constant pressure from their aggressors. With military action at a standstill, calls for diplomacy grew louder from both sides engaged in the conflict.

She turned to her civilian councils to discuss a possible resolution to the growing crises. She would constantly meet with her foreign affairs committee consisting of military generals from the various African kingdoms and civilian representatives alike.

Emissary Adoke was one of her trusted civilian councils on matters related to foreign affairs. He was a mousy man of small stature who balanced his oval lenses on his large nose as he read communiques he received from foreign leaders for the council's listening.

''The monarchs of the Western Coalition are demanding a full withdrawal of our forces in exchange for a cessation of all military action in the Northern territories. They also demand for equal sharing of the disputed territories and a written agreement to permanently put an end to hostilities.'' General Thabiso promptly slammed his fist into the table in swift reply.

''Next, they will demand we roll on our belly's and wag our tails for them. Sovereign, these demands are ridiculous!'' General Thabiso declared. ''These barbarians from the North must be dealt with the same way your predecessor, Queen Nzinga dealt with their ilk centuries ago. We must relay strength by using our biological arsenal.''

''General Thabiso knows fully well that an attack of that nature would directly contravene the 1965 Vienna Treaty prohibiting the use of biological weapons,'' retorted General Sumaina. ''A biological attack would only provoke the ire of the international community.''

Queen Yaa-Yaa had come to appreciate the wisdom of her military advisor; General Sumaina in particular. His calm and collective exterior heavily contrasted with the more militant personalities displayed by his colleagues. While they routinely urged the Queen to make use of their considerable biological stockpile, Sumaina would constantly urge for a more conventional approach to deal with skirmishes in the field.

Upon her mother's passing, Queen Yaa-Yaa had assumed the throne at the tender age of fifteen. She had quickly come to learn of her mother's penchant for winning military skirmishes by using the deadly biological weaponry at her disposal. She would sit Yaa-Yaa down on many occasions to explain the necessity for her actions.

''You will be Queen soon and will have to make hard choices,'' she would say. ''These people only understand strength. That is the only reason why we have survived this long as a people. You will do well to understand this early on, child.'' Despite her mother's warnings, she had sought to distance herself from this course of action in favor of more peaceful forms of conflict resolution.

''And who will come to our aid when their armies invade our borders and murder our people?'' General Thabiso continued forcefully, ''we cannot afford to be complacent as our enemies continue to strike at our borders.'' Queen Yaa-Yaa looked on with interest as they argued amongst themselves. Several Generals sided with Thabiso while others saw reason in Sumaina's warnings and echoed his concerns. The decision however solely rested with the Queen.

She had made her decision. She would extend the olive branch of peace, offering instead to have a meeting with the Western Coalition's Emissary in order to allay tensions in the region. Her decision was met with chagrin from General Thabiso who stormed out of the castle immediately the meeting was concluded.

Despite many of her unpopular decisions, she remained steadfast in her resolve to maintain peace and harmony in her borders. With her mind adrift with these concerns, she would walk the halls of her expansive castle at night when most of her servants had fallen sleep.

She would always return to the painting of her ancestor, Queen Nzinga whose portrait hung prominently in the foyer just above the twin marble staircase leading up to higher levels in the castle. The steely look of Nzinga's eyes made it seem as if she was peering directly into your soul. Her gold crown and elegantly pinned white-laced robe projected the strength she possessed as the Queen of Luanda.

Indeed, stories of her conquests were public knowledge as was her most famous achievement of driving the Eurasian invaders seeking to conquer their lands. Her own mother had made her read a string of historical accounts dedicated to her accomplishments, drilling the legend of the warrior queen into her head. It was with her mother's encouragement that she had become the Queen she was today; stoic yet cunning, capable of making the hard choices when the time came.

Queen Yaa-Yaa knew better than to strive solely for such a goal. What the history books omitted were the bouts of madness the warrior Queen had exhibited on certain occasions. Queen Nzinga was known to take a direct role in the executions of her enemies; a past-time she particularly enjoyed. It was said that she would bring them to a secret room in the castle and torture them through the night before ending their lives in painful ways.

Her reputation for cruelty earned her great respect amongst her peers who aptly nicknamed her, 'The Warrior of the West'. Queen |Yaa-Yaa would gaze upon this portrait in her youth knowing fully well that she would have to make difficult decisions one day as Queen regent.

Mounting pressure from her enemies was pushing the dial towards more drastic measures and it was only a matter of time before the military's push for greater action superseded her calls for peace. Murmurs from her own people also suggested they too wanted firmer action from their Queen. With ever diminishing support from her people, the military would surely be emboldened to usurp her crown at the end of her tenure as Sovereign.

She gazed intently at the portrait of Queen Nzinga once more as if hoping for the lifeless image to gain the ability of speech and counsel her, offering the advice she so desperately needed. When that seemed increasingly impossible, she resorted to contemplating what the old Queen would have done in her stead.

Queen Nzinga would surely have swiftly ordered the execution of her enemies, she thought. She would seek to eliminate those involved in any coup plot against her, sending a clear message that the monarchy would continue to live on, unshaken and enduring.

She would agree that a marital union between herself and another monarch would prove useful in shoring up her claim to the throne but would not allow her power to be subverted by any man. With a couple of months left until the coronation and few viable options before her, she would have to settle with the most viable option in front of her.

The marriage between the two monarchs happened a week before the coronation was to be held. Their union happened in a secret ceremony held in the castle and was witnessed by only a few important people including General Sumaina and several heads of the royal families. King Dinga and Queen Yaa-Yaa both agreed to keep their marriage confidential until after the coronation ceremony took place. It was their intent not to detract from the festivities planned for that day.

Silently, they both knew news of their union would upend the power balance shared between the neighboring kingdoms. Fearing their combined power to be too great, the other monarchs may move to action to prevent their influence from growing. However, waiting until after the crowning ceremony would give them no time to react. They would be forced to accept their new-found union.

The terrorist attack at the coronation however had therefore come as a shock to everyone and launched the united kingdoms into disarray. The continent was thrown into mourning as news of the death of King Dinga swept the land. Meanwhile, the military doubled their efforts to protect the life and safety of the Queen who lay recovering from her injuries.

With the perpetrators of the attack still at large, the kingdom and its bordering provinces were placed on high alert. Intelligence reports from the military placed the blame squarely on the Red Dawn militia group, an organisation working from within Slovian borders who had the full support of its Czar.

General Sumaina held a press meeting to address the health of the Queen. Now that her term as Sovereign was extended, the military would look to her for direction in light of this unwarranted aggression from the Red Dawn.

''We believe this attack perpetrated by the Red Dawn was carried out with the full support of the Slovian King,'' boomed General Sumaina's voice over the radio. His live broadcast was being simultaneously transmitted across the continent. Residents sat dressed in black robes to mourn the loss of King Dinga while they listened for news on the health of Queen Yaa-Yaa.

''I stand here representing our Queen who remains in stable condition at the hospital. She has deemed it fit to transmit her intentions to me…'' His voice trailed off as if the next few words weighed heavily on his tongue. The people who listened waited with bated breath as the General continued the announcement.

''For this unjustifiable act of aggression, today at 5:44 pm, the Sovereign has formally declared war against the Slovian Kingdom and her allies. We will use the full weight of the African Union's military alliance to crush it in retaliation for this most heinous action against our sovereign union.''

The declaration came as no surprise to many who listened to the broadcast. It was only confirmation on the action many people now supported. The Slovian Empire had for years been the singular aggressor across several continents. The attack on their monarch was the last straw and the time had finally come to put an end to their reign.

Queen Yaa-Yaa entrusted most of her military decisions to her generals while she recovered from her injuries. She became increasingly reliant on General Sumaina as she trusted him well above the others. The Agura's stark warning of enemies around her still sat at the forefront of her mind making it necessary to tighten her circle of trust.

With the war raging on across the Atlantic and in Eurasia, she dedicated more and more of her time to conceiving her heir. The Agura had told her that the man to father her child would come from the east, a statement which implied the man to help her conceive her child would come from somewhere within the Aksum Empire.

To conceal her intent, she had several men recruited from the eastern African kingdom to be servants working in her castle. Each night, the Queen would invite one to her bed chambers. All were sworn to secrecy to their nightly affairs with the Queen.

To ensure her actions remained hidden, she routinely replaced them with new recruits received every few months. The men sent away were conspicuously never heard of again.

Her difficulty in conceiving a child began to weigh even more persistently on her mind. She returned to the Agura on an ever-frequent basis for guidance and assistance. The Agura would constantly reassure her that her predictions were sound and would prove true. The Queen would leave her shrine with baskets of herbs and spices with strict instructions from the Agura on how to ingest them.

''These will help strengthen your body once you conceive your child,'' she would say to the Queen but even now the Agura could see the anger and desperation in her eyes. The many years of barrenness had begun to trouble the Queen deeply. In public, she concealed her frustrations behind her colorful outfits and wide-eyed grin but here in private, the Agura could peak behind that façade to see the true face behind the smile.

She offered a wide, forced smile of her own as the Queen departed her shrine again. It would be the last time they interacted with one another, the Agura would make sure of that. Fearing for her life, the Agura departed from her shrine that night, never to return.

As the years went by, the raging war too began to weigh more heavily on the Queen. She had underestimated the strength of the Slovian empire and now had grown tired of the resources she was made to expend on the war effort. She jumped at the potential peace treaty negotiated by her new diplomatic envoy to the Slovian Government, Emissary Tife, and ordered that she be personally be present for the meeting with other world leaders.

Against the advice of her own generals, Queen Yaa-Yaa insisted she too be present for the summit. Other world leaders were expected to arrive, and it would not augur well if she were not in attendance as well. It would be the first time she left the shores of the continent since the attack at the coronation. With most of the details of the peace agreement already hashed out, it would only be a simple matter of signing the treaty which would normalize relations between the warring kingdoms.

It would also be the first time she would meet many of the world leaders in person. She had only seen them in pictures before and was curious what they would look like in real life. Despite being allies in the war, it would be the first time she set eyes on the Chinese regent, Emperor Mo Xuefang in person. She was taken aback by the short stature of the monarch. He had always appeared taller in the pictures she was shown of him.

Sophia Schulze, Premiere to the Prussian Empire was a striking woman in her own right with long blond hair and deep blue eyes. Queen Yaa-Yaa had grown a deep admiration for the woman who had managed to maintain her kingdom intact despite constant territorial disputes with their neighbors, the Austria-Hungarians and the Slovians.

Many had expected her first interaction with the Slovian Czar to be explosive and uncontrolled. Instead, she offered her wide-eyed smile to the severe ruler who sat down across from her. She even accepted an invitation to an execution planned by the Slovians, offering her Emissary in her stead to attend the event.

With the war finally at an end, she could return home to focus on more personal pursuits. Her people would surely welcome her return with much celebration, having forced their adversaries to capitulate on several fronts. She could now focus her efforts towards conceiving a successor and ensuring her legacy lived on.

THE WILDERNESS

A bevy of scattered images ran through her mind before coming into focus once again. The dreams which haunted her for so many years always gained focus at this part.

Her memories had taken her back to the massacre at the coronation. The heavy pour of rain around her diluted and washed the blood which covered the ground. The water slowly began to turn a reddish hue which flowed freely down the asphalt roads.

The carriage carrying the regents was on its side and so was the horse which was pulling it along. It was torn in half from the blast. Its insides were exposed and spilling on the ground while it twitched in its death throes.

She shifted her gaze until she found King Dinga lying lifeless on the ground. The ornate pieces of gold jewelry which was handed to him during the ceremony still hung around his neck and arm. His regal robe was drenched with blood and lay splayed untidily on the ground. She thought she could see the king's finger move momentarily but it was probably from the strong push of the water streams which swirled around him.

Kneeling beside him was Queen Yaa-Yaa. Her crown had been knocked from her head and her beautiful hair was matted to her face. Her hands now hung over King Dinga's lifeless body an inch away from his exposed neckline.

As if sensing she was being watched, Queen Yea-Yaa narrowed her gaze to Tife who lay motionless several meters away. Her expression of sadness quickly turned to anger as her eyes narrowed to a grimace. Tife watched in fright as the Queen began to walk over to her, her eyes glinting with murderous intent….

Tife awoke on the hard floor to the sound of several pregnant women fast asleep. They had found a grotto just large enough for them to settle in. Unfortunately, no extra space meant most of their dogs with them would have to be let go.

Tife dutifully removed their harness which seemed to confuse the sleigh dogs. She raised her hands and let out a large scream which seemed to jolt them into running away. They disappeared into the heavy clearing of snow pouring in thick plumes through the trees. She adjusted the harness of the five dogs left and headed back to the grotto.

Tired and hungry, she returned to the small grotto, covered in a freshly fallen coat of snow and carrying a stack of sticks in her grasp. The women and children lay huddled in a corner as new flecks of snow swept in through the front. They gazed at her with desolate eyes as she spread the wood onto the ground and attempted to start a fire.

The wet pieces of flint she had found produced little sparks as she repeatedly struck them together. She was fully aware that they would not last the night without a source of heat to warm themselves up. Exhausted after their escape from the Red Dawn hideout, they would also need food quickly if they would stand a chance of surviving the frozen tundra.

After several attempts, Tife managed to strike an ember onto the stack of sticks. She quickly fanned the burning edge until a small flame caught on the wood. The women and children hungrily huddled around the fire, desperate for some heat to keep their frost-bitten bodies warm.

Tife sat back on the hard floor. Exhausted and starving, she took the time to take stock of her situation. In the past week alone, she had switched roles from diplomat to prisoner and now caretaker of a group of vulnerable women and children. She was far away from home, deep in enemy territory and unable to reach out to her people over the border. She could only assume they would have sent out a rescue party to find her but without any means to contact them, she was helpless and alone.

Tife recounted her training for the role of Emissary at the Academy for Diplomacy in Luanda. Every year, a select group of fifty-six individuals from across the continent would attend the academy and be schooled in a wide range of topics from conflict resolution to treaty drafting.

Other more extreme topics taught at the school were how to endure pain when being tortured for information by a foreign adversary and life skills on how to survive in inhospitable conditions.

Emissaries were only meant to broker peace however their postings to more violent parts of the world required they be taught skills that would be helpful with their survival in perilous circumstances. Even her most severe of mentors would not foresee she could wind up in a situation so dire.

She looked with deep sadness at the group of women and children who now warmed themselves by the fire she made. Caught between starvation and death, their outlook for survival was grim. She thought of the babies yet to be born in their bellies. At this rate, they would not have the opportunity of taking their first breath out of the womb. The gaunt faces of the children also filled her with deep concern. Their hunger was clearly visible on their emaciated bodies.

As she remained lost in thought, Katrina came close and pressed her tiny face onto her side. Miraculously, she still had her pet cat from the hideout which she now cuddled in her arms. She produced a wide smile as Tife looked down to meet her gaze, returning one of her own.

Looking down at that innocent face stirred something deep within her. She knew she had to survive not only for herself, but for these little ones too small to understand what was going on around them. Tife was determined to have them survive.

''Everyone…everyone please listen to me,'' Tife spoke to them in their native Slovinian tongue as she pressed closer to them, ''the night will soon be upon us and I fear we will not last long in our current location. My people over the border can guarantee your safety if I can only contact them. I can have you all taken to safety and won't mention you are part of the Red Dawn. However, without a means to pinpoint our location, they will be unable to find us.''

The women exchanged glances with each other as if communicating their thoughts solely with their eyes. They clearly knew something Tife did not. She needed them to trust her if they would get out of this alive.

''I understand that it is hard for you all to trust me, but I had no other intent but to make peace when I came to your borders. These unfortunate series of circumstances does not change that. Your Captain trusted me enough to keep you all safe and that is what I want to do. I need your help to make sure of that.''

She looked at each of their faces keenly as they turned their attention to a singular person. An older woman among them hesitantly nodded as if to give approval to the others. Buoyed by her apparent consent to cooperate, the group of women turned their attention back to Tife, eyes filled with information.

''I was given the task of holding a radio in the event of an emergency,'' one woman spoke up as she pulled out a rectangular device from underneath a dirty brown shawl. She looked younger than most of them. She had bright red hair knotted into a long braid running down her back.

''We attempted to contact our second base of operations further up north when you went out for the wood. We received no communication from them which could mean their base was attacked too.'' The woman handed the device over to Tife who reached over to inspect. It was an older radio model with several large, circular dials on its face and a long metallic receiver rising from the top.

''Perhaps you will have a better time contacting your people,'' the woman finished. Tife examined the radio again. With this, it would be possible to send out a message to any rescue party looking for her. However, the range of the radio was clearly short. The radio also had a limited charge stored in its batteries. She would probably have a small window of time to send out a distress signal before they gave up altogether.

''I may be able to send out a message with your radio, but I will have to find higher ground to boost the signal strength. I could use the dogs to reach higher elevation and return as soon I get a response.'' The unease on their face was clearly visible as she finished sharing her plan. It seemed they could not trust her to take the only means of communication and transportation away from them.

''I will go with you, then, '' the woman who offered the radio to her spoke up, returning a resolute gaze to the crowded women. ''I will ensure she keeps her word and returns here to us.'' With everyone comfortable with the arrangement, Tife saddled up the remaining dogs unto their sleigh and together with the woman, departed the grotto deeper into northern territory.

The snow fall had eased off slightly as they made their way up towards higher ground. The woman accompanying Tife had revealed her name was Arial. Together, they balanced on the wooden sleigh which cut through the powdery surface floor.

Part of her training as a diplomat centered on information extraction required to carry her duties accordingly. The academy had several training exercises dedicated to learning techniques to do this successfully. One of which was gaining the trust of your mark. If she was going to have any chance of returning home safely to her grandmother and her family back home, she would have to glean as much information from these people as possible beginning with Arial.

Tife turned to Arial who was staring off into the distance as they travelled further down the plains. The blistering, frigid air ripped into their skins as the winds began to pick up making them both shiver intermittently. Tife inched closer to Arial to share the little body heat she had with her. Arial in turn returned a smile of gratitude to her.

After several minutes, they had made substantial progress up the gradual incline of a mountain side. Tife suggested it would be best they navigated their way up to its highest point before they tried the radio again. Leaving the dogs tied to the base of the mountain, they trudged by foot up the snowy foothill.

''I like your hair by the way,'' Tife began as they walked along the steep incline. Arial turned to give her a weak smile before focusing her attention back on the path. Tife continued, ''you must have been very important for the Captain to entrust you with that radio in case of emergencies.''

''I am no more important than the other thousands of us fighting for our cause,'' Arial replied dryly.

''But you must have held a special place in his heart for him to give you that responsibility. I wouldn't think it otherwise.'' Arial turned back to Tife who walked behind her. A curious grin crossed her face.

''I know what you are trying to do,'' Arial replied, still walking at an even pace up the mountain. ''You think you can befriend me and learn vital information from me. I do not appreciate such tactics as underhanded as that. If you wish to know something, I suggest you just ask me the question directly.'' Tife stopped walking briefly, momentarily taken aback by her candor but quickly resumed.

''Why would Michail trust you enough with the only means to contact your allies. What were you to him?''

''I must say I am impressed he shared his real name with you. He must have judged you worthy of that information. Michail and I were very close once. He was a deeply passionate man committed to achieving freedom for my people. His days as a soldier for the autocratic Slovian government took a toll on him, you see. He carried the burden of the many sins he committed while under their service…'' she trailed off as a strong gust of wind blew across the path raising the settled snow into the air.

''I fell in love with him despite his deep psychological wounds. That love only grew stronger as time went by. But despite my great affection for him, he had his eyes on another.''

''Are you referring to his partner, Galina?''

She nodded in reply, "After her capture, he became obsessed with rescuing her. In the process, he put my life and the lives of his fellow comrades in jeopardy. In the end, it turned out to be a fool's errand.'' Tife could not help but notice the discontent under her voice as she recounted their history together. His rejection of her clearly wounded her deeply.

At that moment, Tife realized the striking resemblance with a child she had seen at the cavern. The girl's bright red hair only seemed to confirm it.

''Is Katrina your daughter, Arial?'' Tife probed. Now it was Arial who stopped in her tracks. She inhaled deeply as she stared off into the distance.

''I have no daughter,'' she replied firmly. ''I disown any child borne from a loveless union. The Captain rejected me so I will in turn reject his offspring.'' She turned to look at Tife now. Her eyes glinted with rage as a singular tear streamed down her face. She brushed it aside with her palm before continuing up the inclined path. The foothill now began to grow steeper as they ventured up the hill.

''Why are you sharing all of this with me?'' Tife asked.

''Because none of us may make it out of this icy tundra alive, '' she replied despondently. ''I have tried to remain positive around the other women, but our current situation does not bode well. I have no problem sharing these things with the walking dead.'' She returned a wry smile to Tife as they arrived at the summit.

The hilltop was modest in comparison to the mountains surrounding it. Its edge overlooked the snow-covered trees littering its base. The peak itself had barely enough space to accommodate both of them. With the winds whipping ever more fervently at this elevation, they braced themselves, holding on to as much ground as possible.

At the same time, Tife fished out the radio receiver from inside her cloak and switched in on. Static replied her as she began to move the dials on its face. She had to tune the device to match the frequency which her counterparts across the border broadcasted on. Her delegation at the summit were made privy to that information before they touched down in the event of an emergency such as this.

The radio screeched in reply as she tuned to the exact frequency. Static greeted her before disparate sounds began to filter in. Her heart soured at the sounds of voices coming through the receiver. She quickly pushed the reply button, speaking as clearly as she could through the speaker.

''This is Ododo-1 requesting for a rescue and evacuation of myself and several vulnerable people in the northern territory beyond the Krepost district in the Slovian colonies. By my estimation, we are about 200 klicks north of that city area in unclaimed territories. Send a team to this location immediately…'' As she spoke those last words through the radio, it sputtered out of life and switched off.

''Do you think they received your message?'' Arial asked.

''I can only hope so,'' Tife replied optimistically. If they indeed sent a rescue team to come find her across the border, they would pick up the transmission and track her location down. All she could hope for was that they found her in time before it was too late.

They made their way down the hill back to the waiting sleigh dogs at the base of the hill. The snow was falling heavily in the area now, blanketing the plains in a new white coat. They promptly mounted the sleigh and with a loud call to the dogs, they began to pierce through the snowy white curtain which fell all around them.

As they neared the location of the other women, Arial pulled hard on the reins of the dogs to veer left, taking them slightly off course. She halted the dogs in front of a snowy rock mound and dismounted from the sleigh.

''What are you doing?'' Tife inquired promptly.

''Saving the lives of the women left in the cave, even if it may be for a short time, '' she announced as she brought out a short blade from underneath her garments. Tife stiffened up as Arial brandished the knife, eying her with anxious eyes.

Tife desperately looked around as snowfall showered around them. With no one in sight, Arial could easily kill her and return to the other women. Her hand tightened around the radio in her possession. It was the only weapon she had against her knife-wielding foe.

Arial ambled forward and took hold of one of the leather reins holding the dogs together. With a swift flick of her hand, she cut through the one holding the last dog in place. She looked up at Tife with unflinching eyes; the knife still held firmly in her grasp.

''I won't be long,'' she said before taking the untethered dog behind the rocky mound, beyond Tife's sight. Seconds later, a loud shriek pierced through the air. Tife waited several moments before Arial emerged again. She had the dog's bloody carcass draped over her shoulder. Its fur had been skinned from its body and she held it firmly across her shoulders.

She dropped the dog's corpse unto the sleigh along with its pelt before stowing away the knife in her clothes. Tife stared incredulously at the woman now covered in blood. With a loud command, the dogs started back up and hurried through the icy plains.

The eerie sound of nightfall swept through the cold air as they huddled for warmth in the grotto. Tife stoked the flame to coax more heat from the dying fire. The cooked carcass of the sleigh dog hung over the blaze. Its bony ribs were now exposed as most of its flesh had been picked clean from its body.

The women and children sat down to eat heartily from the bounty. No questions were asked as to where the meat came from. The people only stood grateful that they had something to fill their bellies.

Arial sat on the far side of the small space, staring eerily at the waning fire. Her eyes stood wide open, reflecting the dancing flames from the warm body. Tife noticed she had eaten little from the cooked carcass and took a piece to her where she sat. With a warm smile, she accepted the meat and promptly ripped into its tender flesh.

''Your daughter deserves a mother, you know,'' Tife said, pointing to Katrina who sat playing with the other children. ''I always regretted not spending enough time with my mother before she passed.''

''The girl deserves someone who can give her the love she requires. I possess none of that to give her.'' Arial turned her face till her eyes locked with Tife's. Her expression was solemn and grim all at once.

''You wish to be reunited with your family, do you not?''

''Nothing would make me happier. My grandmother is well into her years and needs help in her old age.''

Arial grinned in reply, ''I find it interesting that you still think of their well-being despite your current situation. Your position as Emissary suits you well.''

''In all my time as Emissary, I have never understood why your people commit acts of terrorism against your own government. Bombs could never take the position of dialogue.''

''I am in turn confused why your people do not take more firm steps against your oppressive government. You erroneously believe they have your best interest at heart while in truth, your rulers care nothing for you.''

''Our leaders prevented further war and destruction by taking steps to sign an overarching peace accord between the Slovian monarchy and other major powers, '' Tife replied indignantly. Your people's efforts to undermine that has put the entire agreement in jeopardy.'' Arial scoffed momentarily at those words.

''You believe the ceremonial signing of a piece of paper by kings and queens from various empires will suddenly stop their aggression towards one another? Their very existence prevents the achievement of true peace. True freedom can only be won when these oppressive governments are torn down. That is why we continue to fight.''

''I cannot speak for the monarchs within your borders, but our Queen and her subordinates will honor the terms of the agreement signed. She would never use her biological arsenal against any foreign government with the agreement in place.''

Arial lay down to rest on the rocky floor using her hands as a pillow to shoulder her head, ''I do hope you are right, Emissary, '' she replied, ''the entire world is standing at the precipice of a full blown World War, one I fear no one will survive.''

One by one, the small group fell asleep, warmed by the dying embers of the wooden fire. Tife was the only one awake now as she pondered deep into the night. It unsettled her to think her efforts at diplomacy would amount to nothing.

The ramifications of war consuming the planet was something firmly at the back of her mind as she carried out her duties as Emissary. The peace guaranteed by a cessation of arms was the only way to avert a grim future like that from taking hold. She said a silent prayer before giving in to the warm embrace of the lit fire.

Tife was awoken several hours later by the rustling of nearby trees. The wind billowed in the distance carrying with it the brunt of the raging snowstorm. She looked around to see the other women and children fast asleep. Arial herself still lay in the same spot that she had fallen asleep. Tiptoeing past the dogs which lay at the fore-front of the cave, she ventured outside to inspect their surroundings.

Her skin tensed up as the biting cold nipped across her body. The curtain of snow slowly fell around her, contrasting starkly against the backdrop of the pitch-black exterior. She ventured further out, looking for signs of anything around her.

She was fearful that a wild animal may be nearby, stalking their location. After all, the grotto which they resided in looked very much like that of a bear's dwelling. Tife hoped to give the others advanced warning in the event she spotted one.

A dark figure suddenly appeared from behind a group of trees. Several shapes followed suit, emerging through the pitch-black darkness. Tife could not make them out fully through the shadows as they approached her.

As the figures inched closer, Tife could make out the outline of a gun in their hands. She raised her hands in resignation as they circled her.

One of them quickly came from behind and struck her knees from the back, forcing her into the snow. Two others grabbed her roughly by the arms and restrained her. The dogs now began to bark furiously as the dark figures moved into the grotto with the others inside. Arial stood awake now, shielding the others while clutching the knife she had in her possession.

Several gunshots pierced through the air, loudly echoing across the walls of the grotto. The dogs were quickly cut asunder by the barrage of bullets which flew their way. Arial instantly fell to her feet, wrangling in pain as one bullet pierced through her right thigh. The soldier kicked her aside as several more of them rushed into the space.

The women and children huddled as far back into the cave as possible. Loud screams and cries followed as the soldiers separated them one by one, taking some of them outside.

Several women and children had been left behind, including Katrina who sat cowering in a corner, her eyes wide with fright. Tife watched helplessly as five soldiers lined up, blocking her view to the other women and children left inside.

A cocking of guns followed by a sickening mixture of screams and gunshots reverberating through the air. Tife screamed in horror as a pool of blood began to form around the soldier's legs.

Tears flowed freely down her eyes as they dragged her off and loaded her into a truck with the others. Arial was last to be boarded after being thrown roughly inside by two soldiers. She cried violently while writhing in pain as the vehicle started up and began to cut through the roads leading south, back in the direction of the Krepost citadel.

Hours later, they had arrived at a heavily fortified compound. Several perimeter lights were arranged around its edges casting long, yellow beams through the darkness. Barb-wired fencing several meters high lined the walls of the prison's boundary. The truck rolled to a stop at a checkpoint into the prison. After a quick inspection, a large metal gate flung open, allowing the truck to enter the forlorn space.

''Welcome to the gulag, your new home for the rest of your lives, '' an armed soldier announced as they were promptly let out of the truck. Immediately the doors were opened, Katrina leapt out and struck the side of the soldier's head with her foot. Others ran to pull her off as she proceeded to strangle him.

After managing to restrain her, the soldier who had been attacked struck her several times in the stomach and face until she fell unconscious. He ended by launching a wad of spit in her face before ordering her to be taken away.

The frightened group were led to a quarry in the heart of the encampment. Several people were already present, working with pitch forks on the mining site under the supervision of several armed guards. They were made to line up in the center of the site in the full view of the other workers toiling away under the desolate conditions. None stopped for a second to look at the new arrivals as they were paraded like prize sheep at an auction.

A severe looking man wearing a formal, brown military uniform stepped into view. His breast pocket and shoulder pads displayed several medals of varying sizes and shapes. He sported a sharp, rectangular cap which framed his already square and dour face.

On his breast pocket was emblazoned the twin-eagle crest of the Slovian empire. The only facial hair he had was a perfectly trim mustache which sat atop his frost-bitten lips. A long sword also hung down from his waist belt.

The man walked alongside the arranged group of women and children, momentarily taking interest in one of them before continuing down the line. Tife averted her gaze as he walked past her. The man stopped in front of her, lifting her face to his before walking past. After he had inspected all the women and children, he stood before them, standing erect and stiff in the freezing air.

''You all are part of the terrorist cell, the Red Dawn which has been operating within the borders of the Slovian colonies,'' he began, projecting his voice so that even the workers toiling away could hear him. ''We destroyed your largest hideout hidden away in disputed territories up North and have been combing the area for remnants of your cell who managed to escape. ''

''For crimes against our great Czar, his Excellency Nicholas Romanov VI and by extension the great Slovian empire, I sentence you to spend the rest of your days working within the boundaries of this encampment. Let your punishment serve as a lesson to anyone foolish enough to challenge the will of our Czar,'' he pressed his right hand to his chest before shouting, ''FOR MOTHER SLOVIA,'' which was refrained by the other soldiers overlooking the mines.

Tife looked upon this spectacle with deep confusion in her heart. She had dedicated her life towards making peace and inroads with warring empires to avert wars capable of consuming the planet. Her experience these past few days had demonstrated the folly in that endeavor. These world powers were not interested in making life better for their peoples. Instead, they subjugated and tormented their citizenry into submission, forcing upon them a dictatorship they did not benefit from.

She realized she had tried to deny this simple fact for many years, instead believing in the necessity of strong leaders to catalyze development in their territories. Her last bastion of hope remained in the rulership of her monarch, Queen Yaa-Yaa who was clearly different from these tyrants. In only her queenship had she tried to ameliorate the lives of her people, shielding them from wars while ensuring they remained prosperous.

She held on to the hope that she would return back home to her loved ones, that she would not be forced to spend the rest of her life in this cruel and desolate place. She in turn looked upon with pity at her fellow prisoners as they lifted the tools thrown in front of them. These women and children had done nothing to deserve this cruel fate. Instead, they would live the rest of their days serving a tyrannical government. Inwardly, Tife hoped and prayed for a miracle.

REVELATIONS

Queen Yaa-Yaa returned home to a hero's welcome. Her ship was greeted by several parades organised by admirers of the monarchy. People flocked the streets to welcome her return from the peace summit and to herald a cessation of a war with Slovia which had gone on for several years now.

She welcomed the adulation and praise she received as her convoy slowly moved through the streets back to the castle. Inwardly, the Queen vowed that within the time she still had left as their monarch, she would not deal on them another cycle of interminable war as they had seen these past few years.

During their trip back home, General Sumaina informed her of the regretful kidnapping of their Emissary by Red Dawn rebels after the execution in Krepost. She had given the order for an extraction to take place if possible. Any other action would have seen her as weak, unwilling to meet the aggression of the Slovian monarchy with force. She was confident her action would not spark further war. It was not her intent to break the treaty with their empire after brokering peace with them.

The Queen found it curious that high-ranking members of the

military were largely absent from the delegation which welcomed her at the port. She cared little for their approval of her but still demanded their loyalty to the throne, more so now that she had the title of Sovereign to the African Union.

For this very reason did she hold General Sumaina in the deepest regard as only he afforded her with the respect she deserved. The war and its subsequent end had solidified her control of the Luandan kingdom from usurpers within the military ranks. With her power now unchallenged, no one was left within the military brass or otherwise who could seize control of her empire.

With the conflict largely behind her now, she could dedicate all her attention back to her desire for conceiving an heir. She would make plans to have even more men brought from across the empire to her castle if needed. She would not need to conceal her efforts any longer now that her rule as Queen regent was unchallenged.

As they arrived at the castle, General Sumaina brought before her even more unsettling news. The Western Coalition had seized on the peace talks to launch an assault on their Northern Territories. They had managed to launch a successful offensive on the Zaragoza settlement and were making their way southward towards the African mainland. Soon, they would reach their most Northern border. Queen Salma had sent a distress signal to Queen Yaa-Yaa asking for her aid and the full weight of the African Union's military.

Anger welled up inside her as she received the news. Those barbarians from Europe sought to cause her ruin once more and destroy the peace and prosperity she had guaranteed. They were not signatories to the peace treaty signed with Slovia and sought to capitalize on the cessation of conflict between the world powers, ''with our military forces depleted, they believe we will not risk taking firm action against them,'' General Sumaina confirmed.

The Queen stared into the distance as she studied the situation. Her military and funds had been severely impacted from the war effort against Slovia. Now that enemy troops had taken over the Zaragoza territory, it would take a considerable amount of time to launch a successful offensive to retake the lands.

They had entered the foyer of the castle with the painting of Queen Nzinga hanging across the center wall. The ancient Queen had faced a similar situation during her reign of power. The painting's steely eyes reflected the old queen's stiff resolve. During her time, she had taken action to drive away the murdering marauders out to steal their lands. History had come around full circle and Queen Yaa-Yaa would respond firmly as her ancestor once did. She had made her decision.

''Order a tactical retreat and have the military mobilize to deploy our most virulent biological weapon on the battlefront. I want a swift end to this campaign.''

General Sumaina returned a stunned look as the Queen made the command. His tough exterior was replaced with one of deep worry and concern.

''Is there a problem, General?'' Queen Yaa-Yaa probed.

''Not…not at all, my Queen, '' General Sumaina stuttered, clearing his throat, ''I would recommend we move to engage our reinforcement troops stationed in the Americas. Within a few days, I am sure…''

''I AM YOUR QUEEN, GENERAL. YOU WILL DO AS I COMMAND'' the Queen's high-pitched voice echoed across the castle halls.

''As you wish, my Queen, '' General Sumaina answered with a curt bow before leaving the castle residence, leaving the irate Queen behind. The servants tending the halls stole cursory glances as the Queen walked past them up to her chambers. They had never seen her display such raw emotion before.

''What are you staring at? Get back to your duties,'' she ordered them. Yaa-Yaa was simmering with rage as she entered her expansive bedroom. Not only did she have to deal with mounting territorial concerns, but also possible insubordination from her closest ally. She would deal with these problems one at a time, first by having Sumaina's loyalty reaffirmed to her.

Night had fallen on the hallowed castle grounds with most of the Queen's servants sleeping in their chambers. Sumaina had just received word from the Queen that she wanted a private meeting with him and he dutifully made his way to the castle.

Long, rectangular shadows cut across the granite floor as he made his way past the large painting of Queen Nzinga in the foyer and up the stairs leading to the Queen's bed chamber. Two guards stood were poised at the door. They were part of the Queen's private security detail he himself had arranged. They offered him a hard salute as they opened the doors to let him in.

Sumaina found it strange that the Queen wanted an audience in her personal bed chambers as they always had meetings in the office space located on the same floor. Nevertheless, he was duty bound to obey the commands of the monarch and would honor the invitation.

The antechamber leading into the Queen's bedchamber was an impressive sight. Light from the moon streamed freely through the windows bathing the high-aesthetic décor in its white tint. Imported furniture and lampstands flecked in gold and other precious metals adorned the space. At the very corner lay the Queen's bedchamber which stood slightly ajar. A voice pierced the silence as he entered.

''Is that you, General,'' the Queen's sultry voice streamed in.

''Yes, my Queen, '' General Sumaina replied. A silhouette slowly appeared through the door. It was the Queen. She wore a sheer, white night gown which exposed the contours of her voluptuous body. The outline of her supple breasts with its pointed tips stood out prominently from underneath the gown. Lines dipping from her hips seemed to point to the fleshy prize which lay between her legs. In place of her crown lay a mesh embroidered gold head piece which sat atop her curly hair.

Sumaina remained stiff as she walked forward to him but stopped several feet as if to allow for the General's eyes to have a more complete look of her. A lustful smile crossed her face as she inspected him with her eyes.

''Have you ordered the military strike I commanded of you, General?'' she asked softly.

''I did, my Queen, '' came General Sumaina's prompt reply. ''they will launch the strike on the Zaragoza region in the early morning.''

''Excellent. You have served me well, General. Your Queen is very pleased.'' Yaa-Yaa shifted her buxom hips while pursing her lips together. She then proceeded to pace around General Sumaina, scanning his body with licentious desire.

''Your loyalty to me has been called to question, General,'' the Queen whispered tracing a long finger across his uniform, ''You know I do not tolerate insubordination from those around me.''

''You are my Queen, now and always. I have pledged to always serve you well,'' came the General's dry-mouthed reply. The Queen stopped pacing around him to face him directly now. Her deep, brown eyes were filled with insatiable desire as she gazed into his.

''Good, then you will serve me now. I recently learned you originally hail from the Mazighen kingdom in East Africa. The prophecy offered to me by the Agura may yet hold true. Perhaps the solution to my problem has always been before me. Now, come with me...''

The Queen turned around and walked back towards her bedchamber. The light from the moon illuminating her plump and buxom rear. General Sumaina followed closely behind her.

With almost slow reverence, General Sumaina undressed the Queen, taking off her mesh gold hair piece first before slipping the white, sheer gown from her supple body. He undid his belt and removed his uniform, folding it into a neat pile on the chair beside the bed post. He turned around to see the arc of the moonlight cut the Queen's exposed body, revealing its beautiful contours in vivid detail.

A passionate moan escaped the Queen's pursed lips as the General dipped his male member inside her moist lips. Their lower extremities pressed tightly against each other as he rhythmically penetrated her. Her breasts heaved with each new thrust against her. She sunk her fingers into his bare bottom and pressed down, forcing him to lunge deeper inside her.

The rhythm gathered pace as the minutes wore on. The Queen moaned in blissful pleasure as sweat now began to seep from their naked bodies. The General responded by pressing even faster into her.

He slowly moved his hands over to the Queen's graceful neck, wrapping his fingers around it and squeezing it in the throes of pleasure. She bore no mind as she was approaching climax. The room was filled with sounds of sexual delight as both cried out into the darkness, each achieving orgasm at the same time.

General Sumaina's hands pressed even more tightly on the Queen's neck just as his rich nectar poured inside her. He ignored her kicks and coughs of protest as he constricted her neck further. Years of toiling in military service had transformed his hands into callous weapons of war. Taking a life with them were just as effective as squeezing the trigger of a gun.

The Queen's eyes glazed over as spit now ran down her mouth. The kicks had simmered down to twitches as the life was slowly drained from her body. Sumaina made sure to press down on her neck for several moments longer even after he had confirmed she was dead. Finally, he removed himself from her and sat naked by the side of the bed, staring emptily through the window into the cold night beyond.

Hours seemed to pass by as Sumaina sat alone in the sparsely lit room. The old castle did little to drive the cold embrace of the outside air from lingering within its walls. He allowed significant time to go by before reaching for his uniform on the bedside chair. Slowly, he dressed himself, cinching up his belt and fixing his hat atop his head.

He turned to gaze at the lifeless body of the Queen. Her motionless face lay contorted in pain as her dead eyes stared blankly into the ceiling. He made no move to cover her body as he walked out the bedroom door and back to the entrance of the antechamber.

''The Queen needs your assistance,'' he said in a panicked voice as he addressed the two guards posted at the door. Together, they bounded back to the Queen's room with Sumaina following closely from behind.

The two guards walked in to see the Queen Yaa-Yaa's naked, lifeless body strewn across her bed. Before they could react, Sumaina pulled out a knife from his pocket and slit the first guard's throat. Blood gushed from the opening in his neck as he fell to the ground.

The second guard looked at Sumaina with wide eyed horror as he approached him. Before he could reach for his weapon, Sumaina rammed the knife's hilt into his belly several times before taking its sharp edge to his throat as well. The two guards now lay dead on the ground; their blood tainting it in a pool of bright red.

With the guards taken care of, he could concentrate on making the Queen's death look more like an assassination. He took his gun from his side and approached her lifeless body. Wrapping several layers of bedding he found in a nearby closet, he pressed the tip onto the Queen's body and shot twice into it. The normally loud gunshot was muzzled and restricted to the bedroom alone.

Satisfied, General Sumaina walked out of the room leaving the dead bodies in his wake. The Queen's servants would find her in the morning as they attempted to cater for her daily needs. An alarm would be duly raised until word reached him. He would be in his quarters within the military base by then. No one had seen him enter the castle except the two slain guards therefore no one would suspect him of murder.

Behind a painting in the antechamber lay a secret passage cutting underneath the grounds to the forest grove which surrounded much of the area. Monarchs of old had used it to make their escape in the event of a direct siege on their residence. His many years serving as the Queen's closest confidant had naturally made him privy to the many escape routes that existed in the castle which he could access with ease.

Sumaina took no pleasure in taking the Queen's life, after all he had pledged to serve her for many years now. He even honored the more controversial directives from the late monarch who sought to quell the talks of a military coup spoken amongst his colleagues. After he had informed the Queen of the plot, she had in-turn hatched a brilliant plan which required his assistance and coordination for it to succeed.

Seeing her power and influence wane, the Queen intended to usurp the position of Sovereign for at least another tenure by assassinating the incoming monarch, King Dinga, who was to assume the seat. She intended to frame the terrorist sect, the Red Dawn for the murder of the Zulu monarch and therefore have her term extended momentarily. For the plan to work, she would have to be entirely removed from suspicion in the plot. The king's death would therefore have to be public and unexpected.

The crowing ceremony would be the staging point for the assassination to take place. On the Queen's orders, the General had arranged for explosive devices to be planted under their horse-drawn carriage. They would have to be detonated with precision as to only maim the Zulu King, a task which deeply troubled Sumaina.

''I sense doubt in you, General, '' Queen Yaa-Yaa said with concern as she finished laying out the plan to him, ''Are you not able to do this for me?''

''Yes of course, my Queen, '' he replied, ''I must warn you of the dangers of your plan. You may be harmed in the process.''

''Great rewards require great risks. If I am to keep my kingdom, then this action must be taken.'' They were both secluded in the private guest study of the castle, away from prying eyes and ears. The Queen made sure only she and General Sumaina were made privy to the plan.

She gazed out the window, looking across the horizon at the city in the distance. She turned around to meet him and with a wide smile declared, ''I trust your ability to carry out this mission, General. My life is in your hands.''

The night before the coronation ceremony, General Sumaina inspected the horse-drawn carriage himself, affixing the bombs to the side of the cart where the King would sit. During his time as a young officer serving in the field, he had become adept at fixing charges in clandestine locations to eliminate unsuspecting enemy combatants. Now he would use those same skills to ensure the Queen's safety in her radical plan.

It therefore came as no surprise to him when the explosions detonated on the day of the coronation. With skillful precision, he pressed the detonation trigger in succession, each blast made to seem like the attack was random and happening from all sides. Except for a mild concussion, the Queen was relatively unharmed by the attack.

He was easily able to convince the military elite of the details of the complicated plot. The attack was planned and coordinated by Red Dawn terrorists working within Luandan borders. It was common knowledge that these rogue syndicates sought to destabilize monarchies spread across the globe.

The Red Dawn were also known to have significant ties with the Slovian government, making this attack a direct plot by their Czar, Nicholas Romanov VI to overthrow the leadership of the African Union and bring it to ruin.

A convoluted plot for sure, one which demanded proof. Ample confessions supplied from captured Red Dawn agents confirmed Sumaina's words. In truth, they had been men taken in on petty crimes and pressured to give false testimonies in exchange for clemency. General Sumaina made sure that the men disappeared the moment their use had expired.

With the military fully on-board, Sumaina was set to wage a war campaign against the Slovians, a goal he desired given their large cache of biological weapons. He would use this war to attack their stockpile and destroy any prospect for its potential use. Both he and the Queen would get what they desired: the Queen would have her kingdom while he would have his chance to destroy their enemy's biological weapons supply.

He understood the hypocrisy of his actions. The Queen herself had several biological weapons in her arsenal, each more deadly than the last. Her predecessors had stockpiled a considerable amount before their deaths in pursuit of the protection of the Luandan kingdom.

Their use had made them a dominant force on the continent and was credited with the years of stability enjoyed by the African Union. Unlike other world powers, the General knew the Queen would never deploy them and had faith in her leadership.

For five years, the war saw much destruction happen to both the Slovian colonies and the Eurasian mainland. With the aid of their Chinese counterparts, they had delivered a string of defeats against their enemies. However, fatigue began to set in as resources were drained on both sides.

Meanwhile, the General's troops had managed to destroy several biological weapons depots on the Eurasian continent. Intelligence reports coming in indicated the last of their weapons stockpile may be hidden in their North American colonies.

The Queen herself, growing weary from the resources being poured into the war, sought a means to end the campaign so that she may focus on her desire for an heir. With a negotiated peace treaty in progress, the General would have to bide his time again before he could launch a final assault to destroy the last of their supplies. That opportunity came when he received word of the capture of their Emissary in Krepost. He saw this as a chance to launch the final assault he so desperately desired.

His life's work of ridding the world of weapons of mass destruction was finally coming to an end. His mind returned to that fateful day that changed his life forever; the day he saw the effects of a biological agent firsthand and how it slowly killed his squadron. He spent the rest of his life honoring their memories by ensuring no one would befall the same fate.

The biological strike ordered by the Queen had therefore come as a shock to him, putting him in a difficult position. Although he had sworn an oath to always serve her, he was not willing to sanction the use of their biological stockpile on the battlefield.

Disobeying the Queen however would incur grave consequences to himself. The Queen did not tolerate insubordination well. He was mulling over his options when his radio buzzed to life. Providence would shine on him once more that night as the Queen invited him to the castle.

To avert the use of these devastating weapons on the field and prevent a crisis which could potentially cost billions of lives, Sumaina would make the only choice available to him. He would take the Queen's life and seize power to avert the looming destruction. Inwardly, he cringed at the thought of usurping power for himself. He only now sought this path out of necessity and not out of desire.

That morning, a soldier accosted him in his quarters to make a shocking report. The Queen had been found dead in her room alongside two guards, he said. No one had seen her attacker enter or leave the castle.

The following few hours which followed were critical. Sumaina knew he would need to get in front of this as quickly as possible. Arrangements for a continental-wide radio broadcast were promptly made. The announcement of the Queen's death had to come from him.

Before a crew of sound engineers and news reporters he made his address. Silence fell in the room as he entered the small auditorium and sat in the desk placed in front of the expectant audience.

''People of Luanda and the African Union, I have the unfortunate responsibility of reporting a terrible crime which occurred this day on our soil. I regret to inform you that the Queen regent of Luanda and Sovereign of the African Union, Yaa-Yaa is dead.'' An audible gasp filled the room as he uttered those words. The news was immediately carried far and wide across the radio to those tuned in.

''She was murdered in her castle alongside two of her personal guards. We believe it to be the work of rebel soldiers acting within the Luandan estate and are hot on the tails of the perpetrators. We will have them in our custody shortly. I declare that the citizens of the African Union must observe a month-long mourning to honor our fallen Queen. We will overcome this tragedy and emerge stronger.''

''In the interest and protection of our kingdom, a new leader must be installed immediately. As the highest-ranking officer in the Continental African Forces, I hereby declare myself the King regent of Luanda and Sovereign of the A.U. You have my word that I will protect our union and bring an end to the tyranny of our enemies.''

With the address complete, he needed to solidify his control within the military. No doubt General Thabiso would seek to capitalize on this circumstance to gain control for himself within its ranks. He sent out messages to several Generals, expelling them from their posts and promoting their lieutenant officers. This new crop of Generals would swear their loyalty to him and solidify his control.

He now turned his attention to other pressing threats including the war on their Northern flank. The Western Coalition comprising British and French troops were still advancing on their continental borders and would quickly overwhelm Queen Salma's local troops without his aid. Sending word to General Mao, he ordered for a large portion of their mercenary troops in the North-American colonies to be redeployed to the North African border.

''But Sir, that will leave our base and our colonies vulnerable to attack, '' Lieutenant General Mao responded through his receiver, ''Did the Queen sanction such an action?''

''The Queen is dead, Lieutenant. I am now the King regent of

Luanda therefore you will obey my commands now.''

A long pause followed on the telephone before Mao responded, ''I will have the troops ready for redeployment, Sir.''

Sumaina had confidence he could protect the African mainland and its territories without resorting to the use of biological weapons on the field. Temporarily bolstering their troop levels would be sufficient to stop the Western Coalition's advance and safeguard their continental borders.

A few days later, Sumaina would take residence in what was formerly the Queen's castle. He would return to the room where he took the Queen's life, sitting down on the chair next to the bedframe. The blood which had covered the ground had now been cleaned up, leaving no trace behind. The entire room was neatly arranged, giving no impression of the crime he had committed in it just the days prior.

He could still vividly picture the Queen's lifeless body where it lay on the bedframe; the look of sheer betrayal in her face as he snuffed the life from her. He would forever carry the guilt of taking the life of a woman he had long dedicated his life to. The necessity of her death only weighed against the billions of lives which her orders would have caused.

A knock on the antechamber pulled him from his reverie. A servant came to inform him that someone was requesting to see him. It was the grandmother to Emissary Tife, the captured diplomat on Slovian soil.

''She has been coming to the castle every day for the past two weeks asking about her granddaughter. We thought it best not to bother you with such trifling news, but she has been very persistent. Should I let her in, Sir?'' the maid asked.

''Have her meet me in the garden,'' Sumaina replied.

Sumaina walked into the carefully kept castle garden to see an only woman sitting on one of the benches. She looked well into her years, sporting a thick white plume of hair and a walking cane beside her to support her weight. She got up unsteadily as General Sumaina approached her, giving a respectful bow to the new regent.

''My King, thank you for honoring my request to see you. My name is Madame Uvewa. I am Tife's grandmother and only living relative. Poor thing lost the rest of her family years ago,'' she said with a solemn look on her face.

''My servants tell me you have been frequenting the castle in recent days asking about Emissary Tife.''

''She told me she would be returning weeks ago. I haven't been able to get in touch with her ever since. I am very worried about her, my King.''

''It is not unusual for diplomatic missions to last longer than they are originally scheduled for, Mrs. Uvewa. And given the sensitive nature of their missions, we cannot divulge the specifics to anyone, not even her family members.'' He led her through the gardens back towards the entrance into the palatial estate.

''I am sure she is doing fine. I have received no information to the contrary. Be rest assured that you will have your granddaughter back soon,'' he said with an artificial smile before gesturing her through the gates.

''Thank you again for your reassurance, my King. May your reign be long and prosperous,'' and with that, Mama Uvewa ambled out of the castle, leaving a stone-faced Sumaina on its outer steps.

SALVATION

Over the next three days, Tife hoped for death to take her away from her wretched fate. Every day for twenty hours straight, they would toil and break rocks under the watchful eye of armed guards who surrounded them on all sides.
Without being provided any warm clothes, they were vulnerable to the blistering cold air which unceasingly tore at their skin. Even the children were made to work, sorting the mined rock which they chipped loose from the mountainside.

The older women and pregnant ones were given no exception either and were forced to toil in the elements with the rest of them. There were no breaks given between work forcing many to the point of exhaustion. One pregnant woman suddenly collapsed in the snow beside Tife as she struck at the rock with her pickaxe. The soldiers promptly carried her lifeless body away. She would not be seen of again.

Their daily four hours of rest would solely be dedicated to feeding and sleeping. Soldiers carried large plates filled with stale bread and threw them inside their small, poorly insulated cells. The men and women were separated in cells facing each other, each one holding no less than ten people. Fights quickly broke out in each cell as people rushed to get a hold of the food. Soldiers rushed in to quiet them down, often beating offenders with the ends of their guns.

Meanwhile, Tife gauged her surroundings and the cell she was placed in. She had been separated from most of the women whom she met at the caves and was now surrounded with women who looked at her with distrust. She attempted to gather the loaves to share it equally amongst them but was quickly swarmed by them as they made to take as many as they could, leaving many empty handed.

Hungry and alone, Tife shrank back into a corner of the cell desperately trying to keep warm. She looked down to her ripped clothes which gave no protection from the harsh weather and inspected her matted hair.

Hope began to give way to the realization that she would die in this place. Her home in Luanda seemed so far away now as any chance to return there seemed to have disappeared. Any attempt to sleep was interrupted by the sound of neighbouring cells. Eventually, the soldiers came by to take them to the mines once again.

The abuse from the guards were on clear display even as they worked tirelessly outside. Two guards accosted a man as he momentarily stopped working to drink water from a nearby puddle. They struck him repeatedly before stripping him and proceeded to tie him to a post in the middle of the camp for all to see. Tife saw some women be taken away only to return several minutes later disheveled and abused with vacant looks on their faces.

''You there, '' a soldier pointed to Tife as she toiled away, ''the prison ward wants to see you.'' Tife was promptly taken to a room overlooking the prison camp. Warm air greeted her as she entered inside. The room was sparsely decorated, having a metal chair and table on one end. Loose papers littered its surface as did many bottles of wine and beer. A large window cut at one end gave an uninterrupted view of the mining prison camp from above.

Sitting at the desk was the same man who had addressed them when they first arrived. He sat scribbling furiously on several notes before momentarily turning his attention to Tife.

''You are far from home, are you not Emissary?'' he said casually

before proceeding to make several more notes on the papers spread on his desk. Tife could not conceal her surprise as she returned a non-plussed look on her face.
''You know who I am, then?'' Tife replied firmly.

''Of course, is this not your picture?'' the man raised a newspaper article which featured Tife's face prominently in the main section. It was written entirely in Slovian with the headline reading, 'Missing A.U. Emissary to Slovia Suspected of Abetting the Red Dawn Terrorist Cell, Last Seen in Mountains.''

''It would seem that you have been very busy since entering our lands,'' he suggested, now turning his full attention to her.

''That report is false and inaccurate,'' Tife protested, '' I have been held captive for several days now. Your own soldiers attempted a rescue only to knowingly botch the exchange in the middle of it. The crimes your military have committed are long and traitorous.''

''You misunderstand your position, Emissary, '' the man said, now standing up from his seat, ''the Slovian empire does not recognise your diplomatic status any longer. You have been accused of aiding and abetting terrorists. We have it on good word that you were instrumental in helping several of them escape during the raid on their main base.''

''Your soldiers were going to cause the death of several innocent women and children. I acted only to protect lives-''
''The lives of terrorists, nonetheless. You sought to safeguard the lives of rebel scum who have caused nothing but chaos in our borders. That is unforgivable.''

''Then send me back to my homeland for punishment. You would not risk placing the current peace accord in jeopardy with my continued detention.'' The man walked forward till he was facing Tife. The pungent smell of beer and cigarettes lingered on his breath.

''Emissary, you still do not understand your position here. You have been branded an enemy of the state and therefore diplomatic protocol does not apply here. Given your position, your leaders would not dare to cause an international incident now.''

Tife's eyes grew wide with disbelief. Her last strand of hope seemed to have been dashed away in seconds. She knew diplomatic protocol well and understood how tenuous the peace agreement was. The Queen may in fact not seek her extradition back to Luanda if it would maintain the treaty, a possibility Tife did not consider. In that case, she would be left to the mercy of the Slovian army, a fate she inwardly dreaded.

The man returned back to his seat, taking in a long drag from his cigarette and breathing out a cloud of smoke into the room.

''What will you do with me then?'' Tife queried him, realizing her perilous position.

''I just signed your transfer papers. We will be relocating you to a more secure location. You may have information useful to the empire and our Czar. Enjoy your last night at this facility. They will not be as gracious of hosts where you are going,'' and with a definitive nod, the prison guards led Tife by the shoulders out and back into the frigid prison camp barracks.

Later that night, several guards returned to their holding cell with a prisoner in tow. The prisoner had been stripped of her clothes except for her undergarments which were torn and bloodied in several places. A sack cloth had been placed over her head as they dragged and threw her inside Tife's cell. The other women quickly shrank bank at the listless body while Tife approached it cautiously at the sight of a familiar strand of red hair coming from underneath.

She removed the bag to reveal Arial's bloodied visage. Her eyes were black and swollen from multiple blows to the face and her body was scarred in several faces. She slowly opened her eyes as Tife tenderly propped her back against the wall.

''Where am I?'' She inquired weakly as her swollen eyes wandered the cell.

''They took you to the detention area with the rest of the prisoners,'' Tife replied,'' The other women have been separated and placed in other holding blocks. What did they do to you?''

Arial looked wearily at the other prisoners who still shrank back from her, ''the guards took me to a private cell where they tortured and abused me for hours. I passed out several times from the pain. I…'' she paused as tears now began to flow down her face. She wept bitterly into her hands as a thought passed through her mind.

''They killed them all. They killed all those women and children in the cave. I couldn't save them. They killed my daughter, Katrina.'' Tife embraced her warmly as she wept for several minutes. She knew she had no power over this situation and could do nothing else but comfort her. Her leaders had abandoned her to the caprices of a foreign government and left her to a painful fate. She was left broken, alone and effectively stateless. Tife had become the sacrificial lamb to a peace treaty she herself had helped negotiate, a painful recognition to the irony of this situation.

Like clockwork, the prison guards returned that night to take them to the mining site. Under the cover of night, they marched them to their stations and forced them to begin work anew, chipping at the precious metal which the hard rock concealed. Tife, now bereft of hope, dutifully worked away at the rock, knowing she would be taken away in the morning to a fate even worse than this one.

A loud commotion outside the prison walls caught the attention of several guards scanning the area. The guard numbers were substantially lower at night, with many soldiers sleeping in specially designed quarters within the camp. Wind gusts now swept up more snow, blanketing the entire camp in a deep haze.

A loud explosion was suddenly heard at the East-facing wall followed by several more explosions in the night. The prisoners cowered to the ground as a flurry of gunshots pierced through the bitter-cold air. The guards watching them ran off in the direction of the sound, leaving them alone in the work area.

At that moment, a loud, blaring sound erupted in the prison complex. The alarm system had been triggered causing several red flashing lights mounted on each corner of the yard to sound out furiously. The barrage of gunfire mixed with intermittent explosions seemed to be inching closer to them. Tife looked round to the terrified group of prisoners who stood frozen in the cold.

''This way,'' Tife called out to them, pointing to the prison cell housing they had just been taken from. It was the closest building they could take refuge in as the fighting erupted around the base's perimeter. The prisoners hesitated at first but quickly relented as the mix of battle sounds grew more intense.

The entire camp was now a scene of a warzone. The soldiers had forgotten those they were guarding and took positions around the camp to defend against the onslaught from this unknown enemy. Tife used the opportunity to lead the terrified group into the dilapidated housing as cover against the attack.

''What are you doing?'' said a guard viciously as he accosted them at the entrance. He had stayed behind to guard the building while his colleagues repelled the foreign invaders. He pointed his gun menacingly at them as they attempted to enter the building.

''Get back outside, '' he ordered, aiming his gun at them and forcing them to back away from the doors. Suddenly, a hand from inside grabbed his head and struck it against the door post. The hand took the gun from the guard's unconscious corpse and stepped out of the shadows.

Arial greeted them at the entrance. She had been left inside the prison cell unable to work with the rest of them in the mines but had somehow managed to escape during the commotion.

''Come inside quickly,'' she urged them, '' before more of the guards return.''

They all hurried inside, closing the door behind them. The sound of gunfire and fighting still raged on outside. It would only be a matter of time before the battle outside moved into the buildings as retreating prison soldiers took up shelter to protect themselves.

''We have to barricade the doors and windows. Get whatever you can carry and press it against any openings,'' ordered Arial to the terrified group of people. Fearing for their lives, they went to work pushing any desks, chairs, and wooden planks they could find against the door frames.

Once the outer entrance was barricaded, they retreated inside, taking the guard's key and locking the doors leading to the prison cell quarters. Everyone except a chosen few were ordered to enter the cells and to close the doors behind them.

Arial cocked her weapon and pressed herself against the side of the door, ready to defend against any would-be intruder. Tife stood on the other end holding a large plank she had found. Nearly a dozen others placed themselves in strategic locations carrying with them anything they could use to defend themselves.

The battle sounds outside reached a crescendo before descending to a whimper. The sound of boots could now be heard traversing the exterior of the buildings. Several footsteps suddenly stopped in front of their building and proceeded to break down the entry doors, clearing the barricades which had been placed in front of them. The troop of footsteps proceeded to the inner room containing the prison cells where Tife and the others were seeking refuge.

They waited anxiously as the entrance was breached from the outside. The doors were struck repeatedly until they gave way. Tife and Arial kept firm at the sides of the entrance, waiting patiently on the intruders who would attempt to gain access.

''Lower your weapons and come outside. We are not here to hurt you,'' streamed a familiar voice through the doorframe. Tife instantly recognized who it was but could not believe it. She stepped through the door into the antechamber to greet her savior.

Zala was decked in full military fatigue and was flanked by several other men and women holding firearms of every kind. Tife rushed over to her, embracing her fully while the others watched in confusion.

''Zala! How? I thought you were dead!'' Tife cried out in surprise.

''Not dead, just hidden away,'' Zala replied before turning to her colleagues.

''Secure the area, make sure we haven't missed any of their armed patrol guards in the camp. Then round up the prisoners and take them to the transport vans. We only have a few minutes before we must depart.''

Zala led Tife away into a corner so they could speak in private. This time, she embraced her once more, squeezing her tightly before scanning her body curiously.

''I see you have been through quite a lot, Tife. I am sorry for your ordeal.''

''And I thought Michail had you killed back at the State House.''

''A necessary ruse, '' Zara replied, ''I had to be assumed dead to operate more freely within this area. Michail knew that a Red Dawn Spy would be coming from Luanda and only knew to make contact when he saw this symbol,'' she said as she pulled out a single star pendent hanging from her neck. Engraved on it were the initials 'Kℑ', the same symbol on the pendant that Michail had entrusted to Tife.

''My father was the Red Dawn commander to operate within Luanda. He passed this on to me after his untimely death. Since then, I have been able to extract information about the monarchy in Luanda posing as a journalist to the crown while coordinating our underground rebel network.''

''Wait, then you were responsible for what happened at the

coronation ceremony,'' Tife realized as she backed away. ''You are responsible for the death of my father!''

''No, that was not us, '' Zala interjected swiftly. ''We had no role in the attack which killed all those people. I recently uncovered a plot which implicates the Queen and her highest ranking General. Together, they schemed to murder King Dinga who was to be crowned the new Sovereign thereby retaining control of the title. They orchestrated the attack that killed all those people.''

''No, they couldn't have...'' she said but as the image of that day flooded back in her head once more, her recurring dreams attained vivid clarity and focus. She remembered seeing the Queen beside the lifeless corpse of King Dinga, how her hands wrapped around his neck and squeezed the life from the maimed monarch. She had witnessed the Queen take his life but had somehow blocked it from her memory.

''You see? I am telling the truth and I think deep down you know it to be true,'' said Zala as she put a hand on Tife's shoulder.

''They killed my father. They killed all those people...'' Tife replied finally, her eyes glazed now with tears as she now came to the awful realization. Zala wrapped her hands around her once more, comforting her in warm embrace.
The rebels proceeded to round up every last one of the surviving soldiers and threw them in the empty jail cells.

Reinforcements arriving at the base would find their soldiers locked in the cages long after they had escaped. Zala shared her journey over the past couple of days with Tife as they inspected the base together.

''After they faked my death at the State House, I rendezvoused with several rebel commanders in the area. We were coordinating a strategy to dismantle the supply lines sent from the colonies to mainland Europe. The mainland armies would quickly collapse without resources from their colonies.''

''I see. But how did you eventually find me?'' Tife asked curiously.

''Our Northern-most base was attacked by Slovian troops shortly after the base you were held in was destroyed. It was during our escape that we received your distress radio transmission. We combed the area for several hours but could not find you there. We believe your transmission was intercepted by Slovian troops before we could reach you. It was our belief that the surviving hostages were taken to the nearby prison camp and we struck when we thought the security was most lax.''

Two rebel soldiers were seen dragging a bloodied man from underneath a parked truck in the camp. It was the prison ward who had seen her several hours ago. He had been stripped of his uniform and now sported a coffee-stained singlet and underwear. A gunshot wound on his right-side soaked blood into his singlet.

''Rebel scum! I will have all your heads on a pike for this,'' the man threatened in his native tongue as they brought him before Zala.

''Who is this?'' Zala inquired as they dragged him before her.

''He's the prison ward for this facility,'' Tife replied. ''He was going to have me transferred in the morning to another prison. You would have never found me if he had followed through with his plan.''

''I understand your mother tongue, filth and know what you are saying, '' the man continued, ''I already alerted our troops of your siege on this facility. Reinforcements are on their way to this base as we speak. You and the rest of your horde will suffer endlessly for this.''

Arial came walking from the holding quarters when she saw Zala with the prison ward. She instantly rushed over and struck the man with a closed fist, sending him tumbling to the snowy canvas.

''You monster!!'' she spat, rushing to kick the man in the gut as he doubled over on the ground.

''What did he do to you?'' Zala asked curiously.

''That beast tortured me for hours on end. I would be dead if not that he wanted more information from me and still needed me alive. He promised he would kill me himself the moment I had outlived my usefulness.'' At this remark, the man laughed through a toothy, blood-lined grin.

''I will still keep my promise to you,'' he replied with a menacing smile.

''Your sins against my people are long, '' Zala said as she crouched down to address him. She spoke to him in his language now. ''Justice demands I have them decide your fate.'' She walked over to Arial and handed her the holstered pistol attached to her waist.

''Do with him as you wish,'' She replied before standing back. Arial pointed the gun at his head as he lay on the ground. He raised himself so that he was now kneeling in the snow.

''You all fight for a lost cause,'' he began as he grinned through his bloodied teeth. ''You will all share the same fate as your comrades who we hung at Krepost. Each and every one of you will not live-''

The prison ward suddenly stopped speaking as a single shot emanated from the barrel of the gun in Arial's hand. The bullet hit him square in the forehead and exited through the back of his head. He now lay lifeless on the ground as blood from the wound colored the white snow in a deep, reddish hue.

''You will no longer be able to hurt anyone, '' said Arial as she threw the gun aside and returned back to join her people.

One by one the liberated prisoners eager to leave the prison, loaded up into the military trucks. Daylight was nearing quickly, and they needed to leave the prison grounds as soon as possible. Zala organized her rebel soldiers to raid the base of anything valuable before they departed. Storage in the mess halls revealed several cans of food which they helped themselves to.

After helping with loading the food to the trucks, Tife ventured back to the prison ward's office overlooking the yard. Papers alongside bottles of beers still littered the floor and table. She rifled through the papers looking for any information of import. Just then, Zala walked through the door to join her in the small room.

''It is time to leave now, Tife,'' she announced, ''we have a schedule to keep.''

''We are never returning home, are we?'' said Tife aloud as the sudden realization hit her.

''We have nothing to go back to,'' Zala replied. ''With everything you know now, going back there would only risk the lives of the loved ones you have back home.''

''Then where will we go?''

''We have friends in Eurasia. We will travel there by ship to rendezvous with them. Luckily, we have friends at every level of authority there; people who despise the monarchical systems as much as we do and who want to see it end to usher in more democratic institutions.''

''Do you honestly believe we can achieve those goals?'' Tife asked hesitantly.

''We have never been closer, '' Zala stretched her hands towards Tife, beckoning her forward, ''Come now, join us in making a better world.''

The two left the office and joined the others as final boarding was underway. The rebel soldiers doused the buildings and walls with fuel left in storage on the base. As they left the base, Zala gave the orders to light the camp on fire.
One by one, the buildings lit up in a conflagration of smoke and flames. The fire would clearly be visible from several kilometers

away, attracting several Slovian troops to that location.

Tife looked back one last time to the blazing inferno behind her, a visual representation of the life she was leaving behind. She would never see Mama Uvewa again, or Abigail or any of her friends back home in Luanda. What was a simple diplomatic trip had now permanently transformed her life.

The truth before her was clear. The monarchies of the world only brought chaos and destruction upon it. A new way of governance was in order. She would fight alongside these rebels to shake the very foundation of this system replete across the world. She would no longer be a victim to their reign but now would become an instrument of their annihilation.

She raised her head out the window, bathing in the sun as it peaked in the distance. A new day was upon her, one she now greeted with open arms…

Made in the USA
Monee, IL
13 February 2025

12221294R00144